In the epic tradition of Stephen King, Dean Koontz, and Jonathan Maberry, a chilling new masterwork of small-town evil, centuries-old traditions, and newly-risen terror . . .

RED HARVEST

Every year at harvest time, something strange and wonderful happens in the sleepy farm community of Ember Hollow. It comes alive. Truckloads of pumpkins are sent off to be carved into lanterns. Children scramble to create the creepiest, scariest costumes. Parents stock up on candy and prepare for the town's celebrated Pumpkin Parade. And then there is Devil's Night . . .

But this year, something is different. Some of the citizens are experiencing dark, disturbing visions. Others are beginning to wonder if they're losing their minds, or maybe their souls. One newly sober singer with the voice of a fallen angel is tempted to make a deal that will seal his fate. And one very odd boy is kept locked in a shed by his family—for reasons too horrible to imagine . . .

Whatever is happening to this town, they're going to make it through this Halloween. Even if it kills them . . .

Books by Patrick C. Greene

The Haunted Hallow Chronicles
Red Harvest

Published by Kensington Publishing Corporation

Red Harvest

The Haunted Hollow Chronicles

Patrick C. Greene

LYRICAL PRESS
Kensington Publishing Corp.
www.kensingtonbooks.com

First Electronic Edition: September 2018
eISBN-13: 978-1-5161-0830-5
eISBN-10: 1-5161-0830-2

First Print Edition: September 2018
ISBN-13: 978-1-5161-0833-6
ISBN-10: 1-5161-0833-7

Printed in the United States of America

Dedicated to Gavin,
with thanks for many magical Halloweens

Author's Note

This is a dream from a long autumn night. I am helping you to remember—
for better or worse.
This is not the past, though it contains pieces.
Our cell phones and computers are not here.
Safety is not as close as we have come to expect.

A Preamble

"Trick or treat! Rotten meat! That is what we want to eat!" One of the troupe of tweens was out of harmony.

"Hm." Lola, costumed in a short leather nun's habit, smiled and saluted the kids with her wine glass.

She was decidedly not mortified by this variation of the traditional rhyme, and only mildly amused, more interested in the TV party a few rooms away. "Well, no rotten meat I'm afraid, but I think I still have a few…"

She twisted almost sideways and presented a near-empty candy bowl from just inside, dumping the last of the treats into the bags and buckets. "Here you go, kiddies!"

Lola ignored the disappointed expressions the kids cast at her and at one another, her bleary gaze drawn to the figure standing across the street, just outside a vague circle of street light.

The figure, wearing an odd costume of rainbow fright wig, Lone Ranger–style eye mask, and an oversized brown raincoat, wasn't moving, except for his shoulders, which rose and fell as if from suppressed laughter. He hunched over and covered his mouth with both hands, like a toddler who had just stolen a cookie. Did he think she couldn't see him? How silly.

"Is this all you got, lady?" asked the kid in the…whichever superhero wore black tights with green trim. She had stopped trying to keep up.

"Um, well…" She looked inside again. "No more candy," she said. "But how about this for your chaperone?"

From the four canisters of silly string beside the candy bowl—in the event of a prank war—she held one over the heads of the children, to offer it to the man on the street. But he was gone.

"Where's your grown-up?" she asked.

The kids turned to see what she meant. "What grown-up? We're old enough to be without," explained a rubber-worm-infested zombie, quite indignantly.

Her wine glass was empty. She didn't care about the funny skulker anymore.

"Okeydoke, then," she said. "Have at it!" She tossed the silly string at the group, then half waved, half shooed, until they shuffled away. Before closing the door, she decided to blow out the jack-o'-lantern.

Lola re-wined her glass and started back to the den to rejoin her friends in giving old horror movies the MST3K treatment. She was stopped by the doorbell.

She stepped to the door, unsteady on her spike heels. "Sorry! All out! Happy Halloween!"

She moved to walk away but stopped upon hearing a giggle—silly yet eerie—just outside the door. "Hey!" she shouted. "You better not be TPing our lawn out there!"

The doorbell rang again.

"Okay!" Lola grabbed a can of silly string. "I warned you!"

She yanked open the door and poised the canister, finding only blowing leaves, on and all around the front stoop.

She listened for the sound of giggling or leaves crunching under running feet, bracing for a good hearty "Boo!" as well.

"Ding dong ditch," she muttered. "Not even a flaming bag of doggy doo. Kids these days..."

She closed the door—and felt the icy tingle of intuition. Something was very, *very* wrong.

She turned fast.

It was the man from across the street, now less than two feet away.

He had entered through the rear kitchen door.

The fright wig he was wearing, vaguely haloed by the hallway, did its job. From there down, it only got worse.

His Lone Ranger–style mask framed eyes filled with something like joy—but more like hopeless insanity. His face was white, as if bleached.

Then there was the blood.

Streams of it ran down gaunt cheeks to cracked smiling lips from the staples that held the mask on.

The figure raised a meat cleaver with a blade the size of a notebook.

Lola's heart skipped a beat, until she saw that the weapon was mere plastic—a toy. Lola smiled, issuing a relieved, "Whew!"

"*So* funny, Greg." She leaned forward to look more closely at him. "Where's the ol' ball and chain?"

As she reached for his mask, the figure stepped back from her grasp. He lowered the cleaver and slid the toy plastic blade—merely an improvised sheath—off of a very shiny, very *real* butcher knife blade.

The oversized trick-or-treater displayed the implement.

"Oh, my God, Greg." Lola rolled her eyes and raised both middle fingers.

The trickster slashed the knife in a sideways arc, severing the fingers.

She was too breathless to scream, trying to reconcile the sight of her shortened digits and angry that Greg had taken his little joke this far.

Not-Greg squatted to gather the fingers and drop them into his treat bag.

Trying to back away from her own ruined hand, Lola fell like a toddler onto her rump, sucking breath for a scream she would never have time to release.

Chapter 1

Ember Hollow, North Carolina
October 29

"Helen, a few weeks ago, the empty field you see behind me was home to roughly twenty-five thousand Autumn's Pride pumpkins," pronounced local reporter Kit Calloway. "They're all gone now, on their way to markets and homes around the country. But a good many are staying right here in Ember Hollow, where they will be carved and decorated for the town's annual Pumpkin Parade on Halloween night."

Viewers were treated to stock footage of parades past, with costumed bystanders hooting and clapping while spooky floats crawled by with more elaborately costumed performers aboard.

"For, you see, come Halloween, Ember Hollow becomes *Haunted* Hollow, Halloween Capital of the World." The handsome reporter gave a charming raise of his eyebrow. "And this year promises a little something extra, as the town's very own homegrown rock band The Chalk Outlines takes the stage above The Grand Illusion cinemas to play a full set. Now the band has taken the local club scene by storm, but this year, with their performance at the theater, they hope to garner the attention of a special guest."

"Kerwin Stuyvesant—Talent Manager" read the screen caption under a man in his fifties who wore a bright green suit and funny-looking little hexagonal spectacles. He smiled into the camera with huge teeth that made the tiny glasses seem like toys. "The kids have been rehearsing and hitting the gigs hard, and if I didn't believe they had what it takes to make it to the top, I wouldn't have signed on to manage 'em!"

A quick snip of the trio of Halloween-themed punk rockers, awash in strobe-lit fog at some dive club, flashed on the screen before a cut back to Calloway, who concluded the report with a graceful nod. "Helen, as always, I'll be right here in Ember Hollow covering the parade and enjoying the company of these great citizens! Back to you!"

* * * *

Thirteen-year-old Stuart Barcroft woke to the sound of his mother's low humming as she breezed past his door to the room of his older brother, Dennis. He hopped from his bed and hurried into his clothes, eavesdropping on the conversation between mother and brother.

Ma—Elaine Barcroft to you and me—exclaimed, "Oh my word, Dennis! Is that going to wash out of my sheets?"

And he knew Dennis had blood on him again.

As Stuart headed toward Dennis's room, he saw a sheet of sunlight spill onto the hallway floor from the doorway—Ma opening the curtains on his poor brother.

"That makeup is a mess," she huffed, but was not really that sore about it.

At the doorway, Stuart looked his big brother over to make sure he was okay. Dennis, taking a long drink of water from the glass he kept at his bedside, was still in performance attire. His hair, already way too long on top, was disheveled and sticky. Surely exhausted, he hadn't changed out of his stage attire of torn black denim pants and a hospital scrub top spritzed with the offending stage blood, over a black long-sleeve T-shirt with bones printed on the arms.

"Oh yeah, Ma. I checked the package. Washes right out." Despite his exhaustion, he was as patient and respectful with his mother as always.

Spotting Stuart, Dennis raised the glass. "Hey, dude."

"Why didn't you clean it off?" groused their mother. "And you're still dressed!"

When Dennis had moved back in (at the ripe old age of twenty-six) it was into a room his mother had kept essentially as he had left it when he moved out at eighteen. The walls remained plastered with punk posters: Misfits, Black Flag, The Addicts, Sex Pistols, Order of the Fly, Nekromantix, and, of course, Elvis.

"Our gig went over," Dennis explained in a scratchy voice. "Had three encores."

"You're sure that's all?" probed Ma.

"*Ma!*" Stuart called. When she spun with a quick squeal, Dennis and Stuart broke out laughing. Stuart was just trying to get her off Dennis's case. Giving her a start was a bonus.

Ma was a good sport about it. "Just how many scares can I expect this Halloween?"

Dennis gave her a tight hug and a kiss on top of her head. "All of 'em."

Ma took his wrist and pushed up the long sleeves of his black undershirt. "Let me see something."

She turned over his heavily tattooed arm and examined his inner elbow. Dennis pulled away. " What the hell?"

"I hear so many things about punk music people," she said in a grim tone. "Promise me you're not using any hard drugs?"

"*Ma!*" Dennis and Stuart rebuked in harmony.

Ma clapped once, holding her hands together as she gave a satisfied chuckle. "Guess your ol' Ma can still pull off a Halloween prank herself every now and again, huh?"

Dennis walked to his dresser, picked up a crumpled orange flyer, and handed it to Stuart. "I'm a drunk. Not a junkie. There's a diff."

"Don't *say* that!" she rebuked. "You're not either one! Not anymore."

Stuart read the flyer and grinned.

Ma sniffed at Dennis's water glass.

THE CHALK OUTLINES! ON STAGE TONIGHT! read the flyer. It was a rough, old-school mimeograph job, featuring a grainy photo of Dennis with his bandmates, a muscular Hispanic and a petite sneering alt chick, all of them dressed in campy Halloween-inspired rockabilly gear.

"Once a drunk, always a drunk, Ma. That's the deal." Even this sounded cool coming from Dennis.

She patted his back. "You're doing so well, Dennis. I'm proud of you."

Stuart offered an agreeing smile, not sure if he should say anything.

"Now *hurry!*" Ma squealed. "You shouldn't keep Reverend McGlazer waiting."

She kissed him and turned to leave. "Oh! Can you drop Stuart at school? You want to hear how Dennis's jig went, don't you, Stuart?"

Stuart and Dennis snickered at her word choice. "Sure, Ma. No prob."

* * * *

Beaming, Stuart raised the luchador mask off his face and amped up the volume. His favorite part of autumn mornings was this: riding in his brother's tricked-out hearse as leaves blew across the tree-lined streets and swirled in mini twisters, chasing each other under an umber haze.

The trees, fences, and mailboxes along the street all wore such elaborate Halloween decorations, it was like a high-stakes contest. Nylon witches and ghosts floated in the trees, wooden black cat cutouts stood in the flowerbeds, wittily inscribed Styrofoam tombstones jutted from front-yard displays.

Dennis's 1970 Cadillac hearse was a mobile advertisement for his band, with flames painted on the hood, cartoonish chalk outlines of a voluptuous woman's corpse stickered on the doors, and a V8 472 cc engine that could roar like an enraged lion. Stuart loved to ride in it, especially to school.

The familiar punkabilly music emanating from the speakers had Stuart bobbing his head, tapping his fingers on his thigh.

Dennis looked at him, pleased. "You really dig that track, huh?"

"I think it's your best ever."

"Let's hope the record company suit agrees."

"She *will,* dude!" Stuart insisted. "I'd bet on it!"

The chorus began, and Stuart sang along with appropriate facial contortions.

"I better watch you, man," Dennis said. "You'll end up replacing me."

"Yeah, right," Stuart said and scoffed with a sideways glance at his brother. "Maybe I can be in the band one day though. Keyboards or something."

"No way, daddy-o." Dennis shook his head, as he always did when Stuart raised the topic. "College. Then some more college! After that, college. You'll be going to college—beyond the grave!" Dennis goosed his brother, right in that spot under his ribs that made him giggle like a baby. But for Stuart, the appeal of one day being like his brother was near irresistible. "We'll see."

"For real, Stuart. Mom's had plenty of guff outta me. She doesn't need it from her widdle baby bubby."

"Shut up. You're doing okay. Pretty good, actually."

"Maybe." Dennis took his eyes from the road to give Stuart an earnest, penetrating gaze. "But you're gonna do better."

A dozen yards ahead, burly Mister Dukes cast a scowl at them, which seemed reasonable given that he was in the midst of unwinding moist toilet paper from his mailbox. His morning's labor was only beginning; more of the soggy bands lay draped across his shrubs.

Dennis slowed the hearse and rolled down the window. "Morning, Mister Dukes. Ya got hit?"

"Yeah, yeah, yeah." Dukes waved to Stuart as he wadded the tissue into a handful. "Hey, it wasn't you, was it, boys? Be honest."

"Come on, Mr. Dukes." Dennis stayed cool, as always.

"Aaah I'm sorry. It's just … that weird music, and whatnot." Dukes squinted like the concept was a literal indecipherable blur to him. "What d'ya call it? Junkabilly?"

Before Stuart could stop himself, he explained, "It's called horror punk!"

Dennis nudged him. "Easy."

"No offense, boys." Dukes frowned at all the unpapered yards surrounding his. "Guess I'm just too old for all this Halloween crap."

"Never too old for Halloween, Mr. Dukes!" Dennis called, waving. "Hope you make it to the Pumpkin Parade!"

"Maybe." Dukes waved, mumbling something they couldn't hear.

As they pulled away, Dennis gave Stuart a reproachful glare. "Gotta build good rapport with the public, Stuart."

"He doesn't respect our music!"

"Nobody does. That's why it's called punk, genius."

Stuart had this thought and the music to fill his mind for the rest of the ride to Ember Hollow Junior High. If they had stayed at Mr. Dukes's place longer, they would have seen him open his mailbox and find a single piece of orange-and-black-wrapped candy.

Chapter 2

Dennis's father had bought the hearse for him and begun tricking it out before Dennis could even drive. It always drew gawks from parents and students in the drop-off queue, and Stuart loved it. Especially when he spotted a familiar contractor's van in the queue, with its battered ladders and PVC lengths bungeed to the top.

Stuart cracked the window and cranked up the music for the benefit of everybody else, relishing the reactions directed at both the music and the hearse.

Dennis batted Stuart's luchador mask off his head. "I see you sporting that tough-guy sneer there, Robert Blake."

Stuart shoved Dennis's arm, but Dennis smacked his hand down, saying, "Good luck with the costume contest, by the way."

"Think I'll win?"

"No doubt—especially if you ditch the hood."

Stuart shoved both middle fingers in his brother's face, but then found his attention drawn to the contractor's van, from which exited glorious, gorgeous, quirky Candace Geelens.

She was ready for the homeroom costume contest as well, in a homemade green alien bodysuit, complete with ping-pong-ball eyes bobbing on springs atop the tight hood on her head. Beyond the fluttering of his heart was a mild ache; this childish costume would surely make Candace a target of ridicule.

But maybe she didn't give a damn. Stuart hoped that was so, and it only made him like her more.

Dennis must have been watching him watch her. With a light shove of Stuart's head, he said, "That's the new chick?"

"Yeah." Stuart sighed. "Candace. She's not really new anymore. Been here the whole year."

"What? And you still haven't made your move?"

"It's never the right time."

Dennis sized her up. "She's not exactly the cheerleader-poodle-skirt-Barbie type."

"You got that straight. She's all art, no ads." Stuart followed the girl with his gaze as she walked alone, head down. He just wished she would look up sometime and see him (ever so casually) smiling at her.

"Here's a lightbulb," Dennis offered. "Why don't you invite her to the Pumpkin Parade? Tell her your badass brother's playing and needs some cool cats and chicks on the float tossing swag and flying the horns." Dennis made a fist with first and little fingers extended and pushed the "horns" in Stuart's face.

Stuart lit with a spark of hope. "Know what? That might work!"

"You know it will."

"If Ma will let me."

"I'll handle Ma. You handle Candace. And I don't mean literally, pervo." The self-assurance in Dennis's eyes made Stuart question that his big brother could ever have faltered, even in the wake of their father's passing. "Now get the hell outta my ride, ya square. You're cramping my style."

Stuart slugged Dennis on the shoulder and hopped out, putting on his best sneer as the hearse's engine rumbled.

He cast a glance at Candace of course—and found her looking his way. He turned his head fast enough it made him dizzy—and cursed himself for not giving her a cool nod or that smile he had practiced exactly one zillion times.

Then a lanky black kid showed, hanging his arm over Stuart's shoulder. "What's new with you and the weird chick, Stewie?" DeShaun Lott had been Stuart's best friend since either could remember.

"Nothing. I blew it."

DeShaun, costumed as George Washington, cocked his wigged head. "We need to work on your game, man."

"Yeah?" Stuart retorted. "How's your game, Mister Smooth?"

"Okay, we need to work on *our* game. But you get to be the guinea pig."

"*Viva la lucha!*" Stuart pulled his mask over his face and walked from the misty morning chill through the school doors with his buddy.

* * * *

Chief Deputy Hudson Lott, father of DeShaun, frowned at a puzzle of colored glass shards and a fist-sized rock at his feet.

Standing at the four-way stop on Second Street, Hudson scanned the rows of shops on either side: Lefwich Bros. Upholstery, We Nailed It! Manicurists, a thrift store, a tobacconist. He was awaiting a municipal crew en route to repair the traffic light shattered overnight.

Far from busy this early in the day, bored proprietors and cashiers often stepped out to say hello or offer coffee.

When the chief sent him on this—what should have been a rookie task—Lott had to bite his tongue yet again. The chief wasn't trying to cause Hudson grief, after all; he was just trying to avoid any for himself, and maybe even protect Hudson in light of recent events.

Out of the academy, Hudson had popped the question to his high school sweetheart, Leticia, and promptly swept her away to the most autumnal place he could find, simply because she loved the season.

"Ember Hollow is the nation's foremost producer and exporter of all breeds of jack-o'-lantern pumpkins, including Jericho's Wall Super Squash, 'exclusive to the region,'" read the chamber of commerce's pamphlet. This and the town's ambiance, with the annual Pumpkin Parade preparations starting four months in advance, made it about as "autumn" as any place could get.

But it was also about as *white* as it got.

Being a large black man of authority in a sprawling farm town had its challenges, chief among them a constant balancing act between courtesy and obsequiousness—as if there was a need to compensate for his intimidating appearance—and being professional to the point of seeming aloof.

Hudson's keen awareness of when and where he fit on this scale served him well enough—most of the time. But an incident that found him at odds with a senior officer had revealed unspoken racial tensions, within the department and the town.

He shook away the unpleasant recall, returning his thoughts to the present. He admired the decorations that ranged from garish and tacky to understatedly spooky that adorned the shop windows. The young Indian laurel trees rising from brick planters along the sidewalks had gone full orange, their leaves breaking free by the hundreds in the morning gusts and blowing all around Lott. One flattened against his face, as if mocking him for being stuck with such a meaningless duty. He snatched it away.

A massive Ford Galaxie, driven by a tightly scarfed old lady Hudson knew only as Mrs. Dubois, rolled toward the intersection. Hudson checked all directions, merely a show, given the sparse morning traffic, and guided her around the shards.

Then, quiet again.

Hudson's thoughts returned to the incident that had left him in this limbo.

* * * *

Reverend Abe McGlazer stepped back from the church sign to proofread.

VOLUNTEERS STILL NEEDED FOR

13TH ANNUAL PUMPKIN PARADE!!!

Tricksters had been at work the night before, rearranging the letters to read:

MI ASS HURT FROM ANAL LOVE!!!

When Ruth brought him to see the anagram, McGlazer had laughed, a contrast to Ruth's grim indignance.

McGlazer had thought that maybe Ruth, who did volunteer work helping to maintain the church and cemetery, could use a little love herself.

Saint Saturn Unitarian Church, a centuries-old stone structure with a towering steeple, sat atop a sweeping hill amid a historic cemetery, offering a view of the town's main street in front, an eternity of pumpkin and cornfields behind, woods and housing developments on either side. It required a good deal of upkeep, but with horrific tragedies assailing children in all corners of the globe, McGlazer just couldn't pull the trigger on using tithe money for church remodeling projects.

Something about the drafty old sanctuary felt sacred and comfortable, unlike flashier contemporary churches, with their expensive sound systems and plush carpeting. It had been a refuge, after all, to many generations of souls, and possibly, at least one spirit.

A flock of maple leaves blew around the sign and across the grounds, carrying a scent of inevitable decay that the minister did not find unpleasant.

"Reverend!" Ruth called from the sanctuary doors. "Telephone!"

McGlazer looked across the tombscape as he made his way inside, dipping into his pocket for … no longer a flask, thank you, Lord, but a candy or two from the bag he had left in his office that morning.

He followed Ruth through the sanctuary down the hall and into his office, glad to see that colorful bag of candy spilled on his desk.

On the phone was one of the parade's float builders with a question McGlazer couldn't remotely answer. "I have the fire chief coming after lunch," he deferred. "I'll have him call you."

"Something about the parade?" Ruth asked, tugging at her cleaning gloves. She had doffed her denim jacket. Her skirt and simple short-sleeved V-neck flattered her twenty-four-year-old body, a body that had seen its fair share of male attention, as well as abuse, before her recent conversion. Yet she remained undeniably alluring. A large gaudy gold cross adorned her chest.

"Yes, some float issue. How's everything?"

"I've almost finished the sanctuary." She looked him up and down, in that subtle way that always made McGlazer feel judged. "I can take care of in here next, if you like."

"Oh... no, that won't be necessary. I'll just mess it up again by tomorrow. You know how it is this time of year, with parade preparations."

"Yes." She pursed her lips, as if to show she was holding something back.

"Something on your mind, Ruth?"

She took a step forward, her eyes glittering with earnestness. "It's about the parade actually."

"Oh?"

"Dennis Barcroft's band is playing at The Grand Illusion this year."

"Yes."

McGlazer saw Dennis arrive outside the office door and stop upon hearing his name.

"Have you *heard* them?" Ruth made tight fists. "They glorify death and violence."

"Ruth," McGlazer began, "you do know that I'm just advising and recruiting volunteers? I'm not by any means in charge of the Pumpkin Parade."

"Yes, but... I just feel that you could have some influence on who is booked to play."

"I appreciate your concern. The reason I agreed to help with the Pumpkin Parade is that I believe it's a *good* thing, having a night that allows us all to blow off some steam. A little break from our normal lives. It unifies the community."

Ruth's eyebrows rose. "That Dennis Barcroft is a drunk, you know."

"*Ruth!*"

"And his girlfriend dresses like...some kind of"—Dennis entered quietly, right behind Ruth, smiling—"dead slut," Ruth finished.

"Morning, Ruth," Dennis said cheerily.

She jumped. "Oh God! You scared me."

"Hey, uh"—Dennis pointed at her crucifix—"Lord's name in vain, and all that."

She covered the shiny cross and breezed past him.

McGlazer grinned. "Come in, Dennis."

Dennis closed the door and took the chair across from him.

"How much of that did you hear?" McGlazer asked.

Dennis shrugged. "The juicy parts, I guess."

"You know about Ruth. She's a recent convert. A bit overzealous."

"It's cool." Dennis glanced at the candy. "Your pacifier is in full effect this time of year, eh?"

"Ruth threw out my cigarettes, God bless her." McGlazer raised an eyebrow as he tossed Dennis a candy. "So how are you doing?"

"Sober. That's something, I guess."

"It's a big something, Dennis. Any tough moments?"

Dennis gave an ironic chuckle. "Getting up in the morning. Before a gig. After a gig. Pretty much everything around that."

"I spoke to your mother. She was upbeat."

"Yeah. I'm okay, long as I remember I can't let her down. Her, Stuart, Petey. Jill."

McGlazer looked toward the door with a wry smile. "The..."

"Dead slut."

* * * *

Hudson had been sent out with Cabe Naples the night Arn and Beulah Bragg took their longstanding dispute over Beulah's spending habits out into Hewliss Street to air before God and the whole world—including young children who, outside of the crazy people on TV, had no precedent of grown-ups punching and clawing at each other.

Naples always puffed up like a bullfrog around Hudson, transparent in his efforts to out-alpha the larger rookie.

Naples's conversational tones skipped past "soothing" and jetted straight to "hostile" territory, and before Hudson knew it, Naples had forced poor, dazed Arn Bragg onto his stomach and was drawing cuffs. Like a snapping turtle, Beulah jumped to the defense of her husband/sparring partner, jumping onto Naples's back and dropping her fists like tiny harmless hammers onto Naples's meaty back. The senior officer threw her off, while cinching up on the restraint hold he had on Arn.

Hudson didn't have time to consider his next move. He tackled Naples off Arn, wrapping his arms around Naples's neck and behind his head while he hooked his legs over the senior officer's hips.

"You have to calm *down*," Hudson said quietly, almost soothingly. "You're gonna get us both fired. Or worse."

The onlookers were gathering closer, dismayed to see their tax-paid peace officers, their guardian *protectors*, at odds. Hudson realized this was both embarrassing and infuriating for Naples, who struggled in Hudson's grasp like a spooked calf.

"You've lost your mind!" Naples huffed, and then his hand went from Hudson's arm to his own side, and there came the distinct, chilling sound of Naples's weapon sliding from its nylon holster.

Hudson's instincts kicked in and he closed his forearms over Naples' carotids, cutting off Naples's blood supply while he rolled the tangle of their bodies onto Naples's gun side to pin the weapon—if it wasn't too late.

But it was. And Naples, as savvy as any big-city cop, switched hands with the weapon and now pointed it at Hudson's right leg with his left.

With a furious grunt, Hudson rolled a little farther and pinned Naples facedown, trapping his weapon, continuing to apply the choke.

Naples gurgled and went still.

Utter silence, as the people on Hewliss Street watched what must have been a surreal scene: Hudson rising and handcuffing his unconscious partner.

Needless to say, the ride back to the courthouse was a tense one.

In the end, Naples was allowed to resign and move to another jurisdiction, the incident attributed to confusion caused by circumstances in wild flux. The narrative did not remotely approach reality.

The chief acquired an ulcer and gin habit, while locals came to regard Hudson as some kind of brown angel: a man of great physical power and high moral conviction.

But Hudson didn't feel heroic as much as freakish.

He heard a familiar motor and felt a smile crack his officious expression. The Lincoln Mark VII he and son DeShaun had waxed just the previous afternoon now approached, driver's window descending to present a glorious smiling face. "Hi there, officer," cooed Leticia Lott. "How's your nightstick swinging?"

"Ah hell," Hudson lamented. "I didn't want you to see me out here doing this."

"Doing what?"

Hudson held out his hands to indicate "Nothing. Directing nonexistent traffic. Like a rookie." He pointed upward. "Some mischief-maker took out the most boring stoplight in town."

Leticia's brow furrowed at the stuffy term.

"You heard me."

"Well. Don't worry," she consoled. "You'll need all your strength anyway."

"Oh?" Hudson's eyebrow rose now. "Why's that?"

"Because I can't have my big man all worn out when I try on my new holiday-themed unmentionables for him tonight."

She teasingly dangled a bag logoed AMORE INTL from her perfectly manicured thumb and forefinger. She drove away, leaving Hudson with lifted spirits. Aware of activity at his crotch, he realized it was probably best to give the rigid stance a rest and keep his hands in his pockets for a minute or two.

Then came a murmuring from a pair of elderly power walkers in pastel sweats, stopping to gawk at something a block over, coming around the corner of Turner's Wedding Rentals.

It was a girl in her twenties, her reddened eyes as wide as fifty-cent coins, clothes torn, knees scraped. Stumbling toward him, she looked like an extra from a Romero film.

Peripherally, Hudson saw a car turn the corner of Turner's and accelerate toward the girl. He blasted into his whistle.

As the car screeched to a halt, Hudson watched the girl pitch forward. He ran toward her, keying the radio mic on his shoulder. "Dispatch! Need an ambulance at Second Street!"

A small mob of early shoppers and storekeepers poured out and gathered at safe distances. The driver stood halfway out of his car. "I didn't hit her, officer! Least, I'm pretty sure."

Hudson knelt to find the girl shivering, her eyes twitching madly. He recognized her—Belinda Pascal, track-and-field standout from the university. "Belinda? Are you injured?"

Dazed, Belinda did not seem to know. Hudson assessed the scene, remembering faces, conditions, searching for anything unusual. "Doesn't look like you did," he said, firmly addressing the driver. "But I need you to pull over. Gonna need a statement."

"Yes, sir."

The lanky Belinda exploded from her fetal position to become a feral human animal, shrieking, biting, and clawing at Hudson.

"Belinda! Calm down!" Her teeth clamped shut an inch from his restraining hand.

"You can't have my aortic valve!" Belinda shouted, her eyes rolling back in her head, lids blinking at machine gun speed.

Hudson turned her face away and bear-hugged her, pinning her arms to her side. Despite her small stature and his strength, her spasmodic movement made him feel she might break his grip at any second. She was far stronger than Naples had been.

She went still. "Is it really daytime?" she asked with a soft, ragged voice. "It's daytime, baby girl," he reassured. "Just stay still. Got help coming." In his arms, she trembled as her eyes darted all around.

The ambulance siren rose in the near distance.

"Things," Belinda muttered. "*Things...*"

"What?"

"There were...*things*, everywhere. All around. They... they were killing me." She nestled herself against his thick chest.

"What things, Belinda?"

"They were killing me." She didn't seem to have heard him. "A little piece at a time."

* * * *

Stella was too aware of her breathing, sure that it echoed throughout the sanctuary as she strode to the panel behind the pulpit platform and switched on the sanctuary lights. All of them.

She had asked, practically *begged* Ruth to leave them on after morning cleanings, but the young zealot, citing a sinful waste of church resources, always refused, sometimes adding a snippy remark about Stella's irrational fear of the dark reflecting a flawed walk with the Lord.

Approaching forty, Stella had a wholesome beauty that caught the eye subtly and grew more appealing with time, unlike the immediate "wow factor" of the younger Ruth. Their dispute over the lights might have seemed a quibble, but it amounted to much more for Stella. She was intrigued by spooky things. She loved this time of year when the prep for the Pumpkin Parade was at its peak, with the fun of festive frights in the atmosphere. It was the opposite pole of a long childhood period when she had been besieged by night terrors, a time that was easy to recall in pitch darkness.

But since becoming the church's pianist last February when Mrs. Mirschaw moved to some desert town for her rheumatism, Stella had experienced reminders of those youthful night terrors. She didn't remember when they started. Perhaps in her toddling years, when she had seen two large dogs fighting at the park.

Practicing walking with her parents and holding their hands, Stella was probably smiling all the while, until the man and dog—a very large mix of shepherd and chow—approached a little girl and boy with a juvenile Samoyed.

The fluffy pup lunged away from his young keepers and dashed to the hybrid playfully. But the older dog, perhaps poorly trained or going blind or simply in a bad mood, met the newcomer with snarling and gnashing, tearing at the Samoyed's neck and ears, ripping chunks of flesh away. The pup yelped, unseasoned in protecting itself or fighting that wasn't play.

Stella was abruptly hoisted by her father and turned away from the melee—but not in time to keep her from seeing fur and flesh torn, an eruption of blood, and terror on the faces of the little boy and girl.

After her father covered her eyes, she still heard the sounds of trauma, of rage and pain and terror both human and canine, sounds and sensations new to a baby girl.

NEWS FLASH, LITTLE GIRL! CUTE PUPPIES WILL HURT EACH OTHER!

An existential revelation for little Stella.

The night after the incident, Stella had her first nerve-jolting episode.

She recalled her parents running into her room and comforting her, not only on that night but countless following, their patience and sympathy decreasing with each episode.

Well into her preteen years, she had already survived an eternity of nights shivering under a heavy comforter as a cavalcade of imagined *sick things* dashed past her door, or peeked their pointy-eared, glow-eyed faces just around the door frame, surely to see if she was asleep—and vulnerable.

This became something even worse: a fear of abandonment. Nights spent rocking Stella had tested her parents to the breaking point it. They pored over parenting and home remedy books, desperation building as the terrors became an entity that leeched sleep from the household and drove a widening wedge between her parents.

Stella was given little placebos, trinkets to keep the monsters away. Her father, patiently at first, then tersely and tensely, toured the corners of her room with her, armed with a flashlight, uncovering nothing to fear each and every time.

Still, she found herself lying there, alternately squeezing her eyes shut and glancing to see if the child-eating evils of pure dark were gathering at the door—or halfway to her bed, perhaps extending claws...

A ten-year-old girl who still bore childish night terrors was just accustomed to the attention; the "overlove," it was concluded. Thus, continuing to grant it would only ruin her. Whether that was advice from her mother's growing stack of parenting books or an agreement between mother and father to leave her to the nightly ordeal was a question that Stella didn't really want answered.

By then, her parents didn't often argue—but they also didn't hug anymore, or smile. Or sometimes even talk. When they did, they used code words for separation, divorce, the end of her universe.

Then came a family meeting. Her father announced to Stella in a somber tone that she would be staying with her aunt Miriam for the first few weeks of summer, possibly longer.

* * * *

Stuart barely chewed, trying to finish his lunch in the face of DeShaun's assault. But DeShaun drew closer, determined. "Damn *cockroaches,* man. Like, a whole trash bag, just *full,* man, up to the top, and all shiny and glistening, as the funnel gets shoved into the guy's mouth, down his throat..."

Stuart did a good job of acting bored, just staring at the lunchroom walls. It helped that they were almost completely covered with posters and cutouts of cats, witches, floor-to-ceiling poster board trees with neon orange and yellow leaves.

"Then, on top of that, we add *pig guts,* all gooey and rotten..."

In an instant, Stuart no longer needed Zen concentration to no-sell DeShaun's nauseating litany. For a certain class arrived and separated into cliques, scattering about the lunchroom. All but Candace Geelens.

Carrying a cooler bag that she had decorated with sparkly flower stickers, she drifted off alone.

With her googly-eyed alien hood pulled back, her honey-chestnut locks flowed and bobbed like a mare's tail as she walked to a chair near the wall, several seats from a familiar gaggle of students, the big brains who dangled and displayed their grade point averages over the student body like slumlords.

Noisily shoving his chair back, Stuart popped up, startling DeShaun.

"Where are you going, dude?" asked DeShaun. "You *wanted* me to do this."

As Stuart put on his best cool, he detected via their furtive glances toward Candace a sense of nefarious scheming among the brain bullies.

The leader of these well-read rowdies, a gangly chap with a bowl cut named Albert Betzler, nudged his bespectacled neighbor Del, as he scooped a huge helping of mashed potatoes into his spoon, which he then aimed at Candace like a catapult, his finger hooked at the tip, and fired.

Stuart whipped his notebook into the line of fire, intercepting the missile. The mess spread over his crookedly applied Chalk Outlines sticker, and he glared a warning at the rowdies, who glared back with dorky defiance magnified by thick glasses.

Stuart wiped the mess from his notebook on the table's edge and took a seat beside Candace. "Hey."

She gave him a surprised look, unaware she had been the target of a spud bombing. "Um… hi there, Stuart."

Stuart said, "Hey," then repeated it a third time, with a smile. So much for cool.

But *she* smiled. And he melted.

"Can I do something for you?" she asked.

"Yeah." Stuart glanced toward the wall and spotted a sign from god. "Well…there's the uh…"

He motioned toward the poster. "Pumpkin Parade coming up."

"Yeah?"

"So…" Stuart began as rehearsed, "my brother sings and plays guitar for The Chalk Outlines."

Candace brightened. "Oh, I know! Kenny Killmore! He's so darky-dreamy!" She realized her gaffe. "Sorry. That was annoying I bet."

"His real name's Dennis, ya know."

"They're really good!"

"Yeah, well… I'll probably join the band after school. Like, literally this summer."

Candace had taken a bite of her rectangular lunchroom pizza, but now froze midchew. "Sherioushly?" She swallowed. "No fooling?"

Stuart acted casual.

Candace swallowed and leaned toward Stuart. "So. Why are you talking to me?"

"Huh? What do you mean by that?"

Candace picked at her food with her fork. "I just…" She blinked. "Nobody talks to me. So why would the brother of a rock star?"

Stuart thought of the aggro nerds, Albert and company, probably staring tombstones at his back and plotting some Rube Goldbergesque revenge even now.

"That's crazy! You're…" Stuart felt a small terror warn him not to come off too stalky. "What I was saying is, there's a record company exec coming to check out the band and my brother kinda needs me there, on stage keeping the gear tuned." This he had rehearsed. The next he hadn't. "And, well, he says I should bring a chick."

Excitement lit up her brown eyes. "Are you... asking me?"

Stuart shifted, glanced away. "Well, yeah."

Candace's smile bloomed as though she couldn't restrain it. Then, just as quickly, she grew gloomy.

"Jeez," Stuart scratched his head. "Didn't mean to ruin your day."

"No, it's... I don't know. I'll have to ask my dad, but..."

"But what?"

"We might have plans." It sounded false, but like she wanted Stuart to *know* it was false.

"The only plans anybody makes around here are for the parade."

Candace pushed away from the table, leaving her tray.

"Hey, wait, I didn't mean..." Stuart began.

"I'll let you know. Thank you for asking though. I mean it." She breezed away, leaving Stuart perplexed. He turned, meeting the virulent, far-sighted glower of Albert Betzler.

Chapter 3

On Gwendon Street, at the end of a stone walkway splitting the leaf-covered yard of a once-beautiful Victorian house, sat Dennis's hearse. With its spacious rear storage section, the customized funeral car doubled as The Chalk Outlines' official band vehicle.

A battered hatchback belonging to one Pedro "F.U." Fuentes, bassist and bona fide badass, was parked in front, a primered Indian motorcycle piloted by Outlines drummer "Thrill Kill" Jill Hawkins, in the back. Behind that was a BMW with a flamboyant sparkle-blue paint job, belonging to band manager Kerwin Stuyvesant, of giant teeth and tiny glasses fame.

Stuyvesant had recently inherited the house. Rather than have it brought up to code for sale, he volunteered it as rehearsal space.

Farm trucks and teen partiers traversing Gwendon en route to US 70 could often catch snippets of spirited spookabilly music coming from the drafty edifice. Some folks honked either friendly approval or vehement distaste. And some, regardless of their musical tastes, slowed to get an earful of the Outlines rehearsing, just so they might have a "brush with greatness" story, in case the band ever hit it big, as a growing number of Ember Hollow residents thought they might.

The high-ceilinged living room also served as storage space for instruments, equipment, and deliriously campy Halloween/horror stage décor.

Stuyvesant watched approvingly while the Outlines pounded out their club hit "Rumble in Frankenstein's Castle," in full performance mode.

"A man with eyes just like mine
Nephew of ol' Doc Frankenstein
Needs a lab rat, that'll be me
Bring back the ol' doc's legacy

When he does, gonna be a fight
Side by side, slabs and straps,
GO!"

Pedro, classic horror punker with devilock haircut, spiked sleeveless leather jacket, and naked devil chicks tattooed on his massive arms, strangled and banged his bass like it was one of the countless bullies he had humbled during his travels through the juvenile justice system.

Jill battered her drums with equal aplomb. With shocking white hair sporting black electric bolts on either side, skintight leopard-print pants hugging hips that had turned many a driver's head during her travels on the Indian, and a crimson baby-doll shirt with two pentacles that hugged her like a dying lover, Jill was no wallflower-background drummer.

Dennis, his shave-sided pompadour holding steady, issued his growly, wailing vocals and lead notes with absolute sincerity.

"Give my curse the hearse, Doc Frank
Or I swear to God you will die
And your pet monster will fry
It won't be a swell sight."

Kerwin applauded as they finished. "Solid, solid shit, cat daddies. Aaand cat *mama,* of course."

His rhetoric and attire, red-orange suit and gleaming black-and-white patent leather shoes, screamed fifties-era band manager, as seen on television. "Pedro, I'd love to see some more scowl. Maybe stick your tongue out now and then, like, you know, like you're showing the ladies your technique, if you catch my drift."

Pedro flipped him off with a black-nailed finger, as he pulled the pyramid-studded guitar strap over his head.

"Nice, that's real nice," Kerwin said. "What if your sweet Catholic grandmother saw that?"

"Good question! What if she saw me wiggling my tongue around like some square-ass Gene Simmons geezer?" he countered.

Kerwin turned to Dennis for support as the band leader toweled his sweaty hair. "Back me up here, Den Den. We need some more showmanship, am I right?"

As Jill came to Dennis's side for a black-lipped kiss, Kerwin addressed her as well. "No offense there, Jill, but some booty shorts and a spiked bra would do wonders. Don't be shy about"—he leaned in to almost whisper—"stuffing the puppies, you dig?"

She blew a huge bubble that concealed her face, and then sucked it in to reveal a bored expression.

"Or do that," Kerwin said.

"Trust me, Ker," Dennis said. "We bring the sting when it comes to showmanship." He turned to Pedro and Jill. "You ask me, we could be a knife edge tighter late in the set. We need to finish strong."

Kerwin snapped his fingers and pointed at Dennis. "Exactly my next point, baby. Leave 'em exhausted. Empty. Drainsville. Tomorrow, we'll do it ag—"

"Take ten, guys," Dennis interrupted. "Then let's hit it."

Jill sighed. "Denny. Give yourself a break, babe."

"Yeah, maybe she's right, Denny-o." Kerwin said. "I need you guys fresh on the day. Besides"—Kerwin pointed at his watch—"I got a thing."

"We'll be all right without you for a coupla tracks." Dennis plucked at his D string.

"Yeah, man. Go get your shoes polished," suggested Pedro.

Jill and Dennis chuckled when Kerwin took on a terrified expression, shooting a look down at his shoes.

"Wouldn't hurt you to show a little gratitude, Petey," Kerwin said.

Pedro got very close to Kerwin, a half-sneer forming on his face. "Tell you what. We get signed, I'll give you a great big soul kiss. Tongue and everything." He clapped Kerwin's shoulder, nearly knocking him down. "How's that?"

"How 'bout just a fruit basket and a God damned thank-you note?"

"All right, all right," Dennis refereed. "Comedy hour's over. Water up and let's go again."

Kerwin went to the door, giving the house a last-minute, worrisome scan. "Be sure and lock the joint. Right?"

Dennis gestured around at the ancient, battered, yet irreplaceable equipment, then back at Kerwin. "Really?"

"Right. And remember, the basement is strictly off-limits. Could be dangerous."

When Kerwin closed the door, Pedro did not allow even the time it would take for him to tromp down the porch stairs before exclaiming, "*Damn* but he is radio friendly."

"Top forty," agreed Jill. "Till doomsday."

"I'd say top five." Pedro turned to Dennis. "Dude, do we really need his slick ass?"

"He got us this rehearsal space." Dennis closed his eyes to listen as he plucked the D string again. "And the meeting with the suit. So, yeah, I'd say we need him."

A soft creaking noise chirred beneath their feet.

Jill raised a perfect black eyebrow. "You guys heard that, right?"

"Yeah. Spooky." Dennis turned from one to the other with a comically terrified expression. "Hey, Pedro, go check it out."

"Oh. Why sure, chief!" Pedro answered with faux earnestness. "Right after you go dig a grave."

The trio shared a chuckle.

* * * *

On Stella's first day of practice in the drafty sanctuary, with its high ancient arches, granite walls, and stained glasswork depicting the famous faithful as perhaps *too* mournful to be truly confident of paradise, a D note had played far from her fingers.

She furrowed her brow at the key, then plinked it twice to see if it was sticky. She opened the top and inspected the wires, finding nothing out of order.

She continued practice, and by the time she shut off the lights and left, she had forgotten the funny little incident.

In the days following, there were other portents. Shadows, inexplicable fogs, the ever-popular cold spots.

One day late in July, lit only by the overhead from the foyer, Stella was skimming through her notes when she heard a voice. In a whisper fed through the sanctuary speakers, someone commanded her to *"Run!"*

Stella inspected toward the pulpit area, sure that the good-natured McGlazer was playing some prank. No one was there, and the PA's power light was dead dark. Turned *off.*

Then her papers exploded in her face like rabid white bats, and the ethereal voice roared again, much louder. *"Run!"*

The reverberations pulsing in her ears, Stella abandoned her notes and bolted out the sanctuary door, never happier to find herself alone in a graveyard. She wished she could call her aunt Miriam.

She needed almost an hour and a half to compose herself well enough to go back into the church, and then it was through the gymnasium entrance, at the opposite side of the church compound. She briskly made her way to McGlazer's office off the hallway leading to the sanctuary, where she found Ruth complaining to the minister, as she often did. But this time it was about her.

"Well *there* you are," said the girl, raising the jumbled sheaf of Stella's notes. "You left a nice mess for me, didn't you? And the doors wide open too."

Stella just stared at her, at a loss as to how she could explain herself. Ruth had already been volunteering at the church for a few months when Stella accepted the pianist position, and Stella did not know her well. Her personality was, at best, off-putting. But Stella figured that if she, Stella, was having weird experiences, then surely Ruth must be as well.

"Are you all right, Stella?" McGlazer asked.

She was among spiritual believers. Surely her experience would not be outlandish to them, she thought, and told them about her odd experience.

How wrong she had been. "Are you suggesting our church, this holy place, has an evil spirit?" Ruth had scoffed.

"Evil?" Stella hadn't used that word.

"The Holy Spirit? Be serious, Stella," Ruth had rebuked. "The Holy Spirit most certainly would not show itself to only you. He lives in all of us who are saved."

"Just a second, Ruth," McGlazer interjected. "You feel you may have encountered some kind of presence?" McGlazer asked.

Stella was sure this was the end of her stint as Saint Saturn Unitarian's organist. However, McGlazer turned out to be remarkably open-minded, even fascinated by the topic.

He smiled, not mockingly but with a sense of wonder, as she related what she had seen and felt. "I envy you, my lady," he said, to Ruth's clear chagrin. "Please don't hesitate to tell me next time something happens!"

After this, he would occasionally creep into the sanctuary and sit listening during her practices. But the stray notes, the wisps of man-shaped fog and the frigid breezes became more pervasive with every practice. Could the spirit be "practicing" as well?

At home, she had twice broached the subject with Bernard. He was a sensible and articulate engineer, though she still remembered flights of fancy from early in their courtship: planned inventions and innovations. Having outgrown such impracticality, Bernard was not exactly the ideal confidant.

The first time she mentioned the strange incidents at the church was over dinner, framed as a throwaway half-joke. "I do believe we have ourselves a ghost in the church."

She passed him the turkey gravy as she said it. It was his favorite and he already had plenty, but it served as a prop to make her statement seem nonchalant.

"Mm-hm," Bernard had mumbled, mulling over a schematic beside his plate.

"Something sure is hitting some stray keys and whatnot," she continued, bolder. "Making it cold sometimes."

Bernard stopped chewing and raised his face. "Piano, playing by itself? Cold spots? You serious?"

Stella was pleased to see his earnest expression.

Then he said, "Cold spots, in a centuries-old stone structure. Yeah..." He took a bite, smiling. "You're pretty much self-taught on the piano, right, Stella?"

"My aunt gave me lessons when I stayed with her, Bernard."

"For a month." Bernard half-smiled.

"She said I was..."

"Possibly a prodigy," Bernard finished. "I remember. You told me maybe a thousand times."

Her face burning, she returned to her meal. Aunt Miriam's encouragement had been a sort of talisman to which she had clung against the threat of the night terrors, after the summer visit. Even now, she often replayed that gold nugget of encouragement when tackling any difficult task.

After a minute of silence Bernard had called to her. A rare apology?

He had his hand inside a napkin, forming a little puppet with finger-arms flapping at her, making it float toward her, while he issued a high pitched, "WOoooOOOOOoOOoo! Woo woo!"

At Robichaud Reads, the bookstore where she often purchased her paranormal romance books—something else she learned was best kept to herself—Stella found a book called *Communing with the Dead*, authored by one Onyx Darkwolf. Though she had doubts about such "new age" esoterica, she studied it and tried several methods to contact the church ghost, without success.

Then July came, bringing another spate of activity.

Even before entering the sanctuary, Stella heard the D key plinking, plinking, then sustaining with such boldness she thought Ruth or McGlazer must be doing it.

When she entered, there was no one. Yet the note continued.

And when she turned to leave the sanctuary, the door swung closed nearly on her face. The lock clicked.

Stella tugged at the knob, sure that the presence, whatever it was, was all around her, smothering. She cried for McGlazer, for Ruth, for *anyone* to come.

She had never been so happy to see Ruth. The girl, wearing her rubber cleaning gloves, opened the door from the other side and stood staring at Stella, annoyed. "What is all this hullabaloo?"

Stella gathered herself, feeling weak under those icy judging eyes. "Where is Reverend McGlazer?"

"He's in his study, working on Sunday's message." Ruth stepped in, eyes narrowed like a suspicious parent detecting marijuana. "What are you doing in here? All this screaming and banging on the door."

Stella had no answer. But her glance toward the piano was all Ruth needed. "Oh, for heaven's sake! Are you going on about your little evil spirit again?"

Ruth strode to the piano, taking the gold cross from around her neck and holding it out like a tiny sword. "Evil spirit of weakness and fear, I *rebuke ye* in the name of the Lord Jesus Christ! Ye are *cast out* from this holy place and *shall not* return!"

Ruth's delivery was bold and purposeful, more like that of a manic televangelist than the even-toned, rational McGlazer. She held her cross out to the piano, up toward the rafters, then thrust it at Stella herself. "Get thee *away* from this place and from Stella, that her walk may be pure!"

Ruth put the necklace back around her neck and returned to wherever she had been working—but not before a parting shot: "Maybe you could think on the words of those hymns you play. You might learn to live them."

Ruth never said whether she believed Stella about her ghost encounters or thought they were just silly fantasies, but it was clear that, to her, either problem had the same solution.

The rest of July, then August, September, and now October, Stella had not experienced a single errant note, slamming door, or even a fist-sized cold patch.

Whatever the reason, Ruth's impromptu exorcism had worked.

* * * *

After the clamor of the bell, a single perfect second passed before hundreds of costumed children erupted into the late-afternoon sun like water from a bursting dam. Stuart and DeShaun, way too cool for the spastic jailbreak bit, just walked. Stuart did scan the crowd though, craning his neck.

"I see you looking for Candace, Captain Obvious," DeShaun teased.

"Maybe."

"Maybe? Man, you're crushing on her like a steamroller. Do I need to make other plans for Devil's Night or what?"

"No, dude." Stuart continued to scan. "No way I would bail on that. It's a tradition. Our tradition."

Stuart and DeShaun found themselves surrounded on all sides by nerdy thugs.

Albert Betzler and his crew, a small army with thick glasses, assembled with the clumsy discipline of a Mensa alumnus flash mob, all the more absurd in Halloween costumes depicting various historic brainiacs.

"Well, well, *well,*" Albert sang, his cotton-ball Darwin beard bobbing, his rubber bald cap wrinkled and sliding high on his forehead. "If it isn't Ember Hollow's two finest examples of *paraplaneta brunea.*"

Albert's circle of nerds guffawed, while DeShaun and Stuart exchanged a look that was both perplexed and annoyed.

"Cockroaches, diphthong," contributed Albert's right-hand Del, dressed either as Albert Schweitzer or Kurt Vonnegut, possibly even Mark Twain.

"What are you two household pests doing?" Albert asked. "Celebrating your latest D minus in resource English?"

More sycophantic chuckling.

"What do you want, Albert?" Stuart huffed.

Albert pushed up his glasses. "I want you to stay away from my woman."

Stuart was too confounded to speak, prompting DeShaun to ask the first of two obvious questions. "Your woman?"

"Candace, if it's any of your business, George Washington *Carver.*"

Stuart asked the second. "If Candace is your 'woman,' why do I never see you two together?"

"Because she doesn't know it yet." Albert wagged his head as he answered. "I have a grand plan, see. And you're a misplaced circuit breaker in my schematic."

"Look, Albert, if you're going steady with Candace, cool. But I'm not seeing it. So until I do..."

"Not so fast, *Stupidert.*" Albert's chums chuckled like bespectacled hyenas at Albert's wordplay. He accepted their congratulatory pats. "Tell you what. I can be a sport. You let me complete my Venn diagram, if you can comprehend my analogy, and I'll relay her to you when I'm all finished."

Stuart bristled, and might have started swinging then and there if not for the sheer absurdity of it all. "The hell's *that* supposed to mean?"

"Everybody knows mentally unstable pubescent females are quite spectacular, carnally speaking. I happened to read in *Abnormal Psychology Digest* that they have a copulatory need like post-juvenile leporidae. And this *particular* future MIT laureate"—Albert yanked a thumb at his skinny chest—"is going to lose his virginity the right way. To a wild, chaotic, frankly *crazy* little vixen. Specifically, Candace."

Stuart had heard enough, absurd or not. He grabbed Albert's collar and lifted him off his heels. "Better watch your pie hole, Betzler."

"No, no, no, c'mon, man." DeShaun went to restrain him, peeling at Stuart's fingers.

But Albert was far from intimidated. "Like you, I think not, tough guy." He raised a sharpened metal protractor to Stuart's neck.

He and DeShaun glanced around and spotted similar weapons in the hands of the other nerds: ball bearing compasses, giant pencils sharpened to deadly points, an asthma inhaler poised like a can of mace. Albert gave an arrogant chuckle as Stuart released him.

"If that's not sufficient motivation for you..." Albert jerked a smirking glance to the concrete steps at the school's main entryway. Ember Hollow High's star jocks leaned against the wall there.

Bull-like Maynard, four-time MVP offensive lineman, whose sleeveless letter jacket exposed tree-trunk arms larger even than Pedro's. To his right, Tyrell, six-foot-eight power forward, terror of the school basketball team, suitably nicknamed Tyrellosaurus Rex. The monstrous athletes smirked at Stuart and DeShaun.

Maynard held out a football to show the boys the childish Magic-Markered cartoon of Stuart's face on it, captioned with the legend "Stewert."

Maynard punched it, deflating it with a loud pop and a gust of wind that blew his brown locks away from his Neolithic forehead.

Tyrell's turn. The giant, his grin framed by a Van Dyke that would have made Anton LaVey proud, held out his basketball in an overhand grip. A similar unflattering caricature of DeShaun was rendered on it. Tyrell squeezed his monstrous fingers together, forcing air out of the valve like it was a mere balloon. He scowled at Stuart and DeShaun, as Maynard handed him a water bottle.

He bit into it, ripping and chewing the clear, noisy plastic as water exploded from the bottle.

DeShaun and Stuart gaped in astonished terror.

"In case those chunks of gravel you roaches call brains haven't fired the appropriate synapses, I'll give you two guesses whose homework I'll be doing while I'm on the commode this evening."

The other nerds puffed out their bird chests and gathered closer, like a pride of spoiled housecats stalking a pair of escaped parakeets.

"DeShaun?" They all turned to see DeShaun's mom, Leticia, standing outside her car. "Is everything okay, boys?"

Albert stood on his toes between Stuart and DeShaun, putting his arms around them, smiling. "Yes, ma'am! These fine lads were just thanking me for tutoring them after class!"

"Okay..." Leticia gave a perplexed smile. "You boys ready to go?"

DeShaun and Stuart walked out from under Albert's scrawny arms.

"Nice chatting with you, gentlemen!" Albert called.

Stuart and DeShaun got into the car without a word.

* * * *

Candace sat alone on the noisy bus, hunched forward, holding her books on her lap. The books had been snatched away and tossed about the bus more times than she could count, and her tormentors had learned how to hide their actions from the bus driver, stunning Ember Hollow High senior Helga.

Candace would not run or cry out to Helga. She had long ago been taught not to call attention to herself or her family.

Still, her father always blamed her when he had to pay for the books.

She had to remain vigilant during the daily ordeal; there were always projectiles flying about, many targeted at her, such as the spitball that now just missed her left cheek.

She pulled the hood of her alien costume up and forward as far as possible. No matter how many times one of the wet little missiles struck her, it was never any less disgusting.

But for once Candace did not stew in the misery of the daily onslaught. She was joyfully distracted. Today, she carried a tingly anticipation.

Stuart, the sweet rocker kid, super cute with his longish hair—yet also both kind and endearingly self-conscious—had not only spoken to her— *her,* perpetual new (weird) kid Candace Geelens—he had asked her on a date of sorts. She had been pranked before by "admirers," but something about Stuart's lively hazel eyes promised sincerity.

The swirling thoughts of meeting his brother, Kenny Killmore, aka Dennis, and the other Chalk Outlines, of maybe even sharing some easy laughter and normalcy, made it hard to stay on guard.

Even two seats up, her distraction was like the scent of easy prey to Anthony Hoke, a puffy twelve-year-old in a plastic gladiator chest piece, and his sidekick/seatmate Ronnie Crupes.

Sneering, Anthony swiveled to regard her just after Eddie Zarzicki, wearing a black vinyl biker's vest bearing a flame-lettered The Vultures! back patch, whispered something in Anthony's grimy ear.

Anthony, his plastic helmet creeping to one side, gawked at her, his gaze sliding from her bobbing antennae to her developing breasts.

Candace drew her books against her chest.

"What are you supposed to be?" asked Anthony with a derisive chuckle. "A big green dildo?"

Other bus brats guffawed. Ronnie made an obscene gesture for his and Anthony's captive audience. Candace resisted the need to lower her head, knowing all too well the price of showing weakness to emotional predators.

Helga looked back at the uproar, wondering if this would be one of those days when she had to pull the bus over and tear new ones into the rude little shits who regularly tormented the odd little girl named Candace.

Before she could see what was happening, a robust horn sounded, snatching her attention. Outside her window a red 1982 Trans Am revved like an angry bull.

On it sat Ryan, handsome and chunky like Marlon Brando, bad boy enough to keep things interesting, yet never in any real *trouble* beyond mischief typical of a bored small-town boy.

Riding shotgun was his pal Angus, somehow both alarmingly scrawny and irresistibly cute with his frost-tipped hair and tasteful gold necklaces, courtesy of his father's jewelry store on Main Street.

Ryan leaned way over Angus. "Hey, hey, Helga!"

"Ryan!" she called back. "You're on the wrong side!"

"Long as I'm on your good side, baby!"

Helga slowed the bus, scared-exhilarated by her boyfriend's reckless driving.

"We going to the lake for Devil's Night?"

"If you'll get over to your side of the road... *yes!*"

She verged on giddy panic as a sharp curve grew nearer. With a hearty "WHOOOOOOOOO!" Ryan hit the gas and passed the bus like it was parked, thrusting his left arm up to wave goodbye.

Helga remembered the uproar from the guts of the bus.

Candace's tormentors, made bold by Helga's distraction, were taking turns pelting her with erasers and wads of paper, like dastardly cattle rustlers gunning down the righteous marshal in a spaghetti western. They called mean names that coalesced into a chant. "Cra-*zy* Can-*dace*! Cra-*zy* Can-*dace*!"

It grew louder with each repetition, as Candace shrank into her seat, disappearing from Helga's view.

As the chant died down, Anthony started another, until the chorus grew louder than before. "Freaky dildo girl! Freaky dildo girl!"

Helga's cheeks warmed like hot plates. In her distraction, she had failed Candace, who of all her young passengers, was the one who needed her most. Helga was angry with herself—but it was a certain handful of obnoxious brats who would pay.

She hit the brakes hard and fast enough to make them crush atop one another. Then she pulled off onto a tractor road, yanked the E brake for the emphasis of its angry grind, and tromped back to them, fury burning in her blue eyes. "Knock it *off,* you little rats! I told you what would happen if you didn't stop picking on Candace!"

She singled out Anthony with her stare, satisfied to see a shamed expression and a bead of sweat forming at his hairline. "Don't you even *try* to step foot on my bus tomorrow morning, you hear me?"

The scorned mockers gave sheepish acknowledgements.

"I'll see every one of you creepos in the principal's office first thing in the morning. With your parents!"

Of all the shame in all the little faces, none was deeper or more abiding than Candace's.

"Candace, honey, come sit up behind me."

Candace was reluctant.

"Come on," Helga insisted. "I want to talk to you."

In solemn silence, Candace rose. Helga shot another beam of ice-blue condemnation at the transgressors, then led Candace to the seat behind and to the right of the hers.

The students remained corpse-still as the bus moved again. "Candace, sweetie, I want you to know something." Helga's inner voice was as angry as her outer voice was kind, screaming to never again drop her vigilance for the little girl. "All of this, it seems so important now," she told Candace. "But it's not. Okay?"

Sensitive as she was, Candace still bore a dignity and an inner strength that Helga recognized as that of a seasoned survivor.

"Three years ago, I was riding this same bus, on this same crappy route." She turned to show Candace her grimace. "And you know what? The brothers and sisters of these same little buttheads picked on me every day. Because of my red hair."

"Seriously?"

"Yes, ma'am." Helga said. "You think anybody makes fun of me now?"

"No! Every boy at school says you're the most beautiful girl in town! Maybe the whole state!"

"Well, you know what? I think that's nice. But I remember when they made fun of me. The only difference is a couple of years. And I put it all in perspective. I think your costume is great. And I'll bet there's somebody out there who likes you. 'Cause you're already way prettier than I was!"

Candace was paralyzed in disbelief. Helga only smiled. "Go to the school library and check me out in some yearbooks."

Candace began to relax.

The bus remained church-somber until Helga pulled to a stop at Candace's driveway. "Bye-bye, sweetie. Remember, okay"

Candace stood and headed up the aisle. "Thank you, Miss Helga."

"Anytime."

Chapter 4

As Candace exited the bus, her steps echoed on the metal stairs. She brushed at her hair out of habit, to dislodge spit wads. Glum faces of her chastened tormentors regarded her from the bus windows. Anthony Hoke raised a quick middle finger.

The school bus rumbled away. She stared down the long gravel driveway to a plain single-story rental house. The panel truck that had sat hidden under a tarp at the edge of the backyard for the past year was now parked at the back door, the sliding rear door open.

But it was the small cinderblock shed squatting in the shade of a towering oak tree, low orange light glowing from its barred windows, that held Candace's attention the longest.

* * * *

Candace went inside, huffing at all the scattered moving boxes taped and stacked on plastic-covered furniture.

"Candace?" Her mother appeared in the hallway from the master bedroom.

Mamalee Geelens, a wild-eyed, pleasantly paunchy fifty-five-year old with a light Dutch accent, offered Candace the smile that always seemed forced. "Good afternoon, baby! How was school today?"

"Well, it was, uh…" Candace met her mother's circus clown expression. "I want to talk about something."

"Over dinner!" exclaimed Mamalee. "We have so much to do!"

As Mamalee returned to the room, Candace's father, Aloysius Geelens, appeared from another. "Candace. Have you packed?"

"No, Father."

"No?" His tone, never patient, had taken an even sterner edge over the last week. "Do you think you're staying behind?"

"No, Father."

"Go and feed your brother." He spared her only the barest glance, as he tugged the rope to pull down the attic ladder.

Candace hugged her books against her chest as she had on the bus, regarding her father as he took a step up the ladder. "Father?"

Aloysius Geelens stepped back down, pointedly dropping his gaze to her. "What?

"I have been asked to...go somewhere."

Before he could respond, Mamalee emerged again from the bedroom, her ever-present smile stretched to near-demented proportions. "You've made friends, Candace?"

"Yes."

"An outing?" Mamalee put her hand on Aloysius's shoulder. "With a boy?"

"Yes, Mama."

"What kind of outing?" Her father's tone did not offer promise.

"The Halloween Pumpkin Parade."

"No. You're needed here."

He turned to climb the ladder but Mamalee stopped him. "Aloysius! Why do we need her here? If she can get packed in time, she should go!"

"No. We won't have time for play."

"Oh, Aloy." Mamalee's expression had taken a rare and heartbreaking tone of bleakness. "Don't you want at least one normal child?"

Aloysius struck her across the cheek, drawing a yelp.

Candace heard herself gasp as her mother crumbled. Aloysius looked down at his wife with shock. He glanced at his hand, then at Mamalee.

As Mamalee struggled to stand, Aloysius was quick to help her. Mamalee said nervously, "Oh, it's so *exciting* around here these days!"

Aloysius turned to Candace. "You will tell me more over dinner. And I'll consider it. *If* you finish your packing first."

Mamalee repeated her nervous chuckle.

"Now, go and feed your brother," Aloysius ordered. "And take Bravo with you. Everett is very excited today."

Mamalee waved at Candace like a toddler.

Chapter 5

Candace went to Everett's dinner tray and thought of Mamalee's daily ritual of dotingly preparing it, accenting it with loving little details that so delighted him, such as the cute smiling ghost faces she had Magic Marker-ed on the napkin covering the dish, humming to herself all the while. The tray was the lightweight plastic kind meant to be disposable—and harmless.

Candace took the tray and backed through the kitchen door into the backyard. "Bravo!" she called, whistling. "Here, boy!"

The huge black mastiff crawled from his corrugated doghouse and trotted to her, panting, wearing a slobbery smile reserved only for her.

"We gotta go see Everett."

Bravo whimpered a little but stayed at her side as she walked to the orange-windowed shed.

She set the tray on the shelf built onto the side of the steel door and drew the key to the massive padlock. She goaded the reluctant Bravo in first and entered with the tray into a narrow foyer, a partition built between the padlocked door and the main room of the shed that was Everett's room/home.

Muffled music—Terry Teene singing "Curse of the Hearse"—emanated from the crack under the inner door.

Candace breathed resolve, looking to Bravo. He met her gaze with ears held low.

"Everett? It's Candace. I brought your dinner."

Shadows shifted under the door. Bravo growled. Candace patted his head. "It's okay, boy." Then she addressed Everett with her bravest voice. "I have Bravo with me, so... be careful, okay?"

The door opened outward, forcing Candace to step back in the crowded space. She put her hand on Bravo, feeling his hackles rise.

Silhouetted by the dim orange light, Everett stood in his strange stance, his fright wig framing a pale face.

Candace held out the tray, gripping to still her shaking hands. "H-here..."

Everett ignored the tray and stared down at Bravo, chuckling at the dog's warning growl.

"Okay," Candace redirected. "Here it is, Everett."

Everett remained focused on Bravo, kneeling to eye level with him. The dog backed away till he met the wall, then gave an uncertain bark and a half-hearted warning snap.

Everett seemed to measure the dog's sincerity, scooting forward an inch or so.

"Everett. Please. It's only a little bit longer now."

Everett reached for Bravo, who snapped at his hand again, more aggressively, drawing a startled squeal from Candace.

But Everett did not withdraw, did not react at all, except to shuffle toward them another harrowing inch, forcing Bravo to scrunch himself behind Candace.

Everett chuckled, apparently satisfied. He stood, and Candace realized that he towered over her. An adolescent growth spurt had been good to him.

Everett's hands moved, making Candace yelp. But it was only to take the tray.

Everett stared at her, his eyes piercing even in the darkness.

Candace backed away and put a hand on Bravo. "Okay, then. Go... back in... your spooky haunted house now, and... we'll leave."

Everett didn't move. Unnerving titters escaped him.

"Please, Everett."

Everett backed into his room, letting the door creak as it eased shut.

Candace breathed relief, and Bravo whimpered. "I know, boy."

* * * *

Excerpted from Communing with the Dead *by Onyx Darkwolf, with permission from the publisher:*

Section 4: Attachments

The emotional body, and sometimes the analytical body as well, can choose to remain earthbound or even to return to some significant location from their corporeal existence, if there is a sense of urgency or unfinished business. But the location must have such resonance that it is or was a great part of the prepassing phase.

A spirit can seem to be inactive for years or even decades, perhaps longer—if they were accomplishing tasks in other lives or were driven to right some karmic wrong elsewhere before they could exit the cycle and pass on to The Greater Plains.

Some remain in The Inbetween simply because they are afraid of what is beyond. But there are cases in which a spirit being has been blocked from returning by a charged talisman or the specific ritualistic actions of a shaman, saint, or devotee.

In at least four cases, I have encountered spirits who either remained in or frequently visited homes where they had lived for many years, causing consternation for current residents. Some spirits choose to visit the grounds where their body is interred, and in some cases, the spirit's grave serves as the entry point from The Inbetween.

Most such spirits will continue to seek entry into our world, but attempting to communicate with a particular entity who has been blocked is difficult, if not impossible. Even more difficult would be determining and removing the source of the blockage. However, should this be accomplished, the spirit could potentially return with such power that its effects on the material world, having accumulated, would be far beyond normal.

Stella reread the four paragraphs. Though she had experienced telltale signs of a haunting, the new-agey text made her skeptical. It didn't help that her husband could leave his football game any minute, walk into the bedroom, and ask what she was reading.

The last paragraph certainly could apply. She had felt the presence growing stronger as she gave it her fear, and only after Ruth's bold banishment prayer had the activity ended.

Scared as she had been, and often still was, of being alone in the sanctuary, she also felt like she had robbed herself of a meaningful experience. She thought of her summer with Aunt Miriam, of learning to dowse, and how her aunt matter-of-factly spoke of the dead as if they moved and thought and acted still.

With Halloween looming, the topic of ghosts and the spirit world was at the fore, even if mostly in whimsy (except in Ruth's case). Stella was a bit sorry that she had lost a chance to satisfy a long-standing curiosity about the afterlife—and to face her childhood fears as a woman.

Still, Ruth's little exorcism show hadn't seemed like much. Could it really be that was all it took to send the spirit away or block it?

McGlazer was the closest thing to a "shaman" this side of the Cherokee reservation two counties away. Could it be that he had taken some action against the spirit?

* * * *

Homemade pumpkin pies sat at the center of three Ember Hollow family tables.

In the Lott household, where a dash more nutmeg than the recipe called for was the unanimous preference, an elegant candlelit setting with polished silver, crisp white tablecloth, and understated autumnal accents greeted Deputy Hudson, wife Leticia, son DeShaun, and two-year-old daughter Wanda.

Hudson, still in uniform, rubbed his weary eyes as DeShaun took a seat between him and little Wanda. "You wash your hands?" he asked DeShaun.

"Nope." DeShaun rubbed his hands on Hudson's cheek and got the reaction he wanted: his mother's shrill cry of "Not at the table!"

Hudson bowed his head for grace but couldn't resist keeping his eyes open to watch Wanda try to interlace her stubby fingers in emulation of her mother. "Dear Lord, thank you for this nourishment. And…please be with Belinda Pascal; see her through this time of difficulty."

This finished, DeShaun set to spoon-feeding his sister the green mush in her little plastic jack-o'-lantern-shaped bowl. "Whaddup with Belinda Pascal, Dad?"

Hudson glared at DeShaun like he had just uttered the vilest of obscenities. "*SSS!*"

DeShaun was confused.

"What'*sss*!" Hudson emphasized. "What *ISSS* up! She's at home, resting."

"Belinda Pascal's too hot to be all messed up like that."

Leticia withered him with what he called "the ol' miffed Mom eyes." "Your *butt's* gonna be too hot!"

"What did I say?" DeShaun asked.

"My baby boy's too young to talk like that!" she answered.

Hudson returned to DeShaun's query about Belinda Pascal. "I don't exactly know. She's always been clean as a whistle. Said she didn't do anything different." He went on to describe the disturbing incident at the traffic light.

"What do you mean, she saw monsters?" asked Leticia.

"She said devils and monsters had been chasing her the whole night. Jumping out of the shadows. Popping out and scaring the hell out of her. *Toying* with her. She thought *I* was one for a minute there."

Leticia put her hand to her heart, alarmed, and Wanda imitated.

* * * *

Closer to town on Midway, in an older but equally well-kept home, well-used dinnerware surrounded the pie on the scuffed mahogany table of the Barcroft family. Their dining room was decorated with cheap and well-used Halloween party decorations. The pie was smothered in whipped cream from the can, just like Pedro liked it, for Dennis's bandmates had come to dinner, per Ma's standing invitation.

Jill's hair was pulled back and she wore an unzipped black hoodie over her The Slits T-shirt. Pedro had taken the trouble of combing his devilock neatly to the side and donning a button-down shirt that threatened to tear at the seams of the shoulders. "Thanks for having us over, Mrs. B," he said, as he squeezed his bulky frame in against Stuart.

"Well you're always welcome, Pedro! Now who wants to say grace?"

"*Ma!* We're punks!" Since turning thirteen, Stuart protested everything normal or familial.

Dennis cocked his chin at Stuart. "Dude, we say grace every night."

Pedro swatted the back of Stuart's head. "Yeah, buzzkill." Pedro caught Ma's nod and began the grace. "Bless this food and this family and our band, heavenly God, and if it's cool, let us get signed this weekend."

Dennis opened one eye to see Stuart sitting with his cheek on his fist, glancing around in boredom.

"And how about don't let that crummy sucker-in-a-three piece, Kerwin, screw this up for us," Pedro continued.

Dennis discreetly gave Stuart the finger, drawing an elbow to the ribs from Jill.

The second Pedro finished, Jill looked at Stuart. "Hey," she said and kicked him under the table, a smile curling at the corners of her black lips. "Heard you got a lady friend."

Pedro turned to him like a curious cartoon bulldog, while Stuart shot a reproachful stare at Dennis.

"Stuart!" squealed Ma. "That's wonderful news!"

"Yeah." Stuart realized it was pointless to resist. "Maybe."

"Maybe?" Dennis asked. "I thought the parade invite sealed the deal."

"First, looks like I gotta deal with somebody else," Stuart explained.

"*What?*" Pedro washed down his mouthful with a slosh of milk. "An interloper?"

Jill leaned toward him, enthralled. "A rival for her affections?"

A half-smile formed on Dennis's face. "There's a song here."

Stuart stabbed at his potatoes with his fork. "Just some square. I can deal with it. No biggie."

Pedro nudged him with an elbow. "You need me to bop this lame-o for ya, little bro?"

"No bopping!" Ma commanded.

Dennis's expression grew serious, almost morose. He narrowed his eyes at Stuart but spoke to his mother. "Don't you worry, Ma. No bopping. He'll take care of it like a smart guy. Like a guy with a future."

Stuart tucked into his food, embarrassed by his big brother's tough love. Jill smiled at him while Pedro stole his dinner roll right from under his face.

* * * *

Farther from town, Candace and family—minus Everett, of course—ate from paper plates on a cramped folding table surrounded by half-filled boxes, a roll of paper towels in place of napkins, the pie a bakery special from the grocer.

As Aloysius took his seat at the table, Mamalee beamed her permasmile to Candace. "And what do we say, young lady?"

Candace turned to address her father—but in rote manner. "Thank you for our food and home, Father." She allowed a pointed pause before finishing. "Homes."

Both parents gave her a reproachful scowl.

Taking a bite, Candace kept a wary eye on her parents as they engaged in the most forced of small talk.

"Is the attic coming along, dear?" Mamalee asked Aloysius.

"Don't go up there," Aloysius said. "The floor is flimsy." He wiped his mouth and asked, "How was Everett?"

"A little scary, Father."

Mamalee tittered. "What does the TV always say? 'Duh!'"

"He's not afraid of Bravo anymore," Candace stated.

Her parents stopped chewing and cutting.

"I think Bravo is afraid of him now." The mastiff whimpered at her side.

Aloysius's frown was deeper than usual. "Perhaps this will be the last time. This time, it will be done. He'll have it out of his system."

"No, Father." Candace's tone was only matter-of-fact.

Her father bristled as if at a challenge. "What?"

"No," Candace repeated. "It will *never* be out of him."

"Candace!" Mamalee interjected. "You don't know!"

Aloysius pounded the table, startling them. "You will *not* disrespect me!"

Candace had the courage of conviction though, having witnessed Everett's behavior just an hour previous. "It's true though, Father! He will always be this way! And he's getting worse!"

Aloysius stood, the rage of denial painting his weathered features. *"No!"*

Mamalee rose to calm her husband with jittery pats on his arm. "Aloy, it's all right! It's all right. We'll get through this one and then we'll figure it out! Like we always do."

Aloysius sat and returned to eating.

Candace summoned her courage. "I guess it's pointless to ask about the parade."

More silence. Mamalee placed her still-shaking hand on Aloysius's. He cast a brief glance toward Candace, mumbling, "You may go."

Candace was stunned.

"You won't see your friends here again," Aloysius said. "You might as well have a chance to say goodbye this time."

Mamalee's happy mask somehow seemed genuine.

Candace stood and hugged her father, and he even patted her arm. "I will go pack right now, Father!"

She dashed away, her young heart singing.

Chapter 6

It was never clear what the catalyst was. Perhaps a doctor's recommendation, or a marriage counselor's. Perhaps Aunt Miriam herself.

The drive was less than two hours, yet to little Stella, it was a cross-country journey ending in permanent fundamental change. For all she knew, her parents had conspired with the strange relative to rid themselves of Stella by selling her into slavery.

They arrived at a cottage centered on an acre of rolling hills, much like Saint Saturn Unitarian, where neighbors were within view, if not earshot.

Aunt Miriam emerged. Even though it was June, she wore a flowing shawl. It smelled of delicious cooking and fragrant herbs. After an introductory hug, Stella held it to her cheek and announced, "I like this."

"Then we'll just have to make one for you!" Miriam declared, wrapping the shawl around herself and Stella in an affectionate gesture.

Miriam's smiles and scents put Stella at ease. When her parents left, she no longer felt it was the end of all she knew. In fact, it didn't feel like any kind of end at all, but a very important beginning.

Entering the kitchen, Stella saw that Miriam had things cooking, sweet things as it happened. "I haven't seen you since you were a baby! Now I will just have to spoil you!"

Stella giggled, and Aunt Miriam held up a playful hand. "No, ma'am! I'll have no argument about it!"

That was when Miriam handed Stella a handmade floral apron and said, "I've needed a helper for a long time!"

During kitchen duties, Stella stood beside her aunt at the counter, handing her things and answering questions about her life that Miriam asked like it was the most crucial information this side of the Pentagon.

A warm thing encircled her ankles, and Stella met Miriam's cat friend, Sneezy, who slept with Stella that very night, after Aunt Miriam hugged and sang to her and then whispered something Stella couldn't understand but that Miriam said would protect her. In the corner of her bedroom a candle burned, smelling of honeysuckle.

That night her sleep mostly felt like rest. Oh, she had bad dreams, but not nerve-shredding visions of bloody mayhem. And she also had dreams that were just normal. Not as bucolic and serene as Miriam's house during waking hours, not the first night. But they weren't scary or tense either.

Stella learned how to cook amazing dishes and they *did* make her that shawl, just like Aunt Miriam's. Aunt Miriam had a piano that she played every few days, and she gave Stella a few lessons, telling her she had a knack for it and could probably play professionally!

And there was something else very cool.

Aunt Miriam's neighbor Tom Dover came over in his old Scout truck, leading a worried-looking man named Reb. They had on identical-brand overalls, which was kind of funny. Stella was sure they hadn't planned to match. An imagined conversation between the oldsters planning their outfits together amused Stella as she rode in the back of the truck while Miriam squeezed between the two men and they took a rambling drive to Reb's place—something about the well going dry—that gave Stella an unforgettable IMAX view of a beautiful countryside even more rural than Ember Hollow.

Reb's was a true farm, with a smelly old pigpen. The pigs were scary at first, but then Stella saw Miriam, unconcerned with the stench, go up and talk to them, and she saw how they only responded with dumb gazes and lazy ear flicks.

They all crowded into Reb's pump house, where Reb flicked his fingers on a little gauge and shook his head like a doctor giving up on a patient, to show something or other about the pump.

Aunt Miriam walked to an apple tree out front of Reb's house and selected a thin limb, borrowing Tom Dover's pocket knife to cut and trim it to a neat *Y* shape. "Let's have Stella try it first," suggested Miriam. "That okay?"

Reb was doubtful. "What if it don't work?"

"Then I'll just do it," answered Miriam with a smile. "But I think she has it too."

"Has what?" Stella asked.

The farmers waited for an answer that came out sounding mundane. "The ability to find water."

Aunt Miriam got behind Stella and showed her how to hold the divining rod. "When you get close, the front part will pull. You'll feel it."

Stella spun to her, a little alarmed. "What makes it do that? Spirits?"

"It's not just the spirits, sweetie," Aunt Miriam said. "You have to help them."

Right then, Stella realized that spirits weren't just evil entities waiting to haunt or bedevil the lucky living, but rather *people* that sometimes moved among the living, helping or hindering depending on their own circumstances, just like flesh-and-blood folk.

Aunt Miriam gave Stella a gentle shove to start her walking. She stared at the pale stick, hoping this wouldn't somehow trigger her night terrors again.

In just a few seconds, she felt a light tingling in her hands as the tip of the branch rose. She felt it pull to the left. As she obeyed the pull, she became exhilarated, giving Aunt Miriam an excited smile, feeling like she was working with something greater than herself to do a good deed.

Thirty feet beyond the well house, the stick pointed straight down and refused to be moved. Stella was breathless as Miriam took the rod and hugged her. "There's your new spring, Reb."

Reb gave Aunt Miriam a roll of bills, most of which Miriam gave to Stella, and Tom Dover drove them home.

No terrors came to her that night, and life became normal for Stella—except that she knew something most people don't.

The next day, Aunt Miriam called her parents, and they came to get her, relieved, perplexed, more at ease than Stella had seen them in a long time. Stella told them about all the cool things she had learned over the three months she had spent there, including the dowsing.

Stella no longer experienced night terrors—but she also never saw Aunt Miriam again, not even at her funeral. When Stella was sixteen, her mother told her that the spirit world was nonsense, and Aunt Miriam was probably crazy. It was just best not to see her again.

After that, Stella didn't pursue spiritual experiences, except in church—yet another trigger for eye rolling from her parents. At least their marriage had healed, and she still harbored a healthy interest in the supernatural, often reading books about the topic, alongside paranormal romances, and oh, God, don't tell Ruth!—ghost erotica.

These days, Stella slept through the night. Her alarm barely woke her, and when her husband, Bernard, went to rouse her, it required some effort on his part, something about which he often joked. It was as if she were making up for all those years of restless sleep.

* * * *

Stuart absently outlined the lightning-spouting guitar drawn on the back of his composition book as Mrs. Steinborn paced her usual route, two steps down each aisle between desks, then two in front of the blackboard, of which she made liberal use.

A sense of excitement buzzed around school, fueled by early release and holiday fever.

Every year, Mrs. Steinborn ended the unit on Ember Hollow history with its most interesting facts and myths on the day when they were most meaningful. "They arrived midsummer and formed our little town. One day, scouts brought back a variety of robust foods—pumpkin seeds, mushrooms, corn—they had acquired from a band of Cherokee they encountered."

She drew a plump pumpkin with a curly stem. "These bloomed in the fall, and it is said that Bennington, remembering his native country's tradition of making lanterns from carved-out turnips with an ember placed inside, took to doing the same with these strange new fruits, giving us both our town name and the modern tradition of jack-o'-lanterns."

Stuart knew a good bit of Ember Hollow history. His father had sometimes related town legends to him at bedtime, when the story well ran dry. Discussing these in class brought back memories, bittersweet, strangely energizing.

Amid distracted, fidgeting bodies, a prim hand rose.

"Yes, Kelly?"

"Is it true that Wilcott Bennington worshiped demons?" Kelly asked.

Mrs. Steinborn held up her own hand to quiet a smattering of condescending titters, then went to her desk to refer to a memo from that very morning. "Before we delve too far into that, I'm obliged to preface with a disclaimer."

The day after the unit began, an anonymous parent had called to complain about, as the parent called it, the "glorification of heathen rituals."

Kelly's parents were of the southern fundamentalist variety, almost as fanatical as Ruth. They traveled to the next county for Sunday services, rather than expose themselves to McGlazer's liberal philosophy at Saint Saturn Universalist. Teachers often found themselves stumbling around her questions, which invariably led back to the Bible. Regarding the complaining parent, it wasn't hard to connect the dots.

"Who knows what 'disclaimer' means?"

"Neither you nor the school system approve, agree with, or encourage the actions described," Albert Betzler pronounced. "Strictly educational purposes, blah blah."

"Albert, we still raise our hands and wait to be called on," said Mrs. Steinborn.

"Should go without saying," Albert continued, casting a sarcastic face at Kelly that was not unlike Mrs. Steinborn's.

"He talked to the dead, I hear," mumbled Fergus Rhew.

The teacher cleared her throat, faced the chalkboard. "Much of the following has been dismissed as urban legend and exaggeration."

She wrote the words "Circa 1660" on the board in a flowing script that would have been quite at home on any preprinting press document. "Around 1660, Wilcott Bennington, an Irishman who had amassed a reasonable fortune with his import-export firms in Virginia, met a tracker who expressed high regard for the flatlands of a colony then called Carolina. Bennington was under a cloud of suspicion at the time, for a conversation he'd had in a pub, about his religious beliefs."

Kelly's hand shot up.

"Yes, Kelly?"

"He was a heathen?"

"The man we know as our town father built the town's first church, which still stands," Mrs. Steinborn said. "But before that, who can tell us how he wound up here?"

"By boat?" Fergus Rhew said, getting a round of laughter he didn't expect, playing it off like he did.

"The man to whom Bennington spoke in that Virginia pub went to his priest and claimed Bennington stated that he not only believed in the gods of the Roman pantheon but further asserted that Christianity was largely false."

"So, he was a Satanist."

"We raise our hands, Kelly. Bennington denied it and accused his accuser of slander. It was Bennington's word against the other man's."

Mrs. Steinborn drew a tankard on the chalkboard, spilling over with froth, held by a beefy cartoon drunk with crossed eyes and bubbles rising from his head. Despite the detail, it took only a couple of seconds, and drew buoyant chuckles. "In spite of this and Bennington's stature, he was sure he was under suspicion and scrutiny. His tracker acquaintance had already planted a seed in his mind about the pristine Carolina wilderness."

She speed-drew a pine tree and a chubby squirrel. "Bennington recruited families from the employees of his businesses, swearing them to silence, giving the reason of not wanting hordes of unsavory settlers saturating what he hailed as God's own country."

Kelly's hand again. Mrs. Steinborn ignored it.

"Then came the harsh winter no one could have expected. As food supplies dwindled, panic rose and prayers went unanswered, Bennington called the townspeople together at the church-schoolhouse and made a momentous announcement.

"He dumped out a bag of dried pumpkin seeds and bade the villagers eat their fill—which they did. He proclaimed that he had plenty of food to last the rest of the winter and then some, and he was happy to share, as long as everyone agreed to follow him without question."

She sketched a document, furled at top and bottom, a feather quill beside it. "They all signed a pledge, and then followed Bennington to a field in the woods behind his home. There, they beheld hundreds of ripe, hearty pumpkins."

Kelly nearly leaped out of her desk, waving her hand like a stranded castaway.

"Please, Kelly. Let me finish, and then I'll answer all your questions."

"Actually, I have comments."

"In a moment."

Kelly settled, issuing a frustrated sigh.

With a muffled giggle, the kid beside Stuart raised his own sketch, a stick figure of Mrs. Steinborn with twin pumpkins in place of breasts, flashing it around for his immediate neighbors before jamming it under his notebook and hunkering over to giggle silently.

"Bennington came clean about his beliefs, crediting the bounty to the Roman god..." She awaited participation.

"Saturn," Stuart mumbled.

Kelly repeated the name, her tone dripping with disdain.

"He told the people they could worship as they please, and give God whatever name they chose," Mrs. Steinborn continued. "But the church, which he built and owned, would be called Saint Saturn—and he would not be responsible for those who actively shunned the deity."

Kelly was practically standing, her hand as high as it could possibly get, her face a portrait of need.

Mrs. Steinborn pointed to her, and Kelly got her chance to vent. "That's why we won't go to...that church."

Mrs. Steinborn lifted her chalk to the blackboard and drew the symbol for Saturn, something like a lowercase letter *h*, with the top crossed. "There is a school of thought that says Jesus was a coded personification of Saturn."

"But that's just stupid!" Kelly asserted.

Mrs. Steinborn offered no acknowledgment. "The rest of the story is not terribly pleasant—and not part of today's lesson."

"Maybe God cursed those families." Kelly's hand was up again, but she wasn't waiting to be called on. "That must be why bad things happen here," she said. "Like…Stuart's dad."

Eyes all burned into Stuart, Albert's holding a hint of enjoyment. Stuart just lowered his head to his notebook and returned to tracing the lines of the guitar.

Mrs. Steinborn's hand had stopped moving on the board. "Bad things and good things happen everywhere," she said. "And to everyone." She continued, chalking, "Saint Saturn Memorial Park" beside a list of names that all struck Stuart as ponderously multisyllabic.

"I want you to choose at least three names from the list and conduct your own investigation. Who were these people? What was their role in the town's origin? Illustrations, gravestone rubbings, any kind of visual aid counts twenty points."

She set the chalk down, rubbed the dust from her hands, and faced the class. "Be safe at the parade, and…"

The class took the cue and spoke the short chant: "Happy Halloween!"

* * * *

October 30

Parade volunteers raised banners and decked poles, corners, and angles with spiderwebs. Main Street was transforming into Haunted Hollow.

Pedestrians came and went amid a sense of fall frisk, some stopping to greet Reverend McGlazer as he oversaw the loading of pumpkins and hay bales from Mooney's Market onto a volunteered flatbed.

"Rev!" came a hearty call. McGlazer didn't need to turn to know it was Kerwin Stuyvesant, talent manager and small-time real estate mogul, approaching for a "pow wow."

"How goes it, Padre?" Though he was clearly exiting Ember Spirits, Kerwin attempted to hide a large brown bag behind his back.

McGlazer chased away his annoyance. He was tempted to extend a hand and watch Kerwin squirm with the bottles. Amazingly, it was Kerwin who initiated the handshake, nearly dropping his package during the awkward juggling act.

McGlazer couldn't help but grin. "Kerwin, I don't know if you're hiding that bag because of my collar or because of my past."

Kerwin shook his head as though he didn't understand.

"I'm a recovering alcoholic," McGlazer explained. "But also a Unitarian. We're a bit relaxed."

"*Oooooh!* Right!" Kerwin pointed at him with his free hand, bringing the heavy bag around to hold at his hip like a baby. "I read ya, Padre!"

McGlazer felt his throat tingle at the mere teasing glimpse of sealed bottle caps. "Nice batch this year!" McGlazer said, distracting himself. He gestured toward the flatbed. "Wanna come to the hangar and help carve?"

"Sounds like a real blast, but ya know, I gotta make arrangements to pick up the record company rep," bragged Kerwin.

"Ah yes! Very exciting!"

"You know it, daddy-o! I mean, *Padre.*" Kerwin struggled to find small talk. "How's the parade prep coming?"

"Oh, it's going to be legendary!" McGlazer stated in a malevolent British accent, assuming a scary face as he leaned close to Kerwin. "Even in *hell!*"

McGlazer was pleased when Kerwin's eyes grew wide, the Clive Barker reference clearly lost on him.

"Right…" It was Kerwin's turn to change the subject. "So Padre, listen you're, like, Dennis's de facto sponsor, am I right?" Kerwin took a step closer to continue, from the corner of his mouth. "I mean, I get the whole confidentiality trip. But, you know, business is business, eh, Padre?"

Kerwin glanced around, like there might be Russian spies at every corner. "He *is* staying on the wagon, right? I mean, this whole Pumpkin Parade gig is the biggest thing ever for me. *Us.* I need him straight. Dig?"

McGlazer offered an assuring smile. "You've nothing to worry about, Kerwin."

Kerwin gave McGlazer a chummy pat on the shoulder, casting a thankful glimpse skyward as well. "Best news all day, right?"

McGlazer excused himself, grabbing a hay bale, guessing correctly that Kerwin hated manual labor more than either anonymity or lean funds. When the dandy man said his quick goodbyes, McGlazer allowed himself a moment of judgmental contempt—and a longer worry for Dennis's well-being. As hard as "the struggle" was for McGlazer, during this stressful season, it surely was a hundredfold for the sensitive young musician.

* * * *

DeShaun watched Stuart chat with Candace, pleased to note his friend's assured body language.

Candace cocked her head to the side. "Devil's Night?"

"Sure." Stuart smiled. "DeShaun and I are going to the old house on Gwendon Street, where my brother rehearses. Tell some ghost stories."

"Whoa." Candace hugged her books. "That sounds super spooky."

"Well, we could do something el—"

"No!" Candace interrupted. "I *want* to do that! I really do!"

"Swell."

DeShaun rolled his eyes. He was happy for his friend, but enough was enough. Bored with the romance, he looked around—and did a double take when he spotted Albert Betzler and some of his genius gang watching from a section of lockers down the hall, myopic menace in their eyes.

"But…I don't know what to tell my parents," Candace explained.

"That's easy," Stuart said. "Mrs. Steinborn gave us this assignment to get grave rubbings, and you wanna come along. You don't even have to lie. We'll even bike by and meet you at your—"

"*No!*" Candace's interruption was firm, definite.

"Okay…"

"I mean…no, you don't have to come by," she said. "I'll meet you at the end of Zebulon Street."

Stuart flipped his hair. DeShaun cleared his throat, turning his back to Albert.

When Stuart ignored him, DeShaun grabbed his arm. "Come along, Stewie." He shot his eyes toward Albert. "You don't wanna make the young lady late for class, do you?"

Stuart pointed at a door not three feet away. "That's her room right there, man."

DeShaun drew close, speaking through clenched teeth. "Well, then, let's compare notes on that geography quiz, shall we?"

"Huh?" The boys' shorthand was misfiring, a side effect of "the love."

"We don't even take geo."

"Excuse us, Candace." DeShaun tugged at Stuart's arm. "Get your ass over here, dude!"

Stuart called to Candace as he was dragged away. "Okay then! Talk to you after class!"

Candace went to her classroom.

DeShaun dragged Stuart to the lockers like a rag doll, opening one to hide their heads behind its door.

"Jeez, dude! What was that all about?" Stuart groused.

"Albert and his brain bullies have been giving you the 'ol' die eye' this whole time!"

"So?"

"So! I don't wanna become the breakfast of champions, *that's* so!"

DeShaun jerked a thumb toward a terrifying tableau: Maynard, the dinosaurian defensive lineman, standing at his locker, guzzling a protein shake, much of which dribbled down his lantern-like chin. His other meaty fist emerged from his locker gripping a forty-five-pound dumbbell for a quick set of curls.

"What am I supposed to do?" Stuart asked. "Keep it a secret we're going out?"

"Maybe just not flaunt it right in front of Albert's prescription hornrims? Is that so much?"

Stuart turned to walk away. "Let's head to class. You ready for Devil's Night?"

"Ah, yeah." DeShaun didn't mind the change of topic. "Got all the goods. You get the key to the old house?"

"Dennis is giving it to me tomorrow. But we gotta be careful. Their gear is in there."

If they had remained vigilant, they might have noticed Albert's friend, electronics whiz Norman Branwith, hunkered over at his locker, appearing to check his calculus homework but in actuality directing a miniature amplifier ordered from a comic book at them.

They might have seen Norman narrow his eyes with devious satisfaction.

Chapter 7

Ignacio hummed a favorite *Tejano* tune, even though he could not hear himself over the roar of his ride mower.

Ignacio loved his job best during *otoño,* when cool breezes replaced the strength-sapping heat of summer and the weeds became manageable. The fallen leaves weren't much of a problem either, here in the churchyard where only a few trees grew in spaces between graves.

He found comfort in the thought of his coming winter belly, made plump by *cervezas* and steak tortillas. He would easily shed the paunch in the heat of Ember Hollow's next growing season, when it was his savings account that swelled.

He turned the corner around the towering obelisk that was by far the cemetery's largest marker. Moving at a good clip, he ran into something that had not been there the week before.

But the impact wasn't what had Ignacio braking hard to kill the blades. It was the sudden cold, rushing wind that blew his cap off and raised goose bumps.

The wind washed over him and was gone.

"*Ay, ay, ay,*" Ignacio mumbled as he climbed off to check the front of the mower and saw the end of a tree limb sticking out. Slowly, he eased the mower back a few feet, then killed the motor.

It wasn't just a tree limb but actually a cross, almost four feet tall, made from the skinned branches of some hardwood. A deep hole indicated it had been driven several inches into the ground at the center of the big grave, until he came along and dislodged it.

Why? God only knew. The grave was already marked with the biggest, and *weirdest*, tombstone he had ever seen.

Kids playing *vampiro* games perhaps?

But what if it was something else? Something important?

What if he could lose his job over it? He thought of losing not only this contract but dozens of others, due to word of mouth from the surly blond girl who often bellowed instructions at him in English.

He did not know her well, but he sensed something cruel about her, and he knew well the power that blond American women held.

If not for this urgent fear, Ignacio might have seen that cold wind blasting through the leaves and bushes and as-yet-unmown grass, heading toward the church.

* * * *

Ruth sang a medley to herself, pieces of hymns she had learned after her conversion. She shuffled and stacked the papers on McGlazer's desk, errant sheep to be herded into their little steel basket.

She checked for cigarettes; it was her duty. None to be found. She congratulated herself for her work in reforming the poor reverend of his weakness.

Hearing a door open and close in the hall, she watched the shadows in the hallway.

But there was no movement, no sound.

"Hello?" Ruth touched her little gold cross, thinking of Stella's silly, godless superstition.

There came a quiet shuffling, then a period of silence that had Ruth praying for its end.

Then, "Hi, Ruth." Reverend McGlazer.

She came out from the desk, pretending to dust a picture frame on the wall.

McGlazer entered, brushing off his blazer. "Quite a sight at the Bruner hangar today. I hoped you could drop by to see it."

"Hm." More than a hint of judgment accompanied this. "I felt my place was here, keeping up the Lord's temple, doing His work."

McGlazer deposited the contents of his pocket onto his desk and hung his jacket on the chair. "I see. Well, we're very thankful for you."

Ruth stepped close. "Who's 'we,' Reverend?"

"The congregation, of course. And me."

"Shouldn't you include the Lord?"

"Of course. Goes without saying."

Ruth gave a prim smile and returned to her dusting.

McGlazer looked at the freshly straightened desk, his gaze stopping on an unfamiliar little black-and-orange-cellophaned package sitting amid the change and pocket lint he had just dropped.

Candy. McGlazer's sweet tooth beckoned, but this was not the time.

"Is something troubling you, Ruth?"

"Well." She wiped the corners of his framed seminary certificates, keeping her back to him. "Now that you ask… I fear this Halloween thing, with the parade and all…could be affecting your walk with the Lord."

"Oh?" McGlazer almost hoped his lack of sincerity was evident. "What makes you say that?"

"It's just…I don't think all this punk rock and celebrating of the dead is very godly."

"I see. Well, I do appreciate your concern."

She approached him with startling quickness. "Reverend, I care a great deal for you."

She lowered herself, settling on both knees, almost between his legs, glimpsing up at him with doe eyes. Were they moistening with tears? She placed a hand on his thigh. "Reverend?"

McGlazer shifted in his seat. "Y-yes?"

She slid her hand higher along his leg. "Would you pray with me?"

What could he say? "All right."

She tugged his wrists as she knee-walked backward, bringing him to his knees on the floor with her. She put his hands together with hers and closed her eyes. "Lord, please send thine angels to protect us from the darkness and evil that hath fallen upon our land and even now tries to invade our hearts with its wickedness."

She was quiet for long enough that McGlazer opened his eyes to see hers moving as if in REM sleep behind her lids. But then: "Thy beloved servant Reverend McGlazer needs you now, as demons of temptation and sinful choices assail him. Please guide him and keep him on the paths of righteousness."

She was quiet again, as the clock ticked. "In Jesus' precious and holy name, Amen."

McGlazer followed her to a standing position with a mix of feelings. He tried to pull back his hands but found her only squeezing them tighter. "Shall I make the calls to cancel the Pumpkin Parade?"

McGlazer had not felt this kind of pressure since his intervention—and indeed, it made him want a drink, preferably a hearty straight bourbon.

"It would fill my heart with joy to do so, Reverend," she whispered like a lover.

McGlazer was able to break free. "You know, a lot of farmers and merchants are depending on the festival for their winter income."

"The Lord will provide for them."

Better make that a double, barkeep.

"I believe…the Pumpkin Parade is the Lord's avenue for providing."

"No *sir!*" Her sudden stridency somehow triggered the taste of an old favorite, Jefferson's Presidential Select. This kind of stress called for only the best, didn't it? "His word forbids these abominations!"

"I'm sorry, Ruth." McGlazer slumped into his chair, physically drained. "I can't cancel it. I won't."

"Then…all I can do is pray for you. And the people of Ember Hollow."

"Yes. Thank you, Ruth. Now, if you don't mind…"

Ruth gathered her cleaning supplies and whisked out of the room like a scorned child.

McGlazer rubbed his weary eyes and propped his feet on his desk, sure he could sleep for at least a day.

Scratch the bourbon. This called for the crudest, hardest, Tennessee-mountain-made corn liquor.

When he opened his eyes, he spotted the bright orange-and-black-wrapped sweet on his desk, a lighthouse beacon amid the scattered change and lint.

Sweets were his crutch, and he surely needed propping up. He reached for it. As he unwrapped it, a chill wind blew across his face, here in this windowless room. The fluorescent light above went dim, then his desk lamp.

His gaze was drawn—by what, he couldn't say—to the far wall, between the pictures and seminary certificates.

An amorphous whiteness seemed to form, about the size of a man, with indistinct features, wispy-gray eye sockets, an apple-sized "mouth."

McGlazer sat frozen in place. He had to work up the saliva to whisper. "Hello?"

The shape floated toward him, issuing a barely perceptible sound, like a distant moan.

McGlazer shakily stood, all but forgetting to breathe.

Then the white shade winked out of existence, like a witch or genie from a '60s sitcom.

* * * *

McGlazer searched for his reading glasses, to see if there was still some remnant of the indistinct haze. What he saw instead was the candy, launching itself off its open wrapper from his desk like a bullet. It flew into his mouth and all the way back to his throat with such force he thought it had pierced the back of his neck.

He was knocked to the floor, the sudden action barely giving his gag reflex time to kick in. In terror, he coughed and grasped at his throat, rolling to his knees and bending forward to enlist gravity's aid.

McGlazer feared for his life, as the candy burrowed deeper, like a malevolent shelled slug.

Then it stopped in the center of his throat.

* * * *

Ignacio banged the crude cross back into the ground with a good-sized rock, soaking its base from his water bottle to swell the soil around it.

He had sanded the post where the mower had scarred it, and then he "aged" the spot with some dirt and grass.

A quick scan offered relief that the blond had not seen him, nor the minister, nor anyone else.

Ignacio hopped back on his mower and continued his work, praying no one would ever know of his screw-up, and he could keep his job.

* * * *

McGlazer continued to cough and convulse. By centimeters, the candy eased up from his esophagus to be ejected with velocity equal to its insertion, plunking into the empty trash can.

It was another couple of minutes before McGlazer could stop coughing and think clearly enough to pray gratitude as he tried to comprehend what had just happened.

His heartbeat throbbing in his ears, McGlazer rose, wondering if he had really just been…attacked. He saw nothing contrasted against the wall's bare spaces. No floating mass. No "specter."

The candy lay in a puddle of saliva on the shiny bottom of the trash can, appearing innocuous.

Chapter 8

The tall figure paced a room lit by pumpkin-shaped strands hanging over barred and curtained windows.

Plastic jack-o'-lanterns glowed from window sills and floor corners. A crate serving as a nightstand sat beside an immaculately made single bed covered by a quilt with a pattern of grinning ghosts and skeletons. Even the tiny doorless compartment that housed his toilet was strung with lights.

A monster-of-the-month-themed calendar hung taped from the wall. October featured the Headless Horseman. All the blocks were X'ed out, save the 30th and 31st.

This "haunted house," though cramped, was a place of contentment, even joy. Everett had coloring and music and lots of time to make masks of every color of construction paper.

He had plenty of glue, tape, and even scissors—plastic, of course. Magazines and books held pictures for him to cut out or color. These were his teachers, showing him a world of people and animals doing things that mostly were not trick-or-treating, but that was okay. At least they were not making little boys do things that hurt or felt wrong.

Recently, his mommy and daddy had let him have a stapler. He could put his masks together much better. Sometimes the staples stabbed his fingers but that was okay. Each prick brought blood and blood tasted good and reminded him of little bats that could turn into widow-peaked vampires with capes like the one he got last year from that guy who could scream really loud.

Everett stopped pacing to dance to music coming from an antique record player atop a stand beneath the window, its rack loaded with LPs. Almost constantly in use, it now played "It's Almost Halloween" by Panic! at the Disco for roughly the fortieth time that day.

The song always filled him with so much excitement for Halloween! Especially now; his calendar said it was soon!

Everett went to his bin of crayons. Many were intact and unused—but not orange, black, and purple. Yellow got pretty good use too, as did brown and, of course, red.

A very dark red was perfect for his present purpose. He took it to his calendar in an underhand grip and slashed an X through the 31st with a mischievous titter.

The wall behind the calendar and all other wall space was covered with cheap rubber masks or cutouts of black cats and scarecrows, with crayon drawings of Halloween scenes: graveyards full of shambling corpses, shrieking cats, and chain-dragging ghosts or towering mansions with broken windows from which gawked vampires and witches.

Some of the older drawings, their corners curling from age, were crude and childish. The new and crisp ones were a different matter. An art expert might have marveled at their brilliance, given a chance to view them.

He admired the new X on his calendar, then went to his record player to restart the song. It was the only one from the entire record he actually liked.

Sometimes listening to his spooky records and making masks excited him, made him want to get out, even if it wasn't Halloween yet. So, pretending to be Frankenstein escaping his dungeon, he tried. He pushed against the heavy steel door, straining his shoulders and arms until his muscles ached.

The windows had steel bars like a jail where you keep robbers or bad guys. He couldn't just climb out. And Ma and Pa told him why, but it still felt like he was a bad guy sometimes, even though he would never do wrong things to little boys. He didn't want to do those things; he wanted to have Halloween.

But he couldn't get the bars loose, or bend them open like a gorilla. Nor could he jump all the way up through the roof, like a superhero. He couldn't push the walls down with his legs and he couldn't run right through the heavy door or any of the walls.

He had to keep trying. He could never ever stop till the whole world was decorated for Halloween.

The pushing and jumping and straining against the bars was making his arms and legs and back feel strong, like a gorilla. He knew he was getting bigger, could feel his shirts and pants getting tighter around him, but now they were torn at the shoulders and thighs, the seams open.

Pushing the walls and jumping made him feel good. Even when he got tired, he would keep doing it, until he had to fall asleep and dream of talking jack-o'-lanterns who told him how to decorate the world.

He was growing up, like Candace, only she was younger. Maybe he was a grownup now. He hoped so! Maybe he could stay out later for Halloween.

The song stopped. Everett went to restart it.

He sifted through the stack of recently played records lying across the top of the rack. So many memories, so many soundtracks for his endless daydreams and nightmares of perfect Halloweens. "A Nightmare Before Christmas," The Chordettes's "Mr. Sandman," several adult crooners in whimsical costumes on weathered album covers.

Everett hugged the albums against his chest, much like Candace often did with her books. Then he sat on his bed and sifted through them again.

Soon he came to an album with harmless, hackneyed witch and ghost stereotypes rendered on the cover, called *Halloween Songs for Children.*

He set the others aside and held out the LP, folded the cover, and snapped the album in half.

* * * *

Fire rained from the sky.

A manhole cover burst open like a giant jack-in-the-box. A giant snake's head rose from it, stitched atop a tree-thick squid's tentacle.

The thing rose with a malignant hiss, towering over Gary Dukes, its body coiling for a strike—or to gulp him up whole.

Weeping acid tears, Dukes raised the .38 in his shaking hand and fired at the snake, just as it lunged.

A chorus of shrill, squealing roars made him turn to see a half-dozen horned, glowing-eyed baboon creatures high above, swinging from tree to tree via their long arms as they screeched hellsong.

He shot at the nearest one, but must have missed.

Dukes dove away, just as the baboon demon landed where he stood, but now the snaketopus was bearing down on him.

He rolled away, but as he hit the grass it burned under him, pungent smoke filling his lungs.

He leaped up, trying to scream but succeeding only in coughing. He managed to get up and run back to the street. As he came up beside a mailbox, its hatch flew open and a horde of screeching bats emerged, all musk and leather and fishhook teeth.

He swatted at them uselessly—forgetting all about them when he saw a rat-headed alligator clawing its way up through the smoldering lawn.

Dukes tried to steady his hand, for all the good it would do; his gun was turning to drooping rubber.

Behind him, a raging roar filled his ears, promising in the ancient language of predation to grind him to gristle.

Dukes saw it coming: the careening, flaming thing that was half-mouth and half-*hearse*—windshield eyes and a snapping engine hood snout.

Dukes stepped into the middle of the street and took aim with his quivering gun at the burning hearse he saw barreling toward him, its muzzle-hood opening wide to swallow him.

He pulled the trigger, despairing at the bright orange flag that emerged from the pistol, reading *Plorp!* in cartoon letters. The demon car nonetheless veered sideways with a startled squeal, skidding on a bed of roiling blackness. Dukes dove out of the way.

Dennis threw his arm across his mother as he swerved. "Get down, Ma!"

Dennis opened the door and got halfway out, crouching behind the driver's door as Dukes rose and aimed the gun at him.

"Mister Dukes!" Dennis shouted. "Easy, man!"

Dukes pulled the trigger—and the gun clicked empty, to Dennis's relief. The crazed neighbor ran away as if pursued by demons.

"My God! What's wrong with him?" Ma asked.

"He's strung out on something."

Dennis took off after him, as his mother called, "Dennis, be careful!"

Dennis caught up. "Easy, Mister Dukes!" He deftly grabbed Dukes's shoulders and rolled him face up, curling into a protective ball around him as they slammed onto the neighbor's lawn. "It's me, Dennis Barcroft!"

Dennis was relieved to hear sirens, coming fast.

Neighbors appeared and stood at a safe distance, too shocked to try and help. The cruiser driven by Hudson splashed blue and red light across the trees and faces.

Hudson and his partner, Monahan, hopped out as the ambulance's siren drew closer. "Step back, everyone! Dennis, Elaine, you okay?"

"Yeah, dude!" Dennis sank his weight atop the bigger man. "Just hurry! He's ape-shit strong!"

"Just kill me!" Dukes begged in a high-pitched tone that raised stinging goose bumps on Dennis's arms. Then his voice sank to a low moan. "*Kill* me!"

Hudson and Monahan knelt to help restrain the quivering mass of man, waving in the rushing EMTs to administer sedatives, to silence Dukes's morbid pleas.

"Mister Dukes, it's Deputy Hudson Lott, Cronus County Sheriff's Department. Remember me? No one is going to hurt you! Do you understand?"

Soon, Dukes settled into motionlessness, only whimpering occasionally. But the sedatives did not relax his expression of horror. Dennis released him to Hudson.

Ma dusted off Dennis's jacket as Monahan and the EMTs loaded Dukes into the back of the ambulance. Hudson came to Dennis. "What happened?"

"Ya got me, man. We came around the corner and found him freaking out, throwing lead," Dennis explained. "Mister Dukes is such a square, man. I never thought he would use."

"Not so sure he *did* use," Hudson said. "I frankly don't know what to think."

"Are you saying he just…lost his mind?" Ma asked, grabbing Dennis's hand like he was a naive five-year-old who hadn't just wrestled a large man to the ground.

"I don't know. But I do know we've had three other cases like it just today. Mostly children."

"Uncool."

"Decidedly," Hudson agreed. "And no telling who might be next. Can I get statements?"

* * * *

"Creeping crud…" Ruth worked her way out of the thorn-and-vine-infested woods to emerge behind the same house where the Outlines had rehearsed just the previous day, praising herself for not *actually* cursing at the dense, scraggly growth, brushing dirt from her rarely worn jeans. Carrying a duffel bag, she checked up and down the lonely street, then at the old house, sparing a huff of disapproval. Despite this, she approached a basement window hidden behind weeds and overlaid with boards.

She knocked twice at the plywood board covering the window, held in place by a single nail at the corner that served as a hinge.

Angelo Betzler, cousin-once-removed from Stuart's nemesis Albert, appeared. He grinned at her with teeth that, though white as snow, still managed to be hideous, somehow predatory. Smarmy in the cut-off denim vest he wore without a shirt, he raised the window. "Don't you know it's still midday, sugar ass?"

"Cut the shenanigans, Angelo."

Swingin' jazz swam at her from a scratched and cracked single-speaker radio.

She turned to descend a stepladder set against the inner wall, feeling Angelo's eyes violating her backside. "I know what you're doing, Angelo."

"Ain't you supposed to wear dresses all the time?"

"So you'll have a chance to peek at my panties?"

"Seen it all before." He tossed something onto the long table behind him. Ruth noted with disgust that it was a nudie magazine.

She handed him the duffel bag. "You heard any news?"

Angelo stepped to the worktable where an improvised chemistry apparatus like a low-rent Doctor Jekyll getup was assembled beside a large tray and a battered police-band radio.

"Oh, yeah." He plucked a piece of the orange-and-black-wrapped candy from the tray, tossed it up, and caught it. "Six cases." He tossed the candy to her. "I told you this shit would induce serious terror trips. And violent reactions."

"Yeah, well, it doesn't seem to have worked on Reverend McGlazer." Ruth regarded him like he had shortchanged her. "Could anyone have immunity?"

"No way. You sure he ate it?"

"If it's around, he ate it." She glanced at the girlie mag and wrinkled her nose. "Now that he's quit drinking, his sweet tooth is like your... filthy sex need."

Angelo stepped well into her personal space. "Did you see him eat it?"

"No, but it's gone from his desk."

"Try again. Leave another one or two lying around."

"Don't you think that's a little suspicious?"

"What difference does it make?" Angelo tried to touch her hair, but she moved away. "Long as even a handful of them work, you'll get your riot."

"It has to be on a massive level," she insisted. "This has to make the national news. Did you leave some upstairs, inconspicuously?"

"Sure." He brushed her lower lip with his finger before she could swat his hand. "Next time those freaks rehearse, they're bound to run across it."

"Good."

"And you really think all this'll shit-can Halloween?" he asked.

"It will, here in Ember Hollow." She raised his chin, made him look her in the eyes. "And that's all I care about. The rest of the country can go to hell for all I care. And I'm betting it will."

"Lady, you are one gospel short of a testament, if you get my drift."

"Don't you worry, Angelo. When Nico gets out, you'll have access to all his connections. I'll make sure. Then you can sell your drug recipes to them. Me and Fab can retire and open that orphanage." She inspected the dusty walls, waxing dreamy-eyed. "Maybe even right here in this old house."

"That's real sweet sky pie you're baking there, baby." Angelo came almost nose to nose with her and put his arms around her waist. "Does your toy boy know about our connection?"

"No. And he won't." She pushed him away. "Not unless you want him to lead pipe you, like he did that dirty snitch. Now, when will the rest be ready?"

"I already finished the cook." He leaned over the table, inspecting his own craftsmanship. "Just need to wrap 'em." He motioned at the deep metal tray lined with balls of glossy tainted confections.

"Oh…" Ruth's eyes lit up. "You're ahead of schedule, then?" She went to the table and raised one of the candies into the weak light of the bare bulb overhead.

"Yep." Angelo stood and eased in behind her, pushing his crotch against her. "Wouldn't mind getting paid a little early too."

She dropped the candy and faced him. "I suppose you wouldn't."

"But you're not exactly"—he stepped closer still, nearly threatening in his persistence—"*liquid* right now, are ya, baby doll?"

"Next Sunday," she answered, stepping sideways out of his grasp. "After tithe offerings."

Angelo sniggered. "Perfect." He slid to catch up with her again, putting his hands on her hips and pulling her toward him. "But I think a little advance might be in order. Dig?"

She made no expression, offered no encouragement—not that he needed it. As he caressed her hips, she fluttered her eyes. "Oh, yes. I think I do."

He kissed her forcefully, making her kiss him back. Their breathing grew faster, heavier, until she wrestled away.

"What?" He pulled at her top, nearly tearing it at the seams.

"Okay, okay, just…"

"Just what?" His slimy-sensual tone had a note of anger. "I delivered. You're up to bat, honey."

"I know."

She doffed the top, letting him leer at her in her lacy pristine-white bra. "Just turn around, please," she said demurely, her nipples rising.

"Yeah, right," he said with a sickening sneer. "I already seen the goods, baby. Remember?"

"And I'm a lady, Angelo. Don't *you* remember?" She cast her eyes down, covering herself. "Shy…"

"Naw, that ain't how I remember it at all." But he did turn, unhooking his big rodeo belt buckle.

Ruth unhooked her bra and removed it—then wound up the fastening ends in her fists.

"I'm gonna want that big finish like last time, you know," Angelo said, tossing his belt to the table with a clatter.

"Don't worry," she whispered.

In a deft motion, she looped the bra over Angelo's head and yanked it tight around his neck.

Angelo was fighting for air before he could react. Ruth hauled him backward, forcing his back to the floor. He looked up at her in purple-faced, helpless terror, digging at the edges of the tough, twisted fabric. His throbbing erection fell as limp as the rest of him would soon be.

"You tell the devil I'm kicking him out of Ember Hollow!" Ruth hissed into his pain-contorted face.

Angelo gave up on the bra itself, clawing at whatever was in reach. His fingers found Ruth's left breast; he twisted and squeezed the pliable flesh. Ruth howled like a trapped mother coyote but relinquished not one ounce of murderous constriction.

He curled his fingers into talons and pulled, tearing at her nipple. She snarled and bit into his nose, shaking her head like a vicious pit bull until it tore free, trailing strands of flesh and mucous.

She spat it across the floor and shrieked as she redoubled her strangling attack.

Angelo's face was a slick scarlet rictus of agony, like a stone bust from an insane sculptor. But the rictus soon went slack and lifeless, his lecherous leer forever frozen in stupefied terror, his clutching fingers now dead crabs.

Ruth held her grip a little longer for insurance, then relaxed and pulled her bra free, letting his head thud against the blood-painted concrete floor.

She slumped to her hands and knees, exhausted. After catching her breath, she stabbed a scolding finger at Angelo's ruined face. "You tell Satan what I said, you heathen filth!"

* * * *

Elaine Barcroft sat at the table with her trembling hands clasped. She considered calling Reverend McGlazer, or Leticia Lott, but decided against it. They were both so busy right now.

The incident with poor Mister Dukes had left her shaken. Dennis had literally dodged a bullet. As a card-carrying overprotective mother, she wondered if he could dodge any more.

He had survived a daredevil period from ages eight till around ten, marveling over the exploits of motorcyclists and stunt drivers before trying them in miniature, first with toy cars and action figures, then with his own skateboard and bicycle, over rickety ramps and potholes, through stacks of boxes, any variable his young mind could conceive.

When punk rock came along to replace the alarmingly more dangerous and elaborate stunt gags, it struck her and Jerome as relatively acceptable, even welcome. Dennis's thoughts of death and/or madness simply took a more cerebral form, and no parent worth their worry warts could balk at that.

After Jerome's accident, Elaine's understandable inclination toward self-pity had to go neglected, as she sought whatever relief was to be had for her two sensitive and fragile boys.

Dennis plummeted into a blackness that could swallow hell, his only expression shell shock. No music was angry or anarchic or bleak enough to give vent to his grief. It was a kind of rage turned inside out. Jerome's belongings—all the keepsakes she wanted to treasure, to use as conduits to her memories—were collected by Dennis one day. He piled them into the back of his hearse one night at some hour after Elaine's exhaustion had overpowered her grief, and he drove away. He didn't return until midday, and when she asked what he had done, Dennis stared off toward some inner horizon and mumbled that they, the Barcroft family as it now remained, would have to forget that Jerome ever lived. The alternative was to—well, to remember that the last thing he did was to die, and he deserved to be remembered for better reasons.

One of Jerome's belongings was a bottle of Diamante's, and that was the one thing Dennis kept, at least until he finished it that evening.

Stuart's response was a different animal. He did not stuff down his grief, or distance himself from it. He gave voice to it, with frightening sobs that left him breathless and hitching, until he gulped enough air to do it again.

Visiting the grave became impossible; Stuart would only stand and bawl at the silent stone. Dennis stayed in the car.

Hudson and Leticia were there, and let's not forget McGlazer, much less DeShaun.

The couple hovered over them like seraphim, Leticia cooking and cleaning and holding Elaine, while Hudson took care of the lawn, house repairs (Dennis's punch holes in the drywall), and the cars.

DeShaun brought comics and action figures, and coaxed Stuart out of his bedroom and onto the living room floor to watch monster movies on TV. Not the really scary ones though, just the ones that were old enough to be campy, or spooky in a goofy way. The chainsaw massacres and whatnot would have to wait. DeShaun understood this.

The reverend took care of the funeral arrangements and other expenses, from his own pocket mostly. And the Barcrofts survived.

Then the boys picked up instruments again. They wrote songs together, and talked of forming a band, and listened to songs that seemed to celebrate death, even to make light of it. Death lost its power, in a sense, because the boys stood up, turned around, and stared it right in the eye sockets.

On a beautiful spring day, Elaine told the boys she was going to the grave and they asked to join her. They all stood around the marker for a while, and then Dennis squatted to pat it, like he would an old friend's shoulder, and they all silently embraced.

Elaine contained her tears, fearful of smashing the fragile stability they had barely achieved.

At home, the boys practiced on their instruments until well after Stuart's bedtime, but Elaine let them be.

For Stuart, a milestone had been reached, a coming to some terms, if not all. For Dennis, the storm was only beginning.

There was no build up, no one-drink-then-two-then-thirteen phase. Dennis blasted through a bottle one night, paid for it brutally the following morning. Something about this self-imposed cycle appealed to Dennis. He needed it.

"You've got to stop poisoning yourself!" she screamed at him one black morning from the very frayed end of her rope, as he caught his breath between pukes. Dennis only looked up at her with weary eyes, then to Stuart in the hallway behind her, saluted, and collapsed on the cold tile floor, to remain till daybreak.

For a good many harrowing, endless nights following, he at least had the courtesy to stay away until he was sober enough to come home and catch just enough rest and nourishment to fuel him for the next night.

Some nights, Hudson or another deputy would find him, in the cemetery atop a grave, or in a freshly dug one, or behind some building or other, even in a dumpster, as if he was determined to literally throw himself or his life away. The officer would help her get him into bed, even when he smelled of trash or grave dirt, or both. She would thank the officer and if it was Hudson, he would stay with her and pat her while she cried, no matter how long.

Ma was sure the whiskey would kill him soon, and then probably Stuart not long after, and then her. She became superstitious to the point of paranoia, wondering if some random curse, perhaps connected to the town's mysterious history, had targeted the Barcroft family after all these centuries.

Hudson took it upon himself to go to Reverend McGlazer. Elaine and the boys had stayed away from church since the funeral, not from loss of faith but simply from loss of interest.

McGlazer didn't mention this. He just showed up one morning, had coffee with Elaine, and went to Dennis's room, where he propped the young man up, gave him some coffee, and asked him questions, asking, asking, asking, always gentle, till Dennis was ready to answer.

McGlazer, bringing heaping bags of candy with him, began staying with Dennis in his room for hours, waking him at the crack of dawn and keeping him busy until late in the day.

McGlazer got Dennis to play music for him, bringing Stuart in for accompaniment, got him to talk about music, encouraged him to make plans.

What he didn't do was judge, preach, or pander. He became Dennis's friend, and that was what he needed more than anything.

The band came next. Punk rock, horror punk, whatever.

Now, success. Many had scoffed at the Outlines's chosen genre. No one questioned their star power.

Elaine clasped her hands together even tighter to fatigue them, to cease their shaking, and that took many hours.

* * * *

Candace went to the kitchen. Mamalee was bent over and humming to herself as she burrowed into the oven to check her roast. As always, Candace made sure to stamp her feet a bit to give Mamalee, easily frightened at the best of times, plenty of early warning.

"Hi, Mama," she said to Mamalee's butt.

Mamalee rose and greeted her with a squashing hug as she always did. "Welcome home, dear! So glad they let you out early!"

"So everyone can get ready for the parade," Candace explained to Mamalee's fragrant shoulder.

As the hug dragged on, Candace said, "But I do have to get gravestone rubbings for school."

"Oh! That sounds so interes—" Mamalee released Candace to look in her eyes. "Hm. Your boyfriend…"

"*Mama!*" Candace chided.

"It's all right, Candace." Mamalee stroked Candace's arm. "Boys are not evil, you know. Oh…" She cast a dark glance toward the door.

"Stuart's only a friend, Mama. And DeShaun. They're riding their bikes."

Mamalee stroked her cheek. "Yes, sweetie. Go see your friend. You know, you can't tell him…"

"I won't tell him we're leaving, Mama."

"Okay." Mamalee almost made a sad face but forced it back to a smile and whispered, "I'll deal with your father."

Candace was bursting with excitement. Before she could run to her room, Mamalee called after her, "Candace, wait."

The façade of vacant bliss had slipped. Candace saw something else in her mother's face, something she didn't remember ever seeing before.

"I know you understand that we must move every year," Mamalee said in a serious tone. "You understand, but you don't know why. And you deserve to. Sit down and let me explain."

Chapter 9

Candace stepped into the early afternoon, still stunned from what Mamalee had just told her.

She only wanted to forget it, to shut it out and live a normal life.

Life had always been a disappointment, even a quiet horror. Now—disappointment was a word so small it meant nothing at all, and the horror was *louder.*

The scent of Ember Hollow's share of autumn helped her wall it off and put it behind her, if only for the time she would have to be distant from it.

Candace knew she would soon miss that scent, and she would miss Stuart. She considered the place she called home and then Everett's shed, seeing it differently. The heaviness in her heart felt ancient.

She trotted to the end of the driveway, then turned onto the road, feeling stranger by the step. The strangeness was like freedom of a sort, and that freedom was like fear—with which she was well-acquainted.

She felt herself begin to trot, either into the strange freedom or away from it, not caring which. Her trotting became a run, and her run became a desperate sprint, as she let herself pretend that she was escaping the family and the "home" she knew, and maybe even heading into Stuart's arms. Tears streamed from her eyes and either giggles or sobs burst from her lungs as her hair blew behind her.

* * * *

Upon taking his job, Hudson believed that he should remain professional and businesslike not only while in uniform but at church and during off-duty hours.

Leticia had seen him on duty and patiently explained that he need not fear being disrespected, that folks would feel more secure in knowing that he was easy to talk to.

These days, Hudson had good relationships with just about everyone. His friendship with Dennis Barcroft, forged in the wake of the Barcroft patriarch Jerome's passing, was good for both parties. Knowing the lawman liked and respected the Outlines softened their standing with Ember Hollow's more conservative residents, and even encouraged those residents to support the band as it became clear they were beginning to ascend.

Jerome Barcroft had been a retired US Air Force mechanic who served as a sort of technical consultant for local farmers and sometimes repaired their equipment, more as a neighborly gesture and hobby than as a true business.

One would have been justified in assuming Jerome Barcroft was fairly conservative and straight forward in his expectations of his family. But he and his wife encouraged the musical inclinations in their boys without reservation, buying them instruments and records and taking them to shows. Perhaps Dennis's leanings toward punk rock raised an initial concern—but it was *his* interest and his talent, no one else's.

Besides, there was also a healthy injection of rockabilly and tongue-in-cheek humor in this weird mashup called horror punk, and there was nothing wrong with that.

Hudson admired this in Jerome, and he vowed to be the same way with his children. Good thing, since DeShaun turned out to be as quirky as they come in his obsession with B movies and comic books.

When the accident happened, the horrific incident with the grain thresher Jerome was fixing, Hudson was among the first to arrive on scene. Worse than any shooting or traffic wreck, the death of his friend shook him to his core, tore into all his reserves of faith and professionalism.

It was a horrible way to die, and a worse way to lose one's father or husband. From the second he saw Jerome's corpse, the man's family became Hudson's. Thus, it hurt him more than he could express to see Dennis, barely out of his teens, plummet into alcoholism—he finished his father's bottle of Diamante's Deep Dark Rum, and thereafter drank *only* that—to the point of near-suicide. Seeing Elaine crippled with grief yet still trying her best to be a mother, and little Stuart trying to understand the new upside-down world he inhabited, put things in grim perspective.

Hudson teamed with McGlazer, twelve years sober himself, to free Dennis of his suffering, to find him a band and give him a cause.

Hudson already knew Pedro from the juvenile system. The big half-Mexican kid had been in far more than his—or just about *anyone's*—fair share of fights. But mostly against bullies and bigots. Pedro liked heavy music and was often caught using a fake ID not to get alcohol but to get into clubs where metal bands were playing, just to stand alone as near to the stage as he could get.

Hudson arranged a meeting between the boys and was gratified when they hit it off. Dennis gave Pedro a bass, and a very young Stuart taught him how to play it. Soon they were talking about forming a band.

McGlazer placed an ad for drummers and hosted tryouts at the church. Hudson stressed the importance of staying clean if they were serious about music. Jill displayed the most lethal combination of alt beauty and skins-bashing talent any two troubled young fellows could ever hope to see.

Initially, Hudson and McGlazer worried that the boys might fight over her. It was either a testament to their dedication as musicians or the fact that Jill unabashedly, uninhibitedly chose Dennis, that their worries were assuaged. Besides, Pedro had no trouble eliciting female interest, and being in a band would only magnify the effect.

In short time, they were a cohesive unit, with Dennis calling the shots when they played. But they were also closest friends, equal and inseparable away from the instruments, with Pedro and Jill forming a protective shell around the still-reeling Dennis.

It was no surprise that oily-but-mostly-harmless Kerwin Stuyvesant took an interest in managing them. Hudson had seen the report on the bar destroyed by the Outlines one winter night, heard how Stuyvesant smoothed over the trouble and took the Outlines under his managerial wing with just a few silky words.

It was less surprising that a record label would sniff them out.

* * * *

Mamalee put the finishing touches on Everett's meal of baked potato, flayed and garnished, a healthy portion of the tender roast, barely solid at all, summer squash medallions, and, his favorite, a slice of pumpkin pie. She dabbed whipped cream onto the pie and placed two little chocolate chips on top to create a ghost. His pre-Halloween meals were always extra special. The boy would need a lot of energy.

Satisfied, she hummed a happy Halloween tune from one of Everett's records as she set a large plastic spoon to the side and then covered the dish with a thin plastic cake cover. "Aloysius! Everett's lunch is ready!"

She poured milk into a plastic child's sippy cup, orange of course.

Aloysius was grim, as usual. "It smells like dinner, not lunch."

"He's getting big, Aloy. I read about growing boys. He'll need lots of carbohydrates for his big night."

"My God, how you spoil him," Aloysius grumbled.

"Aloy." She waxed serious. "He deserves to be spoiled in *some* way."

"Yes?" Aloysius gestured toward the door, as they all did when discussing Everett. "And what do we do when he is grown?"

Mamalee answered, "He *is* grown, Aloy."

Aloysius rubbed his face, then took the covered tray and the chain leash that hung beside the door.

* * * *

Aloysius glowered toward the orange-lit windows of the cement shed, allowing himself a plaintive huff for the many misfortunes of his life. He saw Bravo's big paws crossed in repose and uncoiled the chain, whistling to wake him. But the huge paws retreated into the dusty dark of the doghouse.

"Come, boy! Stop this nonsense!" Aloysius tromped to the doghouse and reached in to grab the mastiff's thick leather collar, balancing the tray in his other hand.

Bravo pulled back from him with his strong legs, whimpering.

"*Damn* your hide!" cursed Aloysius. "Worthless beast…"

Aloysius set the tray atop the doghouse and reached in with both hands to drag Bravo out. The dog resisted, very strong. "I'll starve you if you don't mind me, boy!"

Gritting his teeth, he heaved Bravo out, only to have the whining dog scoot away again. With great exertion, Aloysius hauled him from the house and whacked him with the slack of the chain, something he'd rarely done since the dog had reached maturity. "You will obey me, *damn it all*!"

Bravo sank to the ground in a peaceful protest that left Aloysius enraged. "Get…*up, God damn it*!"

He yanked at Bravo's collar, causing the dog to whine. Aloysius felt guilty, fearing he had hurt his loyal pet. When he released the choke, Bravo took his chance. He darted away toward the forest.

Aloysius dashed after him a short distance—but the agile mastiff burrowed into the dense brush and disappeared.

Aloysius caught his breath and bellowed, "Get back here, you bastard!" He hurled the chain at the woods.

He knew that Bravo would not return, probably not ever. And how could anyone blame him? Aloysius would go and hunt for him later, with a helping of leftover roast as a peace offering. He needed to calm himself.

With a huff, he picked up the tray. He tromped to Everett's shed, entering the tiny vestibule he had built onto the structure. He closed the exterior door behind him and knocked on the inner door. "Everett! Lunch!"

Scratchy notes from Bert Convy's 1958 hit "Monster Hop" wafted at Aloysius under the door.

Aloysius became angry. "Everett! I have much to do!"

The door creaked open—another assault on Aloysius's patience.

Everett stood there, a crisp, new, black construction paper eye mask stapled to his face, the heavy Dracula cape draped over his shoulders.

"Damn it!" Aloysius said. "You've stapled yourself again. You're going to get another infection." Aloysius reached to tear the mask away, but Everett took a quick step back.

Aloysius regarded him reproachfully. "You're in costume a day early, I'm afraid."

"So happy!" Everett croaked.

Aloysius would not break eye contact—though he wanted to. "You haven't packed at all!"

"So happy!" answered Everett.

Aloysius grunted. "Come and take the food, boy."

Everett took a step forward, but did not take the tray.

"Don't try me today, Everett."

Everett took the tray—then dropped it, his smile never wavering as it clattered and splattered food, startling Aloysius backward.

"What the hell is wrong with you?" bellowed the big patriarch. "Clumsy fool! Pick it up!"

Everett crouched, as if to obey. Aloysius did not see him draw from his waistband, hidden under the cape, a knife-shaped sliver of hard black vinyl—the once-beloved record of children's Halloween favorites Everett had broken earlier that day.

With a huff, Aloysius smacked Everett on the top of the head. "I'm losing my pa—"

Everett rose to a stand, raising the black knife over his head.

Aloysius lunged for the doorknob. His hand was on it and turning—just as Everett drove the vinyl shard between his ribs.

Aloysius pushed the door open as he stumbled out face forward. "Leelee!" he cried. *"Run away!"*

Everett sliced through the flesh between the ribs of his father's back, carving a slit all the way to his spine. He pulled the weapon out and stood over Aloysius, watching with fascination as blood dripped from the tip of the black knife.

As Aloysius rolled onto his back with an agonized moan, Everett snickered down at him. The demented man-child held up his finger, as if to say, *Wait here, please*, and went back into his shed.

Aloysius coughed blood, his punctured lungs failing him when he tried to scream another warning to Mamalee.

Everett returned, smiling as he showed his father a hand-sized construction paper crescent. Aloysius saw the vertical lines drawn on it and realized it was an oversized cartoon smile. In Everett's other hand was his stapler.

Everett knelt and positioned the mask on Aloysius's face, then mashed the stapler into it repeatedly. Aloysius's weak efforts to stop him meant nothing to the strong, adrenaline-fueled teenager. Everett seemed to take pleasure in the paper smile, perhaps the only smile he had ever seen on his father's face. "So happy!"

Satisfied, Everett stepped over his father, and left his shed.

Blood streamed from the edges of the mask to mingle with the growing puddle under Aloysius's head.

Chapter 10

In the bedroom Mamalee hummed, taking books from shelves and placing them in a box as she had a year ago, and a year before that. The last book was a large family Bible with cracked corners, its pages crumbling at the edges.

Furrowing her brow, she smoothed her hand across its tooled leather face, its gothic gold letters, and opened it, knowing she would find the same pictures tucked between its pages as she had ever since Everett was a baby.

A family portrait against a background of blue sky and clouds, the bright-faced young couple with infant Candace and toddler Everett holding one of his many monster dolls.

Mamalee stared at the image but did not see it, instead reliving the memory of Aloysius sitting at the kitchen table with his eyes closed, trying not to hear the screams of a little boy echoing throughout that long-gone first house, in counterpoint with the booming baritone chants of a man yelling in Latin.

Mamalee slammed the Bible shut and dropped it in the box, as if it burned her hand. After a thought, she took it and tossed it in a trash box.

She heard Aloy come in and putter around in the kitchen. Staring at the big Bible, she wondered if God and Aloy shared her disillusionment, the same sense of failure at having children so inexplicably broken that it rendered their protective love meaningless, reduced their lofty wishes for a beautiful future to mere sketches in the sand at the edge of an ever-erasing ocean. "Aloy? How is Everett?"

Wait...

The sounds were faint, yet somehow chaotic, not like the grim sense of order that characterized Aloy's comings and goings.

She switched to a higher pitched, more playful tone. "Bravo? What are you doing, bad doggy? Daddy left the door open, didn't he?"

Mamalee went down the narrow hall, already missing the pictures she had aligned chronologically on the wall a year previous. "Bravo, you sneaky..."

Entering the kitchen, Mamalee felt a sensation like walking into a swarm of hornets.

Though his back was to her, there could be no doubt that the caped, mussy-haired figure standing at the kitchen drawers was Everett.

He turned. She saw that he had stapled one of his masks on again and was collecting sharp things. The points of mismatched steak knives and meat skewers jutted from both ends of his fist.

"Oh, God," Mamalee cried. "Everett."

She backed out of the kitchen. "Where is your..."

Seeing blood on his hands, she erupted into tears. "Oh, baby. What did you *do*?"

"Mama can *fly*!" rasped Everett, as he took a step toward her.

"No." She turned to run and heard Everett take off as well, snickering at the new game. Mamalee squealed as she bashed her way past the boxes in her path, bolting for the front door.

As she lunged for the knob, a steak knife twanged into the wood beside it, sending a jolt of immobilizing terror up her spine.

She saw Everett raising another knife and cut to her left, protected by the foyer wall, screaming all the way, not only out of terror but to drown out Everett's ghastly laughter. Mamalee ducked into her bedroom and squeezed her eyes shut as she slammed and locked the door.

She pressed her back to the door—then stepped away as she imagined a knife piercing it, and her.

The rocking chair had been a gift from Aloysius when Everett was born. She slid it toward the door and jammed its back under the knob.

"Everett!" she cried. "This is wrong! And I want you to know, I'm *sorry,* baby!"

She watched the doorknob, unnerved by the silence beyond. Then came a soft shuffling—he was walking away to...

The window opposite the bed was open. "Oh!"

She went to the window and tried to close it, sinking her hips, hoping the extra girth she had acquired over the years would be enough to budge it. "Come... *on!*"

Just the barest movement—but enough to create downward momentum, closing the heavy frame to within less than an inch.

She scanned out the periphery of the window, from one side to the other. Her eyes and ears strained for any warning as she went back to the door.

Then came a muffled thumping. Her senses scrambled to determine its location.

With the realization came despair. *"Attic."*

The ceiling exploded downward, raining plaster, insulation, and Everett. Giggling madly, he landed in front of her on his face and hands, like an angel ousted from heaven.

Mamalee screamed, turning to the window she had just struggled to close. The opening was almost too narrow for her fingers to get under, but once she did, the window refused to rise even a centimeter.

She dared a glance at Everett and saw him shaking off the plaster debris. He pushed the pieces of insulation and thin particle board out of the way. "No time for puzzles." He collected his knives from the floor, muttering, "Pick up sticks!"

Mamalee hammered her palms against the bottom edge of the window, whooping like a lottery winner when it slid up three inches. She pushed and pushed again, until the window shuddered along its rails enough for her to crawl through. Terror and adrenaline drove her shifting and wriggling through—and plunging to the ground outside.

Mamalee struggled to her feet, tears streaming. "Have to stop him..."

She lunged at the window, fingers forming steely claws to match the window's rigid fit—but this time it slid shut with unexpected ease. She fell face-first, bumping her chin on the frame. Stars whirled in her vision, pain lit up her jaw—then the window shattered behind her. Fingers hooked into her hair, maddened giggles stabbed her ears.

Mamalee cried for help, as she clawed at Everett's hand. With another burst of reckless strength, she yanked herself away, leaving Everett with a handful of curly blond-gray hair as she fell forward. She stumbled up quickly on arms going numb from exhaustion, and she found herself facing the window.

The black shape of her son burst through it like a giant bat, and he landed on his feet a few feet away. "Evvie can fly too!"

Mamalee screamed as Everett hurled his handful of knives, most of them landing in her chest, neck, and stomach. "Toys can fly," he noted.

Mamalee fell to her knees, staring with horror at her injuries, then at Everett. "Oh... my sweet little...shnoogens..." She fell to her back.

Everett came and stood over her, wearing a wide grin.

"Oh baby..." she sputtered. "I know. I *know* it's not your fault." She coughed blood.

Everett knelt beside her as he took from his pocket a crumpled construction paper mask, a madly distorted red-cheeked angel, and positioned it on her face.

"Okay, Evvie. That's fine, that'll be…"

He smashed the stapler into the mask, affixing it to her forehead. She tried not to cry out too much, not knowing if it would offend or encourage him. "Just please, baby. Not Candace, all right? Not Candace."

Everett took on an expression of wonder. He patted her stomach. "Cann…niss?"

Mamalee played along. "Oh…oh yes, baby! She's right there in mommy's tummy!"

Everett reached into his pocket and withdrew another crumpled mask to show Mamalee: a green, bug-eyed alien, complete with pipe cleaner antennae.

Mamalee maintained a bloody smile as Everett placed the mask over her stomach and stapled it there.

Mamalee kept up the charade. "Yes, good boy! Now Candace has her own Halloween mask!"

Everett, his madness-soaked eyes burning into her, raised a second alien mask, larger than the first. "*Canniss.*"

Mamalee realized her last-ditch ruse had failed. "No! No, Everett! She had nothing…"

Everett pushed one of the knives into Mamalee, silencing her.

* * * *

McGlazer considered the tiny feeling of paranoia and dread flitting in his brain like a black-light firefly. Walking along Main Street en route to the sheriff's department, he saw the trees in their waist-high brick planters along the sidewalk dance in an onrushing breeze.

Were there… *knives* hiding among the leaves, pointing themselves at him?

McGlazer felt his heart pump in his ears and a familiar domineering thirst on his tongue.

He said a prayer and went to the little tree—to confront it?

No knife leaves. Nothing unusual.

The cool wind carried an artificial scent of pumpkin from the café that recalled the eerie blast of cold he had felt in his office just before the frustrating tease of briefly seeing the specter—and the subsequent near-suffocation by sweet.

Wouldn't that be a joke of a headline? TOWN MINISTER DIES IN CONFECTION-RELATED MISHAP.

He felt better. Whatever the cause of the brief fugue, it had dissipated. But though the grayish shade in his office and the leaf knives could be dismissed as hallucination, the guided-missile sweetmeat was as real as the gritty sore throat that had him grimacing with each swallow.

Chapter 11

Candace had no first memory of her brother, or a family that was like everyone else's. Everett had always been confined to the basement or the attic or more recently to some fortified shack or barn on the grounds of whatever property they were renting any given year—except for Halloween night, which always signaled a quick move to some other distant locale the very next day.

She didn't see him that much, except from a distance and framed in a briefly open door, until a couple of years ago. At that time, her father had agreed to acclimate them to one another via short exposures, in acquiescence to Mamalee's wishes that they have some knowledge of each other.

So Aloysius had taken her on feeding trips, allowing her to wave to the boy and say hello from a safe distance. Everett always acknowledged her, seeming curious and aware beyond his madness of some connection between them.

Then Father had allowed her to accompany Mamalee as well, for afternoon feedings or to sit outside his door and read stories to him in her high and wavering voice. He seemed to love the harmless Halloween books aimed at preschool kids, and after a few readings, Everett's muffled mutterings indicated he had memorized the book. Mamalee would slide it under the door and Everett, apparently as clever at deduction as he was compulsive at killing, would read them to himself, having discerned by process of elimination and the timing of the turning of the pages which words went where.

His strange behavior didn't initially frighten Candace. When they moved to Ember Hollow and the growing boy was locked into a much stronger structure, she sometimes felt safe in sneaking to visit him alone.

She would sit outside the barred windows and sing along with Everett's records. Soon, Everett too would raspingly sing. But when she tried to speak with him, he was mostly incoherent. The cause of his madness had also destroyed his ability to communicate—unless he just didn't want to.

When Candace went to the mall in neighboring Wilcoxville with Mamalee, she was often granted ten minutes to walk around on her own (and, perhaps, pretend she was a normal girl). She found a quaint music store that sold vinyl records and supported local acts, including The Chalk Outlines. She came across their EP *Lullabies to Die By* and remembered that a boy in her class, Stuart, was the brother of swoon-worthy front man Kenny Killmore, and was pretty darn cute himself. Though she had caught him staring at her, she always figured he was just thinking how weird she was, like everyone else did.

She returned from a few of these excursions with records that she secretly slid under Everett's door, including the Outlines's EP and some vintage Halloween records. Later, she was pleased to hear him listening to them.

At one time, her parents might not have approved of Everett listening to "aggressive" music. But these days, Papa was too deep in discontent and denial. Mamalee shared in the latter with him. They hardly paid attention to Everett's listening habits, or Everett himself so much, now that he was almost—well, pretty much *totally*—grown up.

Bravo had come along four years ago, after Everett showed signs of greater strength and alarming cleverness. Aloysius wanted to keep the dog away from Everett during his developing months, to keep them from bonding, but it wasn't necessary. As a pup, Bravo cowered and whimpered anytime Everett was near. As he grew, he growled and postured defensively when Father went to feed Everett, especially if Candace was around.

Father wanted a guard dog for his little girl, and he was perhaps disappointed that Bravo showed fear of the boy, but having the dog professionally trained would leave too much of a trail. He had to try to do it himself.

The first few times Candace took Everett his food, Father stood near—but he had to force Bravo to stay at his side by choking up on the leash.

Eventually, Bravo was consigned to a doghouse, less a guard dog and more a neglected pet. Candace was not allowed to walk him, but she did go and sit with him, just as she did Everett. She ruffled his fur and kissed him, told him he was a good boy. Sometimes, he laid his head on her lap and dozed. Sometimes, he just sat, eyes half closed, smiling, content to be in her presence.

She told him, in low tones, of her despair. They commiserated about their place in a family that centered around endless smoldering horror.

Father sometimes talked about getting rid of Bravo and buying another dog, a Doberman or German shepherd that was already trained. But Candace and Mamalee both would plead with Aloysius till he relented. Maybe this was a mistake, but for a young girl already traumatized by a crushing reality for which she could never have prepared, every love was a deep one.

There were times when Candace wished her brother was dead. He was a permanent black rainbow arcing over their home, a factor in every single decision.

There were times—when Candace was in bed, or walking home thinking about the bullies on the bus, and wanting to see them hurt even worse than they hurt her—she wondered if there wasn't some murder madness gestating within her soul as well, waiting to bloom. Perhaps, Candace pondered, that was what adulthood would mean for her.

****

Filling out a report on an old, heavy steel Royal typewriter, Hudson cursed both the antique and his own lack of typing skill as he applied correction fluid to his seventh error.

Deputy Yoshida approached, leading Reverend McGlazer. "Hud! Visitor." Hudson looked up. "Reverend, take a seat."

"You're not too busy?"

"Not until the next sweet old spinster or volunteer crossing guard goes cuckoo for no discernible reason." Hudson sipped cold coffee and grimaced. "What can I do for you?"

"Well…" McGlazer seemed to search for words. "It's a little strange." He set before Hudson the mercurial little candy that had tried to kill him and changed its mind, its wrapper unfurling in the open air.

"What's this?"

"I found it on my desk."

Hudson raised an eyebrow.

"I know, I know. I'm always eating candy. But…"

McGlazer was weighing just how much to tell him. "I just got an odd feeling about this one."

He dared not mention the gray shape or the leaf knives, for fear Hudson would suspect him of falling off the wagon.

"About what? Halloween candy?" Hudson scoffed.

McGlazer gave an embarrassed smile, then grew serious and tapped the candy. "Is there any way you could have this analyzed?"

"Looks like it was partially consumed." Hudson scooped it up under the wrapper and examined it. "You?"

"No." McGlazer silently asked forgiveness for the lie.

"I could send it to a lab, but it could be as long as a week before we get any results. Low priority, you know. And I doubt the chief would okay it." With an exasperated expression he jerked his head at a corner office with a closed door. "Pumpkin Parade always stretches the budget—and the old boy's patience—razor thin."

"I see." McGlazer felt some small guilt that he was using his "earnest" expression on his friend and parishioner, the same he used at offering time.

"Well, if you wanna leave it with me," Hudson offered, leaning back in his creaky chair, "I'll see what I can swing."

* * * *

Stuart stuffed a stack of comics titled *Horrifear!* and *Haunt of the Accursed* into his backpack, along with some candy bars and a heavy aluminum flashlight. He hoisted it, then went to the living room where his mother folded clothes while watching a black-and-white soap opera rerun. "See you later, Ma."

"Wait, Stuart," she said, her face going grim, as she sat on the edge of the couch.

Ah, crap, Stuart thought, doing a quick check of his recent activities to see why he might be in trouble. He sat beside her.

"Your history teacher called today," Ma began.

"Mrs. Steinborn?"

"She said another student had made a comment about your father."

"Oh," Stuart said. "That."

"Are you all right?"

"Yeah, Ma. It's not like it was some major news flash."

She pushed his hair away from his face to see his eyes, and Stuart knew she was wondering if he needed a shrink.

"Kelly. She wasn't really talking about Dad," Stuart explained. "Just, she likes to talk about God."

It was a topic Ma rarely touched on outside of singing hymns at church. Dennis had told Stuart she was probably not so sure about all that stuff anymore.

"Well." She cleared her throat and smoothed her skirt. "I'm a little worried about you going to that cemetery without an adult. After what happened to Mister Dukes…"

"Ma, we have to get the gravestone rubbings for school."

Ma tsked. "Such a morbid assignment. Are you still going to the movies after?"

"Hell—uh, I mean, *heck* yeah, Ma. It's the Screecher Feature!"

"Well…" Before she could protest further, Stuart kissed her and slid out the door.

On the street, Dennis rolled out from under the hearse and stood, his face and neck spotted with grease. "The big night has arrived," Dennis said, wiping his hands on a bandana.

"Devil's Night!" Stuart exclaimed—but not *too* loud.

"She bought it?"

"What's to buy?" Stuart mirrored Dennis's "charming hood" bit right back at him. "We *are* getting grave rubbings. And they *are* for school."

"Right. But the Screecher Feature?"

"Okay, so that one was just a little whitey," Stuart admitted. "Are you coming by?"

"We're blocking the parade till pretty late. But after that, we gotta collect the gear. So, just maybe, we'll make the scene. Give you tots one good scare."

"Yeah, you suck, if you do!"

"Don't tear the joint down." Dennis tossed Stuart the key. "More importantly, don't touch our gear!"

"Horror comics and root beer. That's it." Stuart climbed on his bike, regarding Dennis thoughtfully.

"Ah, hell. What's with the look?"

"Candace is meeting us."

Dennis grinned. "You sly hound! Wait. What's the deal? You're making DeShaun a third wheel?"

"Scary stories and root beer, remember? That's all. No mushy stuff. I just…wanted you to know, that's all."

Dennis slapped Stuart on the shoulder. "Tell DeShaun I said to eat one."

Stuart chuckled and pedaled away.

* * * *

Deputy Shavers tended the cell door as Hudson carried a steaming cup to Mr. Dukes, adjacent to a cell that housed three other men.

Darrell "Leechy" Beecham, chronic pickpocket and frequent customer, pressed against the bars between cells. "Hey, will you please put this freako in another cell, officer?" He requested. "He's givin' me the jeebs."

"Shut it" was Hudson's response.

Dukes sat in an upright fetal position against the corner, shivering.

"Mr. Dukes, I brought you some tea," Hudson said. "My wife's brew. Cleansing, she says."

"What about me?" asked Leechy.

"You get to shut your mouth," Hudson answered.

Dukes hugged himself in fear, his eyes darting.

"What is it, Mr. Dukes? What do you see?"

"It's…it's full of…*lobsters.*"

Hudson regarded the tiny teacup. "Did you say… lobsters?"

"Big ones! Oh, God, keep it *away!*"

"Damn…" Hudson muttered.

Hudson set the tea on the floor behind his back. On a hunch, he drew from his pocket the candy Reverend McGlazer had brought to him, loosely rewrapped in its orange-and-black cellophane. "What about this, Mr. Dukes? Have you seen any candy like this? Maybe eaten some?"

As the wrapping bloomed away from it, new fear brimmed in Dukes's eyes.

With no farther to go, Dukes squeezed himself against the wall. "Keep it away! God, it…it *sees my last day!*"

Hudson could not know that, to Dukes, the candy was a restless rolling eyeball, its orange iris shuttering around the black pupil pointed right at him.

Dukes turned sideways, pushing the side of his face into the corner. "It sees my last day!" He swatted at the candy, knocking it across the floor, where it landed at the edge of the separating partition.

Leechy eyed it.

"*Don't!*" Hudson warned.

"Okay." Leechy held up his hands like he was being arrested again. "Wha' 'bout that tea though?"

Hudson considered. "Ah, what the hell."

He handed the tea through the bars to Darrell. "Now you can go get a job tomorrow."

Leechy pumped a dirty thumb into the air. "Sure thing, Officer Friendly!"

Hudson returned his attention to the trembling Dukes, as he addressed Deputy Shavers. "Seems to be less intense now."

"Definitely. Whatever he was on, it's wearing off."

Chapter 12

DeShaun and Stuart took turns bumping one another's shoulders at the corner where a dusty highway turnoff met Zebulon Street.

"You sure you know what you're getting yourself into, man?" DeShaun asked.

"I just think she's a cool chick. Is that such a crime, *Dad*?"

DeShaun gave a heartier bump. "I'm just saying. Remember when this school year started? We made a deal: no girlfriend drama until next year. One more year to just…"

"Goof around," Stuart finished. Stuart turned his hand over to show a tiny scar on his palm, and DeShaun opened his hand to show a matching scar.

"Yeah," Stuart continued. "Ma was going on about how this is the first year I won't be trick-or-treating."

"Mine too."

"I'm not gonna ditch you, man." Stuart gave DeShaun a pretty good slug on the thigh. "Not tonight. Not ever."

"Same here," DeShaun said. But he was staring down at the ground. And he didn't return the playful punch.

"I like her," Stuart admitted. He waited to see if DeShaun was going to laugh at him, but he didn't. "I'm glad you're here, if that makes any sense."

"Is this gonna turn into some weird thing?" DeShaun's face and voice were dead serious, but Stuart detected the sarcasm. "I'm not into you that way."

"Shut up, dude!"

DeShaun cracked up. Stuart punched him on the shoulder a little harder than usual, and soon the boys had dropped their bikes and were rolling around on the ground, wrestling.

As always, they began calling their own action, serving as both co-commentators and mortal enemies. "Barcroft's headlock is clearly too much for the weaker Lott, as you can see, Bob. You can hear the screams of agony," Stuart announced.

"I'm afraid you're mistaken as usual, Mean Gene. Those are gales of laughter. Lott is amused by Barcroft's jelly-like grasp and is about to turn the tables," countered DeShaun.

Eventually, DeShaun wound up on top and applied a claw hold to Stuart's hyper-ticklish ribs, making his friend squint and squirm and cackle. Glancing up, DeShaun grew still, staring at something in the road. "Ooohh…"

He stood up straight and dusted himself off. "Here she comes."

Stuart popped up and grabbed his bike, trying to position himself on it before Candace got a good look at him acting like a little kid. "Huh? She's on foot."

Candace was walking briskly, like those old folks early in the morning at the mall. There was something urgent about this—but then there was always something urgent about her. "Come on."

They took off to meet her, waving like castaways flagging down a helicopter, and soon they were beside her.

"Hey," greeted Stuart and hoped he did not seem too excited.

"Hey," she echoed, still huffing from the walk.

"I figured you had a bike."

"I don't mind walking," she said.

"Well, um…" He considered the situation. "You can ride mine and I'll walk."

Candace seemed almost panicked. "Can't I just ride with you?"

"Well, sure!"

DeShaun grinned at Stuart, as Candace clambered on behind him.

"So where is the cemetery?" she asked, as they took off.

"It's just behind the big old church."

"*Stop!*" Candace yelled it loud. Stuart thought she was hurt.

"Huh?" Stuart hit the brakes and dropped his feet like an ace daredevil, but he wasn't thinking of how cool it was. He was worried about Candace. "What's wrong?"

She jumped off the bike and stepped back. "I don't think I can go."

"Why not?" asked Deshaun.

"I just…" She turned and walked. "I better go home."

Stuart stood scratching his head.

"Well, don't just sit there, brainiac! Go after her!" urged DeShaun.

"I don't know, man. She seemed pretty intense about not going."

DeShaun went after her. "I see how it's gonna be."

Stuart watched as DeShaun glided up beside her, gesturing and talking. Soon, she stopped, and soon after that, she turned to walk back. DeShaun waved at him to come meet her.

* * * *

Entering the drugstore, Hudson stepped aside for a gaggle of babbling children, bottlenecking the door with their new Halloween costumes.

He made his way to the back, where pharmacist Charles Plemmons gave a prescription package and an enthusiastic "Happy Halloween!" to a customer from the raised enclosure of the pharmacy.

"Ho there, Hudson," Charlie called.

"Good afternoon, Charles."

"You need a scrip?" Charlie leaned on the elevated counter. "Big strong guy like you?"

"Actually, I was wondering if you could take a look at something for me. Possibly evidence."

"Oh? Official police business, eh?"

"I wouldn't say official." He slid the candy to Plemmons, on its loose wrapper.

"This a joke, Hud?" Charlie lifted it between thumb and forefinger. "It's just Halloween candy."

"No joke." Hudson's face gave away how serious—and weary—he was. "I know you're not set up for this, but I'm hoping you can toss it in your cauldron and see what floats to the top."

"Ah, a very seasonal way to put it," Charlie quipped. "Is this something like that silly old wives' tale about poison candy?"

"I damn sure hope that's all it is."

"Well, I'll be closing up early for parade prep. But maybe I'll get a minute before I leave."

"I appreciate it, Charles. And, uh, just you and me, okay?"

"Ooh! Secret agent stuff! All righty then!"

Bats fluttered around the streetlight above his cruiser, casting quick shadows across his face. These shadows, like his hunch about the candy, made Hudson feel uneasy for reasons he couldn't explain.

* * * *

Stuart and DeShaun took several steps into the freshly mown churchyard and turned to Candace.

"See?" Stuart spread his arms. "The church is like a whole football field away."

Candace took a few furtive steps.

"All the really old graves are on this end anyway," said DeShaun, motioning toward a patch of stones more white than gray.

"Are you okay?" Stuart asked.

"Yeah." Candace hugged her arms against her chest. "Sorry, guys. Churches just kind of weird me out."

"You haven't met Reverend McGlazer?" DeShaun asked. "He's really nice. Not all yelly or anything like that."

"Haven't met much of anybody since we got here," she explained, still on her guard.

"Where were you living before?" Stuart asked.

"Hm." Candace sounded sarcastic. "Which time?"

"You move a lot?" asked Stuart.

"Yeah."

"Here's the first one," said DeShaun as they came to a weathered, crooked grave.

The boys knelt to take charcoal and paper from their backpacks.

"Good thing we have plenty of extra tracing paper, eh, Stuart?" DeShaun pronounced.

"Oh. Yeah, it is," Stuart enjoined, turning to Candace. "And that's because we thought you might enjoy making some rubbings as well."

Candace took the proffered paper and charcoal. "Okay, yeah."

Stuart gave DeShaun a grateful wink.

"You guys…" Candace gave them an intense kind of smile. "Thanks for inviting me."

"Well, sure," said Stuart, pressing his paper against the old grave. "It's about time you got out to see the great metropolis of Ember Hollow."

"Yeah," DeShaun agreed. "Maybe Stuart can show you some of our town's other interesting attractions."

Stuart shot him a warning glare, even as he said, "Sure, yeah."

"I don't know," Candace responded. "Maybe."

"Are your parents strict?" asked DeShaun.

"It's not that so much."

Stuart finished and rose. "It's okay. That's none of our bees' wax." He gave DeShaun a hearty nudge. "Right, DeShaun?"

"It's just…my brother…" Candace trailed off.

Stuart and DeShaun exchanged a look. "I didn't know you had a brother."

"He's...kinda not okay." Candace was quiet for a long time. "He doesn't get out much."

Candace finished her rubbing and stepped aside for DeShaun.

Stuart held his rubbing up to compare it to hers. "Wow. You're a pretty good artist, huh?"

"I guess it runs in my family," Candace said.

They watched DeShaun finish his. "Come on. Next one is down here."

"You guys sure know your way around this graveyard."

"We've lived in Ember Hollow our whole lives," explained Stuart. "Used to play hide-and-seek here. Easter egg hunts. Stuff like that."

"Must be nice," Candace said.

"Don't worry," DeShaun said. "It won't take you long to get to know it too."

She turned away, looking at the ground.

"Wait." Stuart stopped in front of her. "You're not gonna move again, are you?"

"Change the subject." Candace walked around him, leaving him to watch her in bewilderment.

DeShaun grabbed Stuart's arm, stage whispering, "You gotta make your move, man!"

"What about no girlfriend drama?"

"Screw that!" DeShaun gave him a subtle shove.

Stuart jogged to catch up to her. "Then you *have* to be in the parade with us. With me."

Candace's tears welled. "Can we forget about tomorrow for a minute?"

"Forget? About Hallo-freakin'-ween?"

"I just wanna think about today right now, okay?"

Stuart and DeShaun exchanged another perplexed look. "Sure. No sweat," Stuart answered.

"There's ol' Wilcott," said DeShaun.

They trekked to a towering obelisk with intricately carved angelic figures and unusual symbols around the base.

But even odder than the big stone, something was stuck in the earth, dead center of the grave.

"What the hell?" Stuart asked.

It was a sturdy wooden cross about four feet tall, made from inch-and-a-half-thick hickory. The light coloring of its smooth-sanded skin indicated it had been recently placed.

"Maybe somebody's way of paying tribute to the ol' fella," DeShaun conjectured, tugging at it. "It's in pretty good." Stuart took a turn, with the same result.

Candace gave it a wide berth as she went to examine the towering monument behind it.

"Wilcott P. Bennington the third," Stuart said. "Town Father."

"The house we're going to after this"—DeShaun cocked his head toward the woods to his left—"built right on the site where he settled."

"Yep." Stuart pointed beyond a field past the church. "Right over there."

"It's awesome, too," Deshaun said. "There's lotsa weird rumors about Ol' Wilcott."

"There's a rumor he could raise spirits," Stuart said.

Candace looked over the marker, drawn to the majestic sickle-wielding being carved in various poses around the tall base of the obelisk. She began rubbing the inscriptions.

"But my dad says that's silly," continued Stuart. "'*Said,*' I mean."

There was another unusual symbol: the cross combined with a lowercase letter *h*, set inside a triangle, as Mrs. Steinborn had drawn. Candace did a rubbing of this as well.

"These angels, so strong and peaceful," she said. "Reminds me of my mo—"

Candace's words became a frightened yelp, as a quick figure appeared from behind the monument, like Mama Bates descending upon Martin Balsam.

The figure was Ruth, lunging to snatch Candace's paper.

Candace was startled backward. The boys instantly took protective positions in front of her.

Ruth was furious. "What are you kids doing? Desecrating this holy place?"

"N…No, ma'am," answered DeShaun. "It's a homework assignment."

He held up the homework sheet, and she snatched it too, glaring down at it. "It's *still* disrespectful. This is what happens when prayer is taken out of school!"

She handed the papers back and loomed over the shaken Candace. "Who are you, little girl?"

"C-Can…"

Stuart and DeShaun helped her stand. "Candace. She goes to our school," Stuart said.

"Candace. Why haven't I seen you in church?"

"Uh…" Stuart tried to answer for her, but was at a loss.

"She's…allergic," DeShaun blurted.

"To…pews!" Stuart elaborated.

"Pews, pew polish," DeShaun elaborated.

"Makes her break out in splotches," Stuart finished.

"Oh, really?" Ruth scowled at the boys, then down at Candace. "Why can't she tell me herself?"

"She… her allergy… her throat," Stuart improvised.

Ruth took Candace's hand and pulled her close, putting her arms around the girl. "Come here and let me pray over you, child."

"*No!*" Candace jerked loose and ran for the road, fast as her legs would pump.

Stuart and DeShaun took off after her. "Candace! Stop!"

Ruth watched them with more than suspicion. Perhaps it was hatred. And then she made damn sure the hickory cross was lodged deep and solid.

* * * *

Stuart and DeShaun caught up to Candace. Though breathless, she still stumbled forward as fast as her taxed lungs would allow.

"Candace!" Stuart called. "Stop! *Stop!*"

She broke into tears, her feet barely rising. Still she ran, driven by fear or fury. Her backpack fell off, but she ignored it.

Stuart hopped off his bike and let it crash, jumping in front of her with hands and arms out like Superman bracing to halt a runaway bus. "Stop!"

She slammed into him, knocking him on his back—but remained in his arms, sobbing into his chest.

DeShaun retrieved her backpack and caught up, taking his time.

Stuart let his arms wrap around her, comforting but not squeezing. "It's okay, Candace. Whatever it is, it's okay."

DeShaun knelt and patted her back, and the boys somehow knew to just stay quiet and let her cry.

After a few minutes, Candace stood to walk away. The boys exchanged their hundredth perplexed look.

"Wait!" Stuart called.

Candace stopped but didn't turn.

"Whatever you're gonna do, sooner or later you're gonna need to know how to ride a bike."

Candace turned to him, and there was almost, at least, relief on her face.

Chapter 13

DeShaun ran a few yards ahead and turned sideways as Stuart ran along the other side, pushing the handlebars. He got the bike going, waited for Candace to give the okay, and then released. Candace pedaled smoothly, keeping the handlebars straight and true.

DeShaun held his hands up and let her pedal past him, giving Stuart a thumbs-up and then he ran after her. "Okay, brake!" Stuart called. "Easy this time."

She did, and with just a little shimmy of the handlebars, she eased her foot down to stop. She glanced back at the boys with a proud grin, her head sideways and her eyes just a little squinty in a way that Stuart had never seen before, a way that made him feel... squishy, and he started a song about her in his head.

She stared up the road and when she turned back the smile was gone. "I really have to go, you guys. Wish I didn't."

DeShaun went to get his bike, while Stuart held one handlebar of his for her to practice on the pedals while they talked.

"I totally ruined Devil's Night for you guys," she lamented.

"It's okay," Stuart said. "We're getting too big for that stuff anyways."

Candace was incredulous. "Too big for Halloween?"

DeShaun steered a lazy circle around them, shaking his head. "You ask my dad, kids are too big the day they're old enough to toss a roll of toilet paper."

"Boy, I'd like to toss a few rolls across ol' Albert Betzler's lawn," Stuart said with a grimace.

"Yeah. If it weren't for his giant clients," added DeShaun.

"Albert's mean to you guys too?" asked Candace.

DeShaun and Stuart shared a cynical glance. "Yeah, but in different ways," said Stuart.

"And for different reasons," DeShaun enjoined.

"What does that mean?"

"Might as well tell ya, I guess." Stuart scratched his head. "Albert..." He turned to DeShaun for help.

"I don't know...likes you, I guess?" DeShaun said.

"Albert feels entitled to you," Stuart said.

Candace stopped. "Oh. Gross."

She pedaled faster, like she was distancing herself from the very thought.

"Well, that's a relief," DeShaun said, before Stuart could clamp a hand over his mouth.

Candace stopped like an old pro and turned to them, just as Stuart resumed a casual stride. "Why?"

"Because...it's good to know you have decent taste," Stuart said. "Maybe."

"I like niceness in a boy. That's number one. And Albert is *not* nice."

"What's after that?" Stuart ventured.

"Oh...a few things." Candace said, perhaps recalling what she had considered many times. "Sensitivity. Loyalty. I guess. Mostly..." She stood on the bike and rocked it back and forth. "Sanity."

"Sanity?" asked the boys in harmony.

"That's not so much, is it?" she asked.

"No."

As she started pedaling again, Stuart looked at DeShaun and mouthed the question *Am I sane?* DeShaun shrugged.

"My street is coming up," she said.

"It's okay. We'll take you all the way to your door," Stuart offered.

"I don't think so, guys."

"How come? I mean, it's getting dark..."

"My family is kinda peculiar," she explained. "I don't think...I'm not ready for you to meet them."

"Okay." Stuart waved. "No problem. Um...What about tomorrow night? The parade."

"I'm really gonna try, Stuart."

"Cool. Well..." Stuart backed up, waved again. "I guess, good night then."

"Yeah. Thanks, you guys." Candace's smile was more beguiling than ever, maybe because it seemed so sad, almost fatalistic.

"For what?" Stuart asked.

"A wonderful evening."

"You're welcome." Stuart thought of hugging her. He wanted to, just to be comforting, but he was afraid.

She got off and handed the handlebars over to Stuart, then turned and walked onto Zebulon Street.

Stuart stood holding his bike. It felt like the whole world had shifted on its axis, only no one but him could feel it.

"What *now*?" asked DeShaun.

Stuart looked over at his friend and saw the rock of stability he often took for granted, the anchor his brother could not be when their father died, the awkward kid who had sat down beside him in Mrs. Wong's third-grade class and never left.

Stuart knew DeShaun would die for him, and vice versa, and he almost—*almost*—wished for a chance to prove it.

"We could still make the Screecher Feature, you know?"

"No creepy old house?" asked DeShaun. "You sure?"

"Yeah. I think so." He stared off toward where Candace had run away. "One last Screecher Feature. Before we think it's...cheesy or something like that."

"Screamer Femur it is, then!" DeShaun quipped. "My treat." He turned to ride off, and Stuart was so proud to be his friend right then, he beamed. He was going to buy the crazy bastard all the popcorn he could eat.

Candace saw the boys pedal out of sight and slowed her pace, in no hurry to get home. A strong wind blew leaves across her path, making her stuff her hands into her jacket pockets. She felt a little something and withdrew a piece of black-and-orange-wrapped candy. "Stuart, you sweet, sneaky devil."

She unwrapped it and popped it in her mouth.

* * * *

The long straightaway, flanked by a pumpkin field on one side and a cornfield on the other, was quiet after farming hours, with homes on the hilly terrain overlooking the fields going dark by eight P.M.

A vintage Trans Am, the same that had roared alongside Candace's bus earlier that day, hurtled along this stretch, scattering leaves to either side in rattling waves.

The muscle car's driver, Ryan Fray, wearing a pirate hat, massive gold hoop earring, and a ragged striped vest over his bull-like physique, bounced a rubber spider in the face of the girl beside him—Helga, Candace's bus driver.

"*Eek!*" She daintily held the back of her hand to her face, like the medieval damsel her costume depicted, then shoved the jiggly toy back at him.

"Ah, c'mon!" Ryan thrust it at her again. "You can at least play along!"

"It didn't scare me last year, Ryan," she said. "Or back in grade school."

In the back, Trudy Tornquist's killer curves were on full display in a shiny royal-blue catsuit. Angus, whose inflatable muscle suit was surely an ironic jab at his own scrawny physique, clinked his beer bottle with hers, quipping, "Sad. Guess the honeymoon's over."

Trudy raised her bottle. "Here's to the senior-year itch!"

"Yeah, yeah." Ryan tossed the spider back at them. "Pass me one of those."

As Trudy handed it up, Helga intercepted.

"Huh-uh-!" she teased. "Not just yet!"

"Aw, come on! I just want a sip."

Helga eyed him sideways as she took that sip. "If you're a good boy at the lake."

"By 'good boy' do you mean…"

Helga batted her eyelashes. "I mean *bad* boy."

Ryan's eyes went wide, and Angus raised another toast. "Here's to second honeymoons!"

But Ryan was distracted by something in the road ahead. "What in the blue hell is this creepwad doing?"

Walking with an odd gait in the center of the road: a figure, trailing a flowing black Dracula cape, his back to them.

"Maybe I can scare *this* bozo at least." Ryan gave Helga a mischievous wink as he dropped to neutral, revved the engine twice, then punched it, heading right for the dark meandering pedestrian.

They all saw the figure turn his head toward them, saw the ghastly jaundiced complexion and the crooked grin beneath a simple black eye mask. He was carrying a big sack, or pillowcase, sharp things poking through the bottom. He switched directions, turning to meet them.

Ryan stuck his head out the window, hoarsely shouting, "*Hey!* Happy Devil's Night, asshole!"

"Ryan!" Helga was, once again, not impressed. "Knock it off!"

But Ryan continued, straight toward the walker—who did not slow or run, but only kept walking toward them, grinning like a tiger shark.

When Trudy buried her head in Angus's inflatable chest, he hugged her tight, calling, "Easy, Ryan!"

Ryan's response was a cocky guffaw they all knew well.

The figure stopped and stood stock-still in the middle of the road, waiting.

"C'mon…" Ryan goaded under his breath, though he never eased off the accelerator. "*Move,* asshole!"

Trudy emitted a high-pitched keening, her nails digging into Angus's thin thigh.

Helga grabbed the wheel and veered it hard, just in time to miss hitting the figure by less than a foot.

Despite the sudden shift of direction and the sharp pain of Trudy's claw hold, Angus kept his eyes locked on the odd man as they careened past him. What he saw in those eyes was not a display of bravado. It was not fear, but not exactly courage either. More like…a void.

Over the roar of the engine, Angus heard a sound like that of a jackal calling to its pack during the pursuit of wounded prey.

Then—only blurry chaos, as the Trans Am barreled into the rutted turf of the pumpkin field to their right, sending them tumbling into one another.

An abrupt stop. Senses swimming.

"Damn it, Helga!" Ryan shouted.

"Don't 'damn it' me, you *asshole!*"

"Everybody okay?" Ryan asked.

"Yeah, but… *Shit.*" Trudy brushed at her costume and the upholstery beneath her. "I hope you like the smell of beer."

"Aah, shoot," griped Ryan.

"Well, you shouldn't have done that!" said Helga.

Angus got his bearings and scanned toward where he had seen the bizarre creature.

He was walking toward them.

Giving Helga a nasty look, Ryan put the car in gear and floored the gas. But the heavy Pontiac did not move, no matter how loudly he revved the engine.

With his window cracked, Angus could hear the stranger giggling eagerly with each step.

"Great." Ryan smacked the wheel and turned to Helga. "I should make you get out and push."

"Hey, guys?" Angus said in a low tone.

"Maybe I *will* get out," Helga asserted, "and walk home!"

Trudy looked to see what had Angus's attention, while Ryan and Helga bickered. "*Guys!*" Trudy interrupted.

Ryan and Helga turned to see Everett coming closer.

"O ho *ho*!" Ryan said. "He wants a rumble?"

"Get us out of here, dude!" Angus pleaded. "He doesn't…*look* right."

Ryan, flush with adrenaline and anger, shoved the door open. "He'll look even worse when I get finished."

"Ryan, *stop it!*" called Helga, grasping at him as he stepped out and doffed the pirate vest to display his thick chest.

"You comin' this way, freako?" Ryan challenged.

Helga leaned across the driver seat and screamed, "Ryan, damn it, stop! It was *my fault,* okay?"

Ryan drew a switchblade from his jeans pocket and flicked it open. "Hey, you want some real blood on that shitty, gay costume?"

The man's response was an increased pace. He reached into his pillowcase and withdrew a handful of knives and skewers and steak forks.

Ryan's courage fled. "Shit," he mumbled, hoping he didn't appear as scared as he felt.

Helga scooted behind the wheel and went to work trying to free the Trans Am. Shifting back and forth between reverse and first, she hoped to rock the car out of the muddy mess.

Trudy leaned forward to scream at Ryan. He turned to jump back in the car.

"Ryan, you have to *push!*" Helga shrilled at him. She let off the gas and the car rocked back into the rut that it was only digging deeper.

Ryan hurried to the rear, shoving the car with a mammoth effort. At the back windshield, Trudy and Angus frantically gestured and called encouragement to him—cheerleaders at the most important event in their hero's lifetime.

Ryan took a step back, set a deep three-point stance, and exploded, smashing shoulder-first into the Trans Am the way he smashed tackle dummies and defensive linemen. A hoarse scream roared from his red face as he continued to drive, finally dislodging the big Pontiac with an explosive whoop.

Ten yards away the stranger grinned wider than ever, dropping his sack to break into a full sprint. He was far quicker than any running back—or any sane man—Ryan had ever encountered.

Ryan fell to his hands and knees as the Trans Am rolled onto the road—but got himself up and bolted for the passenger side. He could practically *feel* the pursuer, and all those sharp things, less than a half-dozen paces away.

Helga leaned over and shoved the passenger door open. *"Get in!"*

The caped horror was an arm's length from the Trans Am when Ryan dove into the seat. Helga gunned the engine, not waiting for him to pull his feet in.

Everett swiped at Ryan's foot with his fistful of cutlery—but missed.

In the back, Trudy and Angus shouted a cacophony of strident pleas, terrified when they saw that the stranger wasn't giving up, was continuing to chase the car, inhumanly fast.

Ryan wrestled himself inside and slammed the door.

The madman stopped his pursuit.

Breaths of relief escaped them all.

"*Shit!*" Angus squeaked. "What the hell is *wrong* with that guy?"

There was no conversation, as they all recovered their breath and their senses. Then, while Ryan situated himself in the passenger seat, Helga giggled.

"What's the joke, lady?"

Meeting Helga's gaze in the mirror, Trudy joined in with a clap, leaving Angus to wonder if her mind had broken.

"Men. No sense of irony," she noted.

Ryan shot an impatient glance back at her. "What?"

Helga raised the rubber spider. "That dude had you losers for dinner."

Angus face-palmed. "Aaah...Shit."

"Here's to Devil's Night!" said Trudy, and the mood returned, just that easily, to the relaxed celebration it had been before.

Her interest drawn by the DJ's chatter on the radio, Helga shushed everyone and turned up the volume.

"—show your support tomorrow night, as Ember Hollow's very own Chalk Outlines perform on top of the marquee at The Grand Illusion Cinemas, downtown. These kids are making some serious waves!" said the DJ, as he ramped up "Rumble at Castle Frankenstein."

"Ooh!" Helga turned it up to sing along, soon joined by Trudy.

"I was hunted, far from home

Haunted, cursed to roam

Desperate to be freed

From my insatiable need

To kill by full moon's light"

The boys joined too, all singing in a perfect blend of youthful sincerity and sarcasm, as Helga made the hard right onto lonesome Haunted Hollow Road, toward the pond at its end. The main road and its unnerving pedestrian faded to an awesome story they could tell their friends later, as the pumpkins decayed.

* * * *

Everett watched the shrinking tail lights of the Trans Am, till it turned into the tree-lined gravel road. "Stopped playing. Very mean."

Just a few yards away stood a dusty sign that read: HAUNTED HOLLOW FISHING POND, NEXT RIGHT. And beneath that: CLOSED TILL SPRING.

Everett thought about letters and words and remembered from his spooky books how they connected to each other to tell him things.

He would be playing with his new friends after all, it appeared. He walked after them—until his attention was drawn to something across the pumpkin field. A huge, dark old house, the kind Everett often drew and read and dreamed about, the kind his old records portrayed as party central for the dead and the strange—those like him.

Everett's smile grew wide again, and he trudged across the field.

Chapter 14

Albert Betzler, resplendent in top hat with matching wool cloak and a pasted-on goatee, led the line of costumed Krelboynes to the rear corner of the old Victorian. He cocked his ear toward the house, listened for a minute, then removed his plastic vampire teeth to speak. "Excellent. They don't appear to have arrived yet, so we can execute Plan A."

Two of his gang of four—papier-mâché hunchback Del, still wearing his glasses, and Norman in a plush, full-body teddy bear costume—lifted their masks to take in the delicious autumn air. The house's pervasive mustiness was strong, even outside.

Behind them stood two much larger figures:, Tyrell— a rather chintzy bigfoot—spinning a basketball on one fuzzy finger; and Maynard, dressed as a hulking, hooded executioner, sporting a massive broadax to complete the ensemble.

Hunchback Del raised a chain and capered about, clinking it. "How's this?"

"Absolutely eldritch!" lauded Albert. "Norman?"

They turned to Norman. He took his time donning the fuzzy full-head bear mask that was doomed to be whimsical and cheery in even the half-light of an old house. He tried, though, mustering a muffled growl as he raised round paws and paddled at the air like a sleepy kitten.

Albert stroked his false goatee. "Maynard, may I?"

Maynard tossed the massive ax to Albert, who nearly fell trying to ride out the weight. Once he'd regained his balance, he handed it to Norman. "There."

"Wait! This is *real*!" Norman protested.

"Go to the head of class, Louis Pasteur!" Albert adjusted Norman's grip on the ax to make it seem more threatening, then shoved the bear head back on. "All you have to do is wave it around."

Norman practiced, caught off guard when Albert sprayed fake blood all over both the bear costume and the ax. "Hey!"

"Maintain composure, Norman. The package says it washes out."

Albert tossed the bottle over his shoulder and turned to Maynard and Tyrell. "You guys will serve as our big finale."

Tyrell flashed a fuzzy thumbs-up. Maynard, munching on a protein bar, turned to connect knuckles with the hirsute basketballer.

Albert led them around the corner to the weathered back deck and climbed the short set of stairs. Albert stopped at the back door, causing the others to crowd behind him. "Del, do you have the lock-picking set?

"Um..."

"What? Does that mean no?"

"My dad took it away," Del grumbled. "After I got into his trunk and found his sex books."

Albert took off his glasses and rubbed his temples. "Del, you could have—"

Maynard shouldered past them and punched the door, sending it flying off the hinges and to the floor, raising a rectangular cloud of dust.

"Breathtaking!" Norman exclaimed. The boys entered, stopping just inside the dim hallway to take in the peeling wallpaper and old paintings on the wall.

Del pointed to an old portrait of a mustachioed gentleman who might have been constipated at the time of posing. "Hey! I wonder if the eyes follow you around the room."

Tyrell took it down and poked two long, fur-gloved fingers through the canvas at the eyes, then handed it to Del, like he was delivering a package.

"Um...thanks?" Del held the portrait to his face and peered through both his glasses and the fresh finger holes, glancing back and forth to imitate a scary stalker.

First to enter the living room, Norman was impressed to find The Chalk Outlines' gear packed against the wall. He took off the bear head to exclaim, "Sweet mother of Sagan!"

Albert entered, shushing him.

"Check out all this rock-and-roll stuff!" Norman stage whispered.

Albert beheld the equipment, his default devious expression accentuated by the goatee.

"It's so neat!" Norman gushed. "Like a real rock band setup!"

"Duh. Stupidert's brother is leader of that grotesque musical travesty The Chalk Outlines," noted Albert, his eyes narrowing. "These are their instruments."

Tyrell entered and exclaimed, "Gonzo!" as he opened the coffin-shaped case that held Pedro's bass.

"Wow!" Norman said, forgetting to whisper.

Maynard took a seat behind the drums, barely fitting his bulk in the space fitted for Jill. He picked up the drum sticks and tried to spin them in his fingers. "That hot-ass drummer chick plays with these sticks. Bet she'd like to play with my stick."

"That's rather unambiguous, don't you think?" Albert asked.

"Huh?"

"Never mind. Let's find some hiding spots, shall we? Stupidert and DeShaun will be coming along soon."

A paper bag, barely discernible in the house's thickening shadows, sat on an end table beside the band's gear—the tainted treats from Angelo's lab in the basement.

Marvin, searching for a hiding place, spotted the paper bag. He poked his paw inside and was delighted to withdraw several pieces of orange-and-black-wrapped candy. Hiding the bag under his armpit, he crept to the hall closet.

Chapter 15

Candace walked through the neighborhood, humming to herself. She worked the candy back and forth in her mouth as she strolled, thinking of Stuart's cute, earnest face.

An odd sound drew her attention to a row of shrubs to her left. She stopped and peered into the bushes. The darkest section seemed to waver, then formed a large leafy hand that reached toward her.

Candace recoiled. Then the shrubbery snapped back to normal, like a rubber glove.

Candace gathered herself and renewed her pace. "Silly…"

Within a few steps, she had to slow, as her peripheral vision began shimmering, vibrating. A low scraping sound rose behind her, making her spin—to see nothing. Then glowing green jackal's eyes blinked open and peered at her from within an overturned trash can. Behind it, a large pile of leaves shifted—and crawled toward her.

Candace shook her head till it pounded—but when her vision settled, the leaf blob was still coming—and gaining speed.

The leaves burst apart against the yard's fence, only to reform on the other side. Candace burst into a run.

A garden hose unspooled from the side of a house to her right and rocketed toward her feet. She leaped over it with a squeal as dense shadows writhed and rose and flew and flowed toward her like puddles of evil black ink.

"Mama!" she cried. "Daddy!"

She stumbled as she turned hard onto her drive.

Breathless from the incline, she nonetheless ran like hell, all too aware of the blackness behind her, threatening to swallow her. Twisting spirals of bright burning stars lengthened and focused to stab her from above.

Her house came into view, dim light glowing from the window of her mother's bedroom. She begged her mother to *feel* her desperation and open the door in time for her to dart inside.

A black tidal wave rose around and above her, demon fish snapping at her through its surface.

She made it to the door, hitting and turning the knob with such timing that she hardly slowed at all, as she spun over the threshold and slammed the door.

She rested against it and gulped familiar-scented air. Eyes tightly shut, she listened.

When she opened her eyes, she was confused to see a knife embedded in the door beside the knob.

She wrenched it loose, thinking she might need it if something broke in. The knife melted like burning wax. She dropped it.

Candace watched her hand, waiting for searing pain that never came. She took two slow steps forward, staying focused on the dim light limning the edge of the door to her parents' room.

At the door, she stopped, pushing it open a few inches. "Mama?"

As she eased the door open, an ethereal light flooded her face, warming her, erasing her terror. Lit by a celestial glow cascading through the broken ceiling, Mamalee floated above the bed headboard, peering down at Candace with beatific eyes. Angelic wings spread from her back.

Mamalee raised a finger to her smiling lips. "Shhh." She pointed to the armchair near the window, where the curtains rose and fell from the fall breeze.

Her father sat in the armchair with his eyes closed, a boyish grin on his lips like he was dreaming of a time long before damaged children and annual cross-country moves, perhaps his own childhood.

Candace was happy to see such contentment and heavenly beauty in her parents. "Mama, I was so scared."

Mamalee shushed her again. "Let that slip away, child. Sleep."

Candace shuffled to her parents' big bed, watching in wonder as tiny lights like fireflies emerged from Mamalee's eyes and danced around her head.

She settled into the bed as Mamalee hovered over her. "I will watch over you, my baby. Always."

Candace's eyes fluttered. She was asleep in seconds.

Chapter 16

Full dark fell like an anvil in a Looney Tunes episode.

Hiding behind the line of shrubs against the house, Tyrell, unmasked, spun his basketball on each finger in succession, then back, then every other, like a mirthless, hair-covered Harlem Globetrotter.

Nearby, Maynard lay curled up on the ground, snoring. Tyrell nudged him. "Hey! Wake up, dude!"

Maynard sat up. "What?"

"Get up. I need to stretch my legs."

"Your legs are plenty stretched already, Storko."

"Hee-hee, ho-ho. Come on."

Maynard stood. "Wait a minute. What do you need me for?"

Tyrell appeared sheepish even in the dark.

"Well?"

"This place is a little spooky, all right?"

"Aw, jeez," griped Maynard. "I told you, don't go to that Screecher Feature." They shoved their way out of the bushes.

* * * *

Norman trembled at the sounds of a growling, scrabbling thing lurking just beyond the closet, surely sniffing for fresh meat.

Keeping one hand cupped over his mouth, he held his heavy ax close with the other, ignoring the wet stain darkening the crotch of his bear suit.

The bag of candy lay spilled and forgotten on the floor, along with a single wrapper.

"Not real...Not real...*Oh, God...*" he whispered to himself as a tear crawled down his cheek.

* * * *

Albert sighed as he sat slumped on the dusty old commode lid, flicking his flashlight off and on.

He peeked through the crack between door and frame, saw only still shadows, then turned and went to the grimy mirror, underlighting himself with the flashlight. "It's *alive!*" he intoned in quite a reasonable imitation of Colin Clive.

He turned and studied the torn shower curtain. He yanked it open, wielding the flashlight like a butcher knife as he mimicked a screeching violin.

He sat again, checking his calculator watch, cursing Stuart and DeShaun for no-showing. He stepped out of the bathroom. "Okay, guys. Everybody come out. Norman, go get Maynard and Tyrell."

He went to the instruments, and his devious smile reappeared, partially ungluing the goatee. "You think you can outsmart me, Stupidert?" he mumbled. "Think again."

He kicked over the drum kit, pleased by the noisy, hollow echo. "Hate to defecate on your parade, Chalk Outlines, but..." He mimicked the sounds of violent diarrhea.

The exhilaration he felt was perhaps comparable to his first science fair win, after which he had smirked at that stupid kid who had composed the silly theory about atomic fission and refusion. Ha! What a joke.

He raised the bass guitar from its case and plucked at the strings. "Come on, you guys! Let's Tipper Gore these ghoulish blasphemies against the musical arts!"

He raised the bass high, hefting it like a sledgehammer as he eyed the drum kit. "Norman! Guys! Come on. You're going to miss all the recreation!"

Hearing no response, Albert took a breath and swung the bass into the drums, shattering and scattering them and their stands about the room.

He howled as he bashed the bass into the hardwood floor. Its neck splintered with a screechy twang. He admired the destruction he had wrought, then impatiently dropped the bass, went to the front door, and opened it. "Tyrell! Maynard! Don't you guys want to help me trash these atrocious noise pollution machines?"

Wind blew leaves from the big maple in the front yard that stood silhouetted by the full moon.

"Del?"

No sign of anyone.

"Jeez, where are all you guys?"

He was ready for a jump scare, setting himself to give a stony no-sell. But it never came. "You dimwits can forget about trying to scare me."

Leaving the door open, he went back to the instruments and strummed the neck of the wrecked bass with the toe of his shoe. "Norman? You still in the closet?" He didn't sound quite as self-assured as usual.

Albert walked to the closet and reached for the knob, but stopped on hearing a scream from outside. "What the...?"

Norman burst from the closet, bellowing, candy-colored drool running down his chin—and the ax raised.

Chapter 17

The stalker was a demon-grinned mad hatter. The lid of his top hat erupted like a volcano, releasing a leering white rabbit, which in turn split apart to reveal a flying swarm of razorblade playing cards, all whirling into a formation targeting him. Norman had to defend himself.

He swung the ax, bringing it straight down onto Albert's foot.

Albert's cries joined Norman's in a chorus of horror and pain.

Norman cowered against the wall as the cards buzzed him, nicking his cheeks and neck, then circling to do it again, like the biplanes that had tormented a defiant King Kong on the Empire State Building.

Whimpering, Albert pried at the ax in his foot, yanking it free at last—only to separate a piece of his foot with it. He fell to his side crying, refusing to look at the wound, the blood, the separation.

The boys, immersed in a duet of delirious fear meeting transcendent pain, remained unaware of a new arrival emerging from the shadows of the front room.

Everett.

His gaze fell to the ax on the floor lying just inches from a pool of blood. "Choppy treat!"

The boys saw him and went silent.

Snickering, Everett took the ax.

Albert scooted against the wall and tried to continue—through it, or perhaps over it. Norman scurried on all fours back into the closet and slammed the door.

Everett was digging in his coat pocket for paper masks when Tyrell and Maynard bounded up the back steps and appeared at the doorway.

"What's going on?" Tyrell demanded to know. "Who's screaming?"

Everett spun, swinging the ax in a high wide arc.

Tyrell's head spun off his shoulders and landed in Maynard's hands.

The bull-like bully blinked at the head and looked up at Everett, meeting eyes that were far too gleeful. "Choppy trick!" Everett said, pointing at Tyrell's spurting neck, as the body dropped to its knees.

Maynard turned to run away, trailing a scream.

His legs pumped like pistons as he tucked Tyrell's head under his arm and made for safety, hitting a spin move off the corner of the house but never stopping—until something caught him across the neck, snapping him horizontal. Suspended like a balloon, Maynard only had time to realize he had gained no meaningful yardage before he fell spine-first onto the unforgiving ground.

He attempted to catch his breath, trying to believe he had just been pranked. Struggling to focus, he saw that it was a rope of some kind that had leveled him, stretched from the corner of the house to the trees at the edge of the yard, with leaves or something stuck to it.

Oh—those were little bats and skulls and ghosts. It was a homemade Halloween banner.

And the rope was coming out of a fake body propped against the tree behind it.

No...

It was that kid Del, with a messed-up construction paper kitty cat mask stapled over his face, glasses in place over it. He was tied to the tree by his own intestines, which were strung back to the house's gutter pipe.

Maynard tried to sit up, to cry out, but was too breathless to do either. Sensing something behind him, he whipped his head up and saw his ax—the one he had loaned to Norman—silhouetted against the dim sky, just before it sliced into his skull.

* * * *

At twenty-four, Ruth had seen more than her share of good times—many artificially induced—and the bad times that resulted.

Thanks to a libido as formidable as her personality, she had wound up with Nico Rizzoli, whose sex drive was almost as insatiable as hers. His growing addictions were an added bonus. To Ruth, Nico was the doorway to both worlds, and in the end, with most of her bridges burned, dealing with Nico's arrest left Ruth as something like a war orphan.

Seeing she had nowhere to go, a judge took pity on Ruth and sentenced her to a rehabilitation program, payable in work hours. There, she met new friends from opposite ends of a bleak spectrum.

Many of Nico's former customers had wound up in the same program as Ruth. There were no hard feelings though, as most of these were more interested in Ruth's connections—namely, Nico—and how they could score again.

But there was a minority of users who had dug right through rock bottom and were determined to stay clean. Ruth's roommate, Vickie, buttressed by the Holy Bible as viewed through the harsh filter of fundamentalism, was one.

Vickie witnessed to Ruth, and the girls prayed together for Ruth's salvation, which she declared to all who would listen. The program's overseers were impressed. Soon, Ruth was out of the system and nestled in the Lord's embrace, into which she intended to bring every soul who crossed her path.

There were no fundamentalist churches near Ember Hollow. But Reverend McGlazer of Ember Hollow Unitarian Chapel, a volunteer at the center, had gained Ruth's attention.

His educated, regal bearing, with his veneer of flawed conscience, appealed to her need for both a father figure and a bad boy. As a recovering alcoholic, he could topple into relapse any time—and might need a strong woman. Sexually, she would remain loyal to Nico, of course—unless the Lord led her otherwise.

* * * *

Everett pulled the ruined executioner's hood from the mush of Maynard's head and held it up to the moonlight. Satisfied, he tore off his eye mask, leaving a few staples in his flesh, then drew the cloven hood over his pasty face. He stapled the eye mask onto what was left of Maynard's head, where eyes once were. "Swappies!"

* * * *

The warehouse space just outside of town was donated by Bruner Heavy Equipment every year for PR and good will among Ember Hollow's farmers. Ruth had written and called the company numerous times, hoping to convince them to withdraw their support. She was always rebuffed.

Unlike conventional parades, whose display conveyances were usually small cars with themes built around them, Ember Hollow's were motorless platforms pulled by tractors from local farms or tricked-out high-end hot rods. Far from just street racers, these were serious club cars painted with thematic art, babied and blessed by their hardcore rockabilly owners and drivers. For Ember Hollow's car enthusiasts and those in the outlying counties, the Pumpkin Parade was the highlight of the season, an excuse for competitive rodders to show off their dedication and artistry.

A 1966 Olds Toronado from all the way up in Point Pleasant, West Virginia, with a sparkling purple paint job airbrushed with leering pumpkins and tombstones, would take the lead in this year's parade, followed by East Coast Killer Kustoms's HellHearse, the Carolina Corpsemobile, and a good forty more mechanical beauties.

St. Saturn Unitarian's Cemetery Terrorium display was to be pulled by a battered rust-brown 1941 Chevrolet COE truck, the roof of which was cut out for McGlazer to wave and toss candy crosses from it as he boomed his well-practiced baritone laughter. He would be dressed as pagan priest Lord Summerisle from the cult film *The Wicker Man,* as portrayed by Christopher Lee. Few would catch the reference—which delighted McGlazer to no end.

Gathered outside the Bruner open warehouse where the Halloween parade mobiles were built and stored, the drivers and mechanics could not resist some wide-open revving of ear-crushing, eight-cylinder brawn.

The rich smell of a petroleum grade far purer than typical square fare greeted—and offended—Ruth as she struggled through a bay door, arms loaded with a box of diner food and a bushel of apples. She wrestled her load to a long table of pumpkins, then dropped off the apples and searched for Reverend McGlazer.

He and Hudson Lott watched burly workers raise a Volkswagen Beetle-sized plywood-and-metal-tubing spider on a cable web over its display float.

Spooky stereophonic cackling rose and fell from a trailer fashioned into a huge casket, with blood painted like running streams at the coffin lid's edge. Someone inside adjusted the volume.

Ruth whispered to herself. "Oh…Oh, Holy Father. This truly is a demonic blasphemy."

She strode toward McGlazer, stopping to frown at a fortune-teller-themed covered wagon with arcane-looking symbols and poster board tarot cards pasted to the sides.

Stella, sporting a wig of long grayish hair, came around from the front of the float, almost colliding with Ruth. She emitted a yelp. "Ooh, that was a good one!" she said.

"*This* is your contribution to the parade?" Ruth asked.

"Yes! Watch this!" Stella reached inside under the carriage's cloth cover, felt around, then hit a switch that caused an animatronic ragged cackling corpse to emerge from the rear of the carriage, startling Ruth.

"Ha!" Stella exclaimed. "I guess we're even now!"

"Vengeance is *mine*, sayeth the Lord," grumbled Ruth, as she walked away in a huff.

* * * *

Blood-soaked boots trudged across the dusty, stripped pumpkin field, stopping at a lonesome pumpkin that had been skipped over during the harvest.

Everett reached down and lifted the gourd, breaking it from its brittle stem. Raising the pumpkin, Everett placed two bloody fingers on spots where eyes should go. "See all the Halloween!"

He dropped it into his bag and peered off toward the chocolate-colored, tree-lined horizon, beyond which he knew was the fishing pond where his playmates had gone.

Chapter 18

"—need to make a new spider, that's all. That thing weighs a ton," noted Hudson.

"Yes, but it's just so *gruesome,* don't you think?" McGlazer said. He took in the creature's blood-dripping mandibles, mirrored eyes, and grasping legs.

Ruth cleared her throat to interrupt.

"Hello there, Ruth," greeted Hudson.

"Deputy Lott," Ruth said.

"You can call me Hudson, you know."

"I believe formalities with regards to authority are a safeguard against hooliganism, if you don't mind."

Hudson raised eyebrows and hands in resignation.

"What do you think, Ruth?" asked Reverend McGlazer.

"I've explained my feelings." Ruth fingered her gold cross necklace as she gestured toward the table behind her. "I brought you some dinner and apples from Peterson's farm."

"Oh! Ruth, you're the best. Thank you so much!"

"Mm-hm. I'll go attend to some church matters now."

"Nice to see you, Ruth," Hudson said, adding, "Er, Miss Treadwell."

Ruth turned to leave but slowed when she heard Lott say to McGlazer, "Oh! About that piece of candy you brought me…"

She went to the table to unbox the food as she eavesdropped.

"I really don't think there's anything to it, but I did take it over to Charlie Plemmons at the drugstore," Lott said.

"Ah! How is Charlie?" McGlazer asked.

"Busy. Holiday sales and all. He said he would take a look at it after closing."

Ruth's heartbeat quickened.

"Please give him my thanks when you see him."

"Yeah, I'll be heading over in an hour or so," Hudson said.

Feeling panic rising, Ruth stroked her little cross. She hurried away—only to be stopped at the bay door by Kerwin. "Well, *hello*, O Ruthless One!"

Ruth suppressed most of her irritation. The rest, Kerwin ignored. "Excuse me, Kerwin. I'm in a hurry."

"Just a sec." Kerwin's smile morphed into his cartoon conspiracy expression. "We need to talk biz."

"What is it?" Ruth asked.

"Your, uh, little operation going all right?"

"We're finished."

"Oh?" Kerwin craned his neck to see what Hudson was doing. "So… your boyfriend's moving out of the basement?"

"He wasn't—he's *not* my boyfriend."

"Oh?" This brought a light of lascivious hope to Kerwin's face. "Didn't know you were single."

"I have a boyfriend." Ruth imagined calling down lightning to burn Kerwin to a pillar of smoking ash. "Just not here."

"You, uh…" Kerwin pointed up. "You're not talking about the Lord, are you?"

"I have to go."

"I just need to make sure you guys are cleared out by tomorrow, like we agreed. The band's gonna be moving around in there and I don't want—"

"I promise," she interrupted. "Now please…"

"*If*"—Kerwin's face grew the Lon Chaney *Phantom of the Opera* grin he thought was charming—"you'll have dinner with me. After the Outlines get signed. You know." He hung an arm on the door frame just as he surely thought James Dean might do. "I'll need a plus one for the celebration."

"I don't…" Ruth realized there was only one way to end this conversation. "Okay, of course.

"It's a date then!" Kerwin rubbed his hands together.

She shoved past him, feeling his gaze on her.

* * * *

With only the Trans Am's headlights and a lone streetlamp over the pond providing light, Angus and Trudy sat at the end of a small pier over the isolated fishing spot, passing a bottle. They had graduated to liquor: Diamante's Deep Dark.

Helga and Ryan had stripped to their underwear upon arrival, but Angus, citing the cool temperature, was still in costume. Trudy remained clothed too. "Well?" she cooed.

"Well what?" Angus imitated.

"Are you warm enough to get in yet?"

"Hold on." Angus took a huge guzzle.

"Easy!" Trudy jerked the bottle away, spilling a good bit. "You're not supposed to drink and swim!"

Angus watched the other couple cavort in the dark water, and he patted his inflatable muscles. "That's why I'm wearing my floaty!"

Trudy stood and put her hands on her perfect hips. "What? You mean those muscles aren't real?"

She unzipped her body suit and stepped out, presenting to Angus a body he found even more fantastic than he had spent many showers imagining. All he could say was "Uh…"

"Ooh! Chilly!" She said with an almost innocent smile. "Have fun with your play muscles." She jumped in.

Angus set down the bottle and followed, feet-first.

Helga and Ryan held each other, treading water together. Ryan craned his head and got a good eyeful of Trudy. "Great ghosts of Mars!"

Helga forced his face toward her. "Huh-uh, bad boy. You only have eyes for me. Remember?"

"Yeah, but you're not naked."

"Yeah, and maybe I won't ever be if Trudy is what you want to see."

"Aw, babe! You're *killing* me here! Give me something!"

She blew bubbles at him. "I'll give you something."

"Really?"

"But first"—she swam back from him—"you need to get me a beer."

Ryan swam for shore like a school of piranha was after him, splashing Trudy and Angus on the way. He climbed out at the pier and trotted toward the Trans Am.

Helga watched Ryan go, enjoying the sight of his brawny silhouette until he became lost in the headlights. She turned to watch Trudy and Angus play.

Helga grinned as Trudy took a deep breath and ducked underwater in front of Angus, who said, "Oh-ho *ho*! You naughty little mermaid."

Helga swam to the pier and pushed herself up, propping her elbows on it, kicking her feet in the water languidly as she squinted toward the Trans Am, seeing nothing but glaring headlights.

Nearby, Angus felt around in the water for Trudy, a puzzled expression on his face. "Hey, where'd you go?"

Helga shielded her eyes. "Ryan!"

She heard movement from the Trans Am, then: "Got 'em! Getting the beer!"

She heard the trunk lid open and rested her chin on her arms, bored.

Angus was still searching for Trudy. "Did the Gill Man get you, Trood?" he asked. The question was supposed to be a joke, and yet, he didn't sound very amused.

Angus called again. Helga met his gaze, and neither was comforted by the look they exchanged. Angus swallowed air and dove.

Something rose behind Helga like an amphibious jack-in-the-box, scaring a scream out of her. It was Trudy. Helga turned and splashed her friend. "Oh, you *bitch!*"

Trudy and Helga began to wrestle. Angus surfaced and watched, not even noticing the shadow that fell over them.

The girls turned toward the silhouette framed by the Pontiac's headlights.

"Throw me one," Trudy called.

Helga swam back to the pier, propping her arms on it as before. "Today, how 'bout?"

A heavy boot descended on Helga's hand, pinning it to the pier. She emitted an angry yelp. "*Stop* it, you asshole!" Helga tugged at the foot with her free hand.

Behind her, Trudy squinted.

Everett's ax descended, severing Helga's arm. She screamed. Trudy joined in.

"Be a *seal!*" said Everett.

Angus rose from the water just in time to see the bizarre figure lopping off Helga's other arm.

That demented giggling was unmistakable. It was the creep from the road, now wearing a ragged black hood.

Helga fell into the water and sank, red clouds blooming from her stumps.

Trudy swam toward Helga to help—but then saw Everett's ax rise again in the glaring headlights. She could not swim closer.

Helga popped up, her bloody stumps flailing, her terrified eyes locked on Trudy. "Hel...hel...help...*me!*" She gulped water as she cried out.

Angus, making for the shore, called, "Trudy! Come on! You can't save her!"

"Screw you, freako!" Ryan shouted behind Everett and smashed a beer bottle over the stalker's head, sending him to his hands and knees.

Ryan jumped into the water to save Helga, as Everett shook off the effects of the blow.

"Hurry!" Angus shouted as he climbed out. "*Hurry, Ryan!*"

Trudy swam to the far end of the pond, as far away from Everett as she could get.

Ryan plummeted into the red water, torpedoing like crazy to reach Helga. She was just visible in the dark, cloudy water, but the moon and rising bubbles helped him stay oriented.

"*Shit,*" Angus muttered, as he scrambled toward the killer—who was rising to one knee.

In the lake, Ryan got his arm around Helga and pumped his legs to bring her to the top.

Angus dashed for the ax. Hoisting it, he pitched forward, surprised by its weight. He regained his balance just as Everett stood.

Angus swung the ax like he had his bat way back in Little League. Everett caught the handle just below the blade and seemed to find this development as humorous as everything else.

In his other hand, Everett held the neck from the beer bottle Ryan had shattered over his head. He thrust it into Angus's throat. Blood poured from the bottle's mouth onto the pier.

"Treat treat treat!" said Everett.

* * * *

Ryan popped up from the water and grabbed onto the pier, pulling himself up with one hand as he held the shock-addled Helga in the other arm.

Then he saw that Everett was back on his feet. "Ah *shit.*"

Everett arced the ax blade, lodging it in Ryan's thick neck muscles with a *thunk*, then pushed the boy down into the bloody brine.

Angus, emitting horrid croaking sounds through the broken bottle, died at Everett's feet.

With his one good arm, Ryan fought to yank loose the ax blade from his throbbing shoulder, as water filled his lungs. Helga descended to the bottom, trailing clouds of blood from her stumps.

Everett held Ryan under, turning to see the pale naked form of Trudy escaping into the woods, heading toward the road.

He released the ax, watching it sink, and withdrew two construction paper masks: a happy seal and a smiling pirate. He dropped them onto the surface.

Everett's attention was drawn to Ryan's gleaming gold hoop. He knelt and ripped Angus's ear off, then took the hoop, tearing it out through the lobe.

He pushed it through his own unpierced earlobe, excited by the pain, then took up his bag and went after Trudy.

Chapter 19

"You should've asked me first," complained Kerwin from the hearse's backseat, where he was mashed against the door by Pedro's big frame. "What if they burn it down or something?"

Pedro had plenty of room on his right side, but he couldn't resist needling the mouthy manager.

Jill rolled her shadowed eyes at Kerwin as Dennis again explained. "I told you. They have flashlights. *Flashlights,* Kerwin. You can't burn down a house with a flashlight."

"That's not the point and you know it, Dennis," Kerwin said, turning to Pedro. "How 'bout you scooch it back over to your side a bit there, Mister Beefy Body?"

"How 'bout you kiss my casket, cuadrado?"

"It's a big deal to them," Dennis explained. "They're good dudes. Breaking up the joint is the last thing on their minds."

"Still. You know, I told you. That basement can be dangerous."

Jill glared at him. "Cram a tampon in it already, buzzkill. You told us to make ourselves at home, remember?"

"Yeah, but I didn't mean the basement," mumbled Kerwin.

"All this pants pissing has got me wondering," Dennis said. "You stashing something?"

"No!" Kerwin's voice took on a shrill quality. "I mean, there's nothing in the basement. It's just that I'd be liable if...you know."

Dennis responded with a dismissive snort. "We're the only ones using it. Are we gonna sue our manager?"

"No! I just, you know, wouldn't want the little chaps to get hurt."

"Yeah. 'Cause you're such a conscientious citizen," Pedro scoffed.

"Maybe I *am*, Pedro! Maybe I have a sense of civic responsibility," Kerwin pronounced. "Now how about reeling in those sides of beef you call arms and giving me some breathing room?"

"How about you go dig a grave, pencil neck? Your *own*, for instance."

"Can the bullshit, everybody," Dennis ordered. "We need to stay tight. The house is fine, Kerwin. You'll see. We get our gear, we set up, we crash."

"Jeez," Kerwin muttered. "Wish I had a stiff drink right now,"

Jill drilled Kerwin with a glower.

"What? I'm thirsty!" Kerwin justified. "And stressed! And…" He glared at Pedro. "Cramped."

* * * *

At rehearsals Kerwin would snap his fingers, bob his head, and raise an occasional thumb at the band members, certain they were getting better because of him.

Born into a family with significant real estate holdings, Kerwin rarely had to do anything more demanding than phone a property manager and sign checks. The result was a lifetime of bored entitlement filled with attempts at making his name in some niche of the entertainment industry.

During his filmmaking phase, he had connected with a young graduate hoping to expose the IRS via a scathing documentary. The kid had no business acumen whatsoever. It was an easy matter for Kerwin to funnel the film's budget into "business expenses," like gas for his BMW or lavish lunches with young actresses.

Armed with the hapless student's show reel and his own mouth, Kerwin had no problem finding wealthy investors.

As both producer and accountant, he made this meal ticket last a few months, until the student walked away in frustration, not only from the film but from filmmaking.

For Kerwin this was just a temporary interruption of expendable income. Another would come along soon enough. Starving artists floundered in every corner of the world, a good many of whom either were or *attracted* eager young ladies.

Along came The Chalk Outlines.

In the waning days of the documentary scam, he had accompanied the filmmaker and some friends to a dive bar called Planet Six, just outside of Ember Hollow's town limits. The clientele leaned toward trust-fund college students and savvy farm girls scouting for educated city boys.

In short order, the film school boys became blitzed, while Kerwin paced himself through three martinis, enjoying the procession of denim shorts and tight camisoles before the club manager took the mic and introduced the evening's entertainment.

Kerwin found himself enthralled with this band's aggressive yet somehow poignant presentation, if not with the music itself. But it was Thrill Kill Jill with her shocking white hair, spiked collar, and tight T-shirt bearing the logo of a voluptuous murder victim's lines that first caught his attention.

But then there was Pedro, with his tattooed triceps, traps blowing out from his thick neck like a basilisk's frill, and demonic grimace.

And finally, Dennis, billed as Kenny Killmore: lean physique and matinee idol looks—if said idol was a vampire, of course. His guitar and vocals spoke of defiance warring with despair.

This unholy trio was a perfect storm of punk attitude, camp, and pro wrestler charisma.

Kerwin, more of a Crosby, Stills, etcetera kind of guy, had seen punk acts before. He might have been willing to admit they…*alarmed* him. But this mutation of punk and rockabilly was new to him. He found himself tapping his toes to their slick sick style, and soon, his gears were turning.

Any form of cult entertainment will have its detractors, some aggressive. Within minutes of the Outlines' intro, boos rose. Farm boys stood to pump their thumbs down, square chicks bitched to one another that they couldn't dance to it. Then came a flying ashtray that missed Dennis by an inch—and crashed behind Jill.

The music stopped. Kerwin tensed as he watched Kenny Kilmore set himself to address the crowd.

He first produced a pack of cigs from the front pocket of his black jeans, slapped one out, and lit it with an old-school wooden match. He tossed the smoking match into the half-empty beer mug of a scowling patron and exhaled the first puff.

The singer adjusted the microphone. "I see a lot of 555 out there."

Kerwin would later learn that 555 was a term extreme musicians used to refer to average folk, not unlike "square."

"You guys don't want to hear us play?"

"*Fuck no!*" shouted a farmhand. "I wanna hear George Jones!"

"What about you, fella?" He was addressing the fortyish man who had hurled the ashtray.

"You guys suck," he said. Several patrons shouted agreement.

Dennis took another puff. "How 'bout this then? We go ahead and play our set, and if you don't like it, ya tell us after."

Boos.

"Or...we come down there and kick the shit out of each and every one of you."

Their collective voice was indecipherable, but it didn't matter. Kerwin knew it was time to get to a safe place, and he almost didn't make it.

Dennis removed his guitar and pounced into the crowd like a panther, followed by Pedro, then Jill, her face a terrifying visage.

Kerwin found a cozy corner behind a poker machine and watched as body after body hit the floor. Pedro was as powerful as he appeared, and Dennis had the piston precision of a Mexican boxer.

But Thrill Kill Jill—she was both a wonder and a terror to behold.

With no discernible fight training, she nonetheless sent large men falling or scrambling for the exits with her flailing black nails and stiletto-heeled boots, even as her clawed hands closed around any bottle in reach.

Within minutes, the band had cleared the bar, reducing most of the cheap stools and tables to kindling.

That done, they dusted off and went to work packing their gear. As sirens grew closer, the bar's manager found the courage to approach them, swearing they would never see a dime from the gig.

"Sounds fair," said Dennis.

But then, the manager had to press it. "You gon' pay for all this shit too! And muh lost business!"

"Hold on!" Pedro countered, but Dennis waved him down.

"Listen, man," Dennis said, calm as ever. "We told you these dudes wouldn't like our sound. You said you didn't care, 'cause you had a cancel and needed to fill the spot. We agreed at our regular rate..."

"I don't give a damn!" the manager shouted. "You started this fight!"

Pedro grabbed the manager by his greasy apron and dragged him over to where the shards of the ashtray lay, as Dennis addressed him, ever the iceman. "See that, bro? See how close it came to my drummer? You coulda handled that. But you left it to us. So *we* handled it." He looked at Jill, then Pedro. "Maybe we oughtta charge *you*."

When the police came in, the manager found a new vein of courage and mined it. "Officers! You see this assault?"

The Outlines offered no resistance to the police, knowing when they were licked. But just as the handcuffs came out, so did Kerwin. "Gentlemen, please! None of this is necessary!"

He went to the manager. "I think we can agree mistakes were made by all parties tonight, hm?"

He broke out his ostrich-hide checkbook, the one that matched his boots, and asked, "Who's got a pen?"

"Who are you?" Pedro asked.

"I'm the guy who's gonna save your beefed-up bacon tonight, my friend!" Kerwin explained, adding, "Then I want to buy you kids breakfast, and talk about your future."

Chapter 20

Ruth chewed at her nails, stopping to shake the pain away from the exposed quick. She wiped her fingers on her top, then fondled her crucifix. "Lord, help me be prepared and poised in doing Thy will."

She parked her car at the rear of the drugstore in shadows behind the dumpster and stepped out, opening the first two buttons of her top as she walked toward the front of the drugstore.

Coming to the storefront, she peeked in around the "closed" sign and knocked at the glass. "Gosh darn it," she muttered to herself, and knocked harder. Movement from the rear shifted the shadows.

Ruth shone a sweet smile at Charlie Plemmons, as he came down the aisle and unlocked the door. "Hello, Ruth. I'm just finishing up. Everything all right?"

"Well, mostly," she said in a breathy tone. "I'm so sorry to bother you after closing time. Just have to take care of a few last-minute things for the parade."

"Can't wait till morning? I'll be opening early."

"Well…there are some girly things I need too." Ruth blinked.

"Oh. Say no more. Come right in."

"Thank you, Charlie." She pushed the door closed. "I'll get that for you. You go finish up." She locked it.

"Go ahead and gather what you need," Charlie said. "Register's closed, so just remember the prices. I know you're good for it."

"Oh, thank you." A shy, innocent blush.

"I'll be up in the pharmacy for a bit." He turned toward the back. "Working on something for Hudson, so just let yourself out through the back."

"There is something else though." Ruth arched her back a bit, thrusting her chest toward him. "A bit...unusual."

"Oh?"

"One of the parade wagons has a scary dummy that's a doctor. An evil, deranged doctor, like a global warming scientist."

Charlie furrowed his brow. "Reverend McGlazer didn't mention that one."

"It was sort of last-minute. Anyway, it would sure set the scene if he had"—she lifted her hands—"a big scary syringe."

"Oh." Charlie didn't seem to notice her delicate sensual hands. "Most of 'em come with the needles already affixed, and that could be a hazard."

"Oh, that would be perfect! Authentic you know. He'll be...hanging high, so no danger."

"Hm. Don't know about that. Seems like a bad idea."

"Well, I was going to dull it down anyway," Ruth explained.

"That's not as easy as you think. Maybe I should call McGlazer." He turned and took a brisk step.

"No, please. He's so busy. I promised him I'd take care of this."

"Just let me see if we have one without the needle."

Ruth gritted her teeth in frustration and paced a short line along the aisle, whispering, "Help me, Lord."

She stopped and examined a wall of kitchenware: knives, pots, pans, meat tenderizing hammers. *Confound it! All so messy.*

She reached for a long kitchen knife in a plastic package and tore at the package, frustrated by the crackling noise. Then, she spotted a miracle—in an easy-open cardboard blister pack, edged with light from the street like a divine signal, a turkey juicer. A thick syringe for injecting basting juices into the bird via a handy, thick-gauge needle, it would more than serve her purpose.

Ruth snatched it from the hook, just as Plemmons appeared around the corner.

"Here we are."

Ruth hid the package behind her back as Plemmons presented a small diabetics syringe, its business end neutered.

"Oh! Thanks, Charlie."

Plemmons noticed her blouse for the first time. "Oh. Say, your, uh, button there."

"Hm?"

He motioned. "Seems to have popped open."

"Oh! Why, I'm so sorry. I just can't seem to keep it closed." Ruth's face might have gone red. "I'm so embarrassed."

"Please," scoffed Charlie. "I'm old enough to be your father. Sewing kits on five, if you need one." He headed back toward the pharmacy enclosure.

Ruth watched him go, tearing open the turkey juicer.

* * * *

"Well, will you looky there? Still standing!" Pedro faux-gasped as he leaned far into Kerwin's personal space to feast his eyes on the old Victorian in mock wonder.

"Yeah..." Kerwin acknowledged.

Jill turned to him. "What now? You still look buggy."

Dennis hit the horn, startling him. "Son of a *bitch*!" The manager raised his hand to show them it was shaking.

"Relax already, will ya?" Dennis said. "Just giving them a heads-up we're here, so we don't scare the bejeesus out of 'em."

Kerwin hopped out. "You'd think you nobodies would wanna show a little more respect to the guy who's putting you in front of a God damned record label suit in less than twenty-four hours."

Jill smacked the back of Kerwin's head from behind, making Kerwin think Pedro did it. "Knock it off, already!"

Pedro just flipped him off as he followed him up the path to the door. Kerwin unlocked it and led them inside.

The inside was as black as soot, its musty atmosphere invading their noses like rushing water.

"Ho there, Stevie!" Kerwin yelled.

"It's *Stuart*, squarewad," corrected Jill.

"Stuart? DeShaun?" Dennis called into the dusty gloom. "Sound off!"

"They better not be in the basement," Kerwin mumbled.

Jill groaned. "Enough with the basement already."

"Ooooh shit," Pedro said.

"What?"

"Who's got a light?"

Jill drew her Zippo and sparked it, cursing at what it revealed.

"Ah, no." Dennis's shoulders sunk. "No way."

They beheld, in the dancing flicker, their smashed instruments.

"Shit in a sandstorm," Kerwin said.

Dennis raised the remnants of his guitar, clutching the curled broken strings. "My custom Gib."

Kerwin turned on them like a mocked prophet whose promised afflictions had come to pass. "I told you! I *told you*! You shouldn't have let those kids come in here by themselves!"

"Stuart..." Dennis ignored the outburst and went toward the dark hallway. "Where are you guys? *Come on!*"

"We're screwed!" Kerwin cried. "Damn you and your stupid brother!"

Pedro spun and grabbed Kerwin by the lapels. "Better issue some retractions, big mouth." He lifted Kerwin off the floor like a baby. "Yesterday."

Dennis stalked back into the room, glowering up at the suspended Kerwin. "They better be okay, little man."

"Hey, hey *hey*!" Kerwin mollified. "No need to get testy, guys!"

Pedro dropped him.

"I'm gonna check the basement." Jill was halfway down the hall when Kerwin called, "No!"

She spun on her bootheel and paced back to jerk his tie, drawing him face to face. "Your little basement fetish is really starting to toast my tits, douche face."

Kerwin found himself crowded into a threatening half-circle of Outlines. "Maybe it's time you spill on exactly what is the big deal anyway," Dennis demanded.

Before Kerwin could try to answer, the hall closet door creaked open.

They all crowded close together, their disagreement forgotten, and backed away from the darkened doorway.

A pale and skeletal face, disembodied in the darkness, lurched at them with a moan. Small hands reached out. Then the figure collapsed. "Some kid." Pedro lunged to catch him. It was Albert. "He's hurt!"

Jill found Albert's flashlight on the floor. She flicked it on and examined the boy.

"That's not Stevie, is it?" Kerwin asked.

Norman emerged in his bloody bear suit, squalling and swatting at the giant insects of his mind's eye.

Dennis wrapped the boy in a restraining hug. He removed his bear mask and beheld a face that belonged on some poor soul huddled in a forgotten corner of some ancient asylum. "Shit!"

"This kid's hurt *bad*, man." Pedro gathered Albert up. "He needs a hospital."

"Hey, kid!" Dennis held up Norman's lolling head. "Is Stuart here?"

Neither Albert nor Norman was in any shape to answer, the former a rag doll from blood loss, the latter still trapped in a tortured fugue of hallucinations.

"Get 'em in the car," Dennis said. "I'm gonna sweep the place."

As Pedro turned with the shivering Albert, Dennis stopped him. "Dude."

"Yeah?"

Dennis picked up the rest of Albert's foot from the pool of blood where he had found it and handed it to Pedro, who said, "Right. I'll toss it in the cooler with the sodas."

Dennis took the flashlight from Jill and headed toward the basement. Stopping at the door, he grabbed the gape-mouthed Kerwin and dragged him. "Since it's so damn sketchy, you can come along to protect your investment, right, Ker?"

"Shit," whispered the manager.

* * * *

Had they skirted the outside, Dennis and Kerwin would have stumbled upon the corpses of Maynard and Del and the events of the following twenty-four hours might not have been such a tragedy. Instead, they tromped down the basement stairs, Dennis followed far behind by a less-enthusiastic Kerwin.

Finding no signs of Angelo and Ruth's chemistry project, Kerwin gulped his relief, as Dennis noted, "Doesn't seem so dicey."

"Yeah. I, um…forgot I had some guys come and fix the…ya know, ceiling."

"Yo, Stuart!" Dennis called.

"I think he would probably be too smart to come down here," Kerwin said.

Dennis gave him a cold, distrusting glower, holding it for an uncomfortable aeon.

He returned to inspecting the murky room, settling the flashlight beam on something in the far corner. "Hello…"

"Wh…what?" Kerwin stammered. "Didja…find something there, Denny?"

"Did I ever!" Dennis said, walking to the corner, his form hiding the find from Kerwin's straining eyes.

Dennis turned and tossed something on the worktable, shining the light on it. It was Angelo's girls and cars mag.

Leaning one hand on the table, Dennis opened it and perused. "This is what you've been so squirmy about, Kerwin? A boob zine?"

"Huh? …Oh." Kerwin leaned in to see, relieved. "That what that is?"

Dennis's darkened face was a sculpture titled *Dubious*. "So, you come down here to spank it." He shoved the magazine at Kerwin. "No one gives a shit."

"Yeah. Heh-heh!" Kerwin's nervous cackle echoed in the empty room. "I'm like a horny teenager or something, right?"

"Stuart's not here," Dennis said. "Let's get those guys to the hospital."

"Yeah, of course!" Kerwin was eager to leave. "Mind if I, uh, sit up front? Just don't want, ya know, blood on my suit, or…"

"You won't have to worry about that, daddy-o. You're hoofing it over to the neighbor's house. To call the sheriff."

"Huh? But that's gotta be…"

"Quarter of a mile, minimum. Better double-time it."

Dennis went back up the stairs, leaving his manager to form a resentful scowl in the dark.

* * * *

Returning to the candy Hudson had dropped off, Charlie Plemmons poured some fluid into a test tube, then dropped a bit of the candy into it. The reaction was nothing like Charlie had ever seen.

Something white, like a tiny serpent, grew from the particle, squirming in the fluid for a second before dissolving. "What in the bloody blue?" he whispered to himself, before a knock at the pharmacy door distracted him. Ruth called to him.

"Yes, Ruth?"

"I have a question about something."

He went to the counter and raised its heavy steel door.

Ruth squeezed the syringe behind her back.

"What is it?"

"Well…it's one of the, um, feminine products."

"I'll do my best to help." He showed no intention of leaving the pharmacy enclosure.

Massaging the crucifix, Ruth was close to uttering an internal profanity. "I'll, um, go get the package. It'll be easier." Ruth shuffled down the aisle, gritting her teeth. She stood still, then, "You know what? I figured it out! Thanks, Charlie!"

She heard his sigh of relief as the metal door came back down—but Charlie left it a good eight inches open. "Darn your hide, Charlie Plemmons," she murmured. "The devil must be watching over you."

In the enclosure, Charlie returned to the candy, stunned to see the test tube bubbling over, smoking. "Great jumping jack-o'-lanterns!"

Ruth grabbed a step stool from a half-completed Christmas display.

She padded to the pharmacy counter and set the stool under it, then pulled back the stopper on the turkey baster and put it between her teeth. She eased up onto the stool and worked her way under the sliding door with the calm stealth of a sociopath.

With tweezers held in a steady hand, Plemmons positioned another fragment of the candy onto a slide and placed it under the lens of a microscope. He squinted into the lens, adjusting the magnification.

What he saw made him take a step back from the eyepiece.

Ruth eased to the pharmacy floor and snuck toward him. In the half-light she did not see the little box in her path. She kicked it, startling Charlie. He spun to find her raising the syringe. "Ruth? What are you doing? That's not a toy, you know."

Ruth ignored his statement. "So glad you're a church member, Charlie." She jammed the syringe into his chest. "Make that *were* a church member."

She pushed the plunger, filling Plemmons's heart with air.

He clutched at his chest.

Ruth withdrew the syringe as though raising a pen from a shopping list and cocked her head to watch him die. "Praise Jesus. Nice and clean."

But then Plemmons flopped over and fell face-forward onto the counter, smashing his hands into the glass containers, cutting massive gashes into his palms that drizzled blood.

Ruth's annoyance rose to near-profanity levels again. "No!" She reached for him, but he was already pushing away from the table and stumbling into a shelf full of liquid-filled glass containers, which all crashed to the floor. Plemmons landed face-forward and hard, into the puncturing shards.

Ruth glanced heavenward. "You gotta be kidding me."

Plemmons rolled over and took hold of a huge piece of glass jutting from his neck. He yanked it loose, sending a pulsing spray from his jugular several feet. Ruth's gaze followed the stream to the puddle it was forming on the floor. "Oh, you dirty rat."

With a furious scream, she stomped on his throat, only succeeding in driving out an even thicker spray.

But at least he was dead.

Ruth calmed as she stroked the length of her little gold cross, frown huffing at the mess like a woman whose housework is never done. "Thank the Lord you got all these cleaning supplies here, Charlie."

The lights of a car washed over her from the front lot.

"Judas *crud*!" Ruth hissed, as she switched off the pharmacy's fluorescents and dashed down into the drugstore, hiding behind a display of Halloween makeup. Peering around the corner, she watched the front door.

It was Hudson Lott, squinting into the drugstore.

Lott knocked on the window with his flashlight, then took a massive key ring from his belt and began working his way through it. He tried one, but it did not work.

Ruth went toward the door, biting her lip as she thought of a plan. She slid the turkey baster into the back of her waistband.

The next key worked. Lott was opening, about to enter.

"Deputy Lott!" Ruth called, halfway down the aisle.

Hudson almost went for his sidearm. "Ruth! You're gonna kill somebody one of these days. Creeping up on 'em like that."

"Oh." Ruth made droopy lips. "Sorry."

"What are you doing here?"

"I was just…helping Charlie." She gestured toward the rear exit. "Taking some trash out back, and I heard your car."

"I swear. You got a monopoly on all the goodness in this town." Hudson's compliment was genuine.

"Aw. You're sweet to say it."

"I came to see him about something, but it's all dark in there."

"Oh, he had to run an errand. Asked me to stay around till he got back."

"Hm. His car's still here." Hudson's brow furrowed as he scanned the shadows. "You sure everything's all right?"

Casting her eyes down in imitation of demureness, Ruth spotted a bloodstain on her white shoe and hid it behind the other foot. "Oh…"

"What's going on?" A hint of suspicion edged his voice. "Is there something…" He moved to step inside.

"Wait!" Ruth said, and when he turned his assessing eyes on her: "Charlie and I were talking. He… he needed somebody to talk to, and I was just trying to help. He's in no state to talk to anyone else. We were pray—"

"Hold on." Hudson raised his big hand. "Ruth, I've known you a long time. Are you up to something in here?"

"Why, no! I just…"

"You do know Charlie's a married man, right?"

"Oh." Ruth realized what he suspected, and adjusted. "Yes. I…" She lowered her head. "*We*…let things get out of hand, I suppose." She tried to summon some mist to her eyes, but it had always been dicey with that tactic. But she did make her voice crack. "I mean, one second we were hugging and praying together, the next we—"

"Not my business," Hudson interrupted. "But it's a God damned bad idea, I'll tell you that!"

Ruth registered appall at the profanity, but held her tongue. "I know. You're right, Hudson. Is it all right if I call you Hudson?"

"You just go tell Charlie to get himself together, because I'm going in there. And I don't need to see this kind of irresponsible behavior from either of you!"

Ruth nodded like a chastised six-year-old. Behind her back, she thumbed up the plunger, filling the baster syringe with air.

A sudden shout from outside startled them both—Hudson's patrol car radio. "Attention all units, we have an injured boy en route to County General via Hennison Road in a civilian vehicle," called the dispatcher. "Need an escort with sirens to meet."

"Damn." Hudson trained severe eyes on Ruth. "I gotta go. I'm coming back in half an hour and everything best be straight as a pin, you read me?"

"Yes, sir!"

Hudson rushed away.

Ruth patted her heart like an old woman. "Oh Lord. Thanks for Thy... mysterious movements, I guess?"

Chapter 21

Shivering, Trudy fought to stay quiet, to stifle her sobs and muffle her barefoot stumbling through the underbrush.

She almost squealed when a constellation of stings burst in her right foot, from a small prickle bush. She clasped her hand to her mouth, rubbing her foot into cold wet soil.

Then a blessed sight—vehicle lights. She was close to the road!

Trudy looked behind her, relieved to not see Everett. Perhaps he hadn't pursued? She took a chance, cupping her hands and screaming: "Help! Help me!"

But the car continued on, fading into the night. Trudy pranced to the next thick tree, then to another, hiding to glance behind her.

Another car, and she was closer by a precious three or four yards. *"Please stop! Help me!"*

She felt around at her feet and found a fist-sized stone. Hoping to hit the road or even the car itself before it was out of reach, she hurled it. But in her pain and hurry, her throw fell far short. "Damn it!"

No time to waste on tears, she continued to work her way over the cold stones and sticks, cringing with each step. She almost tripped over a stump, but she stayed on her feet. She was almost to the road.

A third car came along, an old truck.

Ignoring her pain, Trudy waved and screamed as she reached the edge of the road at last.

Then darkness became darker, suffocating. Everett's heavy Dracula cloak descended over her. She kicked and screamed as Everett wrapped the cloak around her. As the truck slowed, Everett turned to give a friendly wave.

* * * *

Ruth searched the vitamin and mineral shelf until she found a bottle that read:

RED EYE

THE SANDMAN SLAPPER!

"Lord Jesus God, give me strength," Ruth entreated. "It's gonna be a long night."

She opened the bottle and swallowed a handful of the white tablets, then set to work. Pushing one of the pharmacy's six rusty shopping carts, she gathered heavy-duty trash bags, a squirt bottle of heavy-duty cleaner, rubber gloves, a push broom and dustpan, and a hacksaw, and she took these to the pharmacy platform.

Humming her medley of hymns, she swept the broken detritus into one corner, then dragged Charlie's body over to the same pile.

She sprayed and mopped the blood spillage, jammed debris into trash bags, and turned to regard Charlie's cadaver, ripping the cardboard sleeve from the blade of the hacksaw.

A little over forty minutes later, she jammed the doubled, full trash bags into the back seats and spacious trunk of Charlie's Crown Vic, then slid into the driver's seat. On the dash was a smiling little hula girl figurine. "Lord Yahweh, I guess it was your will for Charlie to pass away. He was clearly a pervert."

She ripped the little figure away and stuffed it into the trash bag beside her, then drove into the darkness of Ember Hollow's maze of farming roads.

* * * *

With a hoarse scream and great burst of adrenaline, Trudy wrestled and kicked the cape away. Everett covered his eyes at the sight of her nakedness, giving her a chance to scramble into the road.

Everett looked between his fingers as he drew a meat cleaver from his bloody pillowcase, aimed it with a flourish, like a carnival knife thrower, and hurled it into Trudy's spine.

Her breath taken by the pain, Trudy could not scream. But she maintained her momentum, running for her life on cold asphalt.

Everett plopped onto his butt and covered his eyes with his bloody hands. "All fall down."

Trudy ran, feeling the safe distance growing. Then—numbness working its way down the back of her legs. She fell, pain blasting her knees and palms.

Wailing, she crawled, trying to breathe away the pain, hating the cold pavement for favoring the evil thing chasing her. She heard Everett chuckling, trotting toward her.

She crawled faster, feeling warm streams of blood crawl down her sides from the cleaver wound.

Her left leg went limp. She cried in vain for it to work, as Everett's uneven cadence grew louder. She was ready to give up, when car lights appeared in the distance, heading toward her.

Hope filled her heart. She pushed up on her hands to scream. "Here! Help! *Help me!*"

She knew Everett was closer, but the car was faster, and its approach gave her a burst of adrenaline. "Hurry!"

Then the car turned off on some dark side road, and all hope drained from Trudy's heart, just as Everett's bloody boot appeared beside her face.

Everett knelt, turning his face away as he draped the cloak over her naked bleeding back. He moved the cloak off the cleaver, positioning the cloth around it to cover as much skin as possible.

He worked the cleaver out of her spine, and not delicately.

As Trudy cried, Everett stroked her head.

He turned her to her back, making her lie on one half of the cloak while covering her lower half with its corner.

He put his hand over his eyes and straddled her, opening his fingers to expose her breasts, as he carved deep *X*s through them with the cleaver.

Trudy issued a hoarse scream, as her own hot blood sprayed her face.

Everett took a mask from his pocket—a happy horse with grass in its mouth—and placed it on her face. He drew his stapler and set it against her face—but it clicked empty.

Everett put the stapler back in his bag and with a quick short stroke, landed the point of the cleaver in her forehead to pin the mask to her face, where it rustled from the breeze.

* * * *

"Hang on, everybody. I'm gunning it." Dennis Barcroft, in addition to being a soulful musician, had a decent knack for the art of fast driving— since he had quit drinking, at least.

Bolstered by the urgency of the two endangered boys in the back, he put every ounce of those skills to work, working the chrome skull shifter while Jill held the pale Albert, and Pedro restrained the shivering, blithering Norman in his lap.

"Jeez, what coulda happened?" Pedro wondered aloud, speaking up over the roaring engine.

"Neither one of 'em is talking, but Fuzzy Wuzzy there is acting just like Mister Dukes," Dennis noted.

"I sure hope Stuart and DeShaun are all right," Jill said.

"Call me Pollyanna,' Dennis said, "I got a feeling they are. But I'll call Ma from the hospital."

"Not to be a Kerwin," Pedro said, "but what're we gonna do about our gear? I mean, are we finished or what?"

"*Shit*," Dennis said. "That's the $666,000 question, Petey."

"Well…" Jill said.

"Well, what?" Dennis said. "Now's no time for the coy act."

"I got that cousin in Craven County in a black metal outfit," Jill went on.

"Oh, yeah!" Pedro snapped his fingers. "Scarlet Frost!"

"Scarlet Frost." Dennis cocked up an eyebrow. "Those cats scare even me. But if I recall, their shit's tricked up to fit our theme well enough. Skulls and scars."

"They have some extra shit they bought in an estate sale and customed. I could give him a call," Jill said. "Maybe they'll lead foot it over here and lend us something in time for the parade."

"Just let 'em know we only need the instruments, not the flaming goat heads on pikes, or pig-blood-filled Super Soakers," Dennis said—dead serious.

"We'd have to uptune everything," Pedro noted.

"No crap, Kolchak," agreed Jill.

"Now we're talking." Dennis took a hard curve at seventy, but seemed for all the world like he was on Sunday drive. "Jill, you call your cuz from the hospital. See if they'll throw us a bone."

"Sure. Only they're gonna want something in return, ya know?"

"No doubt."

Pedro chuckled. "Like what? Our souls?"

A moan escaped Albert, making Norman cry out in response.

"Hang on, little bud!" Dennis called, accelerating. "Only a coupla more miles."

* * * *

Ruth hummed along to an old scratchy-sounding hymn playing on the radio. "So wonderful, Jesus! I am blessed to be doing your holy work!"

She checked the mirror and the road ahead, then turned the wheel, taking Charlie's car off the road and onto a weed-clogged roadbed, unused since the last time Ruth and Nico, thoroughly cranked on speed, had trysted there just a few days before his arrest.

Under this heavy canopy of virgin forest, even the moonlight hardly penetrated.

Deeper into viney darkness by inches, Ruth drove the car under a low thicket of laurel bushes and exited.

She ripped a flashlight out of its plastic package and clicked it on. "There we are. The light of truth shining my way!"

She turned to consider Charlie's car. "I'll deal with you later, Charlie. The least you deserve is a Christian burial."

She trekked back to the road, the uppers singing in her veins.

Chapter 22

A tentacled monster the size of an RV writhed toward a voluptuous bathing-suited girl cowering on a beach towel, its beak-like mouth clicking, all displayed in glorious black and white on the number-three screen of Main Street's The Grand Illusion Cinemas, soon to host a performance by The Chalk Outlines.

DeShaun and Stuart took turns dipping into a massive bucket of popcorn, their eyes glued to the screen.

DeShaun spotted something in the row ahead of them, several seats over. With a sly grin, he nudged Stuart and pointed at a young couple making out.

DeShaun and Stuart shared a look that was at once disgusted, curious, confounded, and mischievous.

Stuart held up a piece of popcorn and squinted to aim, setting up his shot like a free throw.

The popcorn arced and landed amid the young couple's faces.

The girl pulled away with confusion.

The boy turned toward Stuart and Deshaun and found them focused on the screen, their faces as stony as those of royal palace guards.

From behind, a hand clapped onto DeShaun's shoulder. "I didn't do it!" DeShaun shouted.

He stopped on seeing it was just the usher, an older boy from their school named Shuley. "Jeez, pop a Ritalin already," said Shuley. "I just came to tell Stuart his mom called."

"Huh?"

"She said you gotta come home right away. One o' your school chums had some kinda accident or something."

* * * *

Standing outside the emergency room, Dennis smoked the one cigarette he allowed himself every few weeks, doubting he would finish it, even before Pedro emerged through the automatic double doors. "*Damn it! Come on, brother!*" rebuked the bass player. "Those damn things are as good as bullets!"

Pedro snatched the cig from Dennis's mouth, dropped it, and crushed it with his black boot.

Dennis knocked another from the pack and lit it. "What's the scoop?"

Pedro grimaced. "Stumpy's gonna pull through. They're even saying they can reattach. I'm the same blood type so I ponied up a pint."

"Swell. Now he's part meathead Mexican. How's the other kid?"

"Doc's clueless. 'Cept he's showing the same signs as a coupla other patients from earlier today, just like your neighbor."

"Weird." Dennis blew a plume and squinted at the sky. "Hudson's doing the Kojak bit."

"What'd you find out about Stuart?" Pedro asked.

"Ma said he was on his way home from the movies."

The doors whirred again, and it was Jill. She walked past a couple of townie squares sitting on a bench. They gawped at her strange beauty with no degree of subtlety.

"Please say you've got good news!" Pedro demanded.

"They're flooring it right after their gig. Should have all the gear here in a coupla hours."

"Phew! That's goodbye to one headache."

"Yeah, but we can also say goodbye to getting any shut-eye tonight," lamented Pedro.

A battered station wagon arrived, easing to a stop at the curb beside them. Kerwin emerged from the backseat, where a massive red Chow dog sat wagging its tail and panting. "What's new, kiddies?"

"Oh, swell!" Pedro gushed. "Our hero has arrived! I can feel complete now!"

"Ha-ha." Kerwin waved away his ride. "You're a paragon of subtle irony, Petey." He drew a lint roller from his interior pocket, ripped away the top layer, and rubbed the dog hair from his suit. "So all is copacetic, right? I called the sheriff, probably saved the kid's life?"

"Yeah, you're a regular Clark Kent," Jill said with a smirk.

"If I was, I'd spin Earth backward and save all our gear," Kerwin quipped.

"And the kids too. Right?" Pedro said.

"Oh, yeah! Goes without saying!" Kerwin said.

"Jill got the instruments covered," Dennis said. "Got stuff coming from her cousin."

Kerwin's big grin appeared. "Bombastic! So I don't have to cancel the record company suit!"

"You cancel the suit, I cancel your face," Pedro answered.

"All right, no need to be so violent all the time. You kids need anything? Den, you sure this, maybe, wouldn't be a good time for an exception to the rule?"

Dennis dead-eyed Kerwin. "What are you asking, Kerwin?"

"I mean, just this once. A little"—Kerwin made a drinking motion—"glug-glug, you know?"

Jill grabbed Kerwin's lapel and raised her fingernails to his face. "You asking for a quick and painful body mod?"

"Easy." Dennis pulled her away from him. "Everybody's under a lot of pressure. I got an errand so let's just take a powder and meet up in a coupla hours to set up, okay?"

"Yeah, yeah. That's a good idea," Kerwin agreed. "Sheesh. My poor suit has had it today."

Jill and Pedro gave him the evil eyes as they walked away.

Kerwin, fuming to himself, continued to brush at his coat lapels. "Just wait'll I bleed you freaks dry," he mumbled.

* * * *

Out in the house a door creaked, stirring Candace from a dense, dreamless sleep.

The candles had burned out, leaving her in darkness save for a sliver of space between the bedroom door and frame.

She rubbed her eyes, blinked away sleep, and focused on the bedroom door. It seemed to twist. Then she remembered the things that writhed to sinister life when she was walking home. Logic told her they must have been part of a dream. Fear told her it was far worse than that.

From out in the house came sounds of movement. A light clicked on, brightening the sliver and throwing a dim luminescence across the bedroom's angles.

Candace looked over at the chair beside the bed, where she last saw her father sitting.

In the jagged spill of light, she saw not the beatific smiling figure from earlier but a bloodstained corpse with a stapled-on neon-paper smile.

Candace convulsed, as if she'd just touched a naked wire.

Aloysius's eyelids snapped open—but there were no eyes behind, only twin glowing crayon smiles, smaller versions of Everett's artwork.

She felt her stomach churn. Then she heard Everett's distinctive snicker out in the kitchen. Heart hammering, she turned to get down from the bed. Her gaze fell upon Mamalee.

She was crucified onto the wall behind the bed, two sheets hung behind her to form wings, a halo of orange construction paper nailed into her skull. Mamalee was no longer the ethereal angel who had welcomed her before but a cruel mockery.

Mamalee's mouth creaked open, ejecting a swarm of huge flies, their machine-like buzzing surely loud enough to draw Everett.

Candace felt tears streaming down her face. She covered her mouth and blasted a muted scream into her palm.

Footsteps in the hall—Everett was coming.

She skulked to the closet, slipping on a piece of debris from the ruined ceiling before ducking inside and easing the door shut, leaving a tiny crack.

Everett entered the room, dragging his bulging pillowcase of tricks, treats, and terrors. He placed a new candle in the little votive and lit it, but only after wasting five matches.

The quivering glow made the corpses ghastlier.

Everett smiled up at his mother and waved, then at his father, before taking a Halloween book from his pillowcase and going to sit on Aloysius's lap. "So happy," he whispered.

One of the flies from within Mamalee flitted through the cracked closet door. Candace saw that it had a tiny version of Everett's face, smiling with the incomprehending dementia.

The real Everett held the book up to Aloysius's unseeing eyes, then put it in his stiff hands. Everett sat still for a while, as if he could hear his father reading.

Candace kept her hand pressed to her mouth, breathing only in short shudders as she tried to shake away the distortions, the undulating shadows, the Everett-fly that could not, *must* not ever be real.

She grasped that she had been drugged, that these visions and inconceivable beings were illusion. Yet the insistence of these phantasms was stronger than her will, draining her of vitality and courage.

Everett stood from his father's lap, stretched his arms, and put the book back in his treat bag. He stood on the bed and hugged his mother's waist before reaching up to caress her cheek. He took bloody jewelry from his pockets, a necklace, which he clasped around her neck, and a too-small ring, which he shoved onto the first knuckle of her outstretched left hand.

The flies buzzed around his head, but he didn't seem to notice.

Everett took the earring from his ear and skewered it through Mamalee's earlobe.

He examined Mamalee's stomach, then put his ear against the dead woman's belly, listening. "Canniss?"

He drew a carpet cutter from his back pocket and ripped into Mamalee's stomach, reaching in, probing the dead woman's guts. Flies descended to cover the viscera, and Candace strained every muscle in her body to keep from vomiting. The little Everett-fly lapped up these sweet tears, easily evading Candace's efforts to swat him.

"Hell..." Everett stuttered. "O? Can-niss?"

He shoved his face into Mamalee's stomach, his voice muffled when he called out, "Can-niss?"

Candace swooned and slumped to her side on the closet floor, just in time to miss seeing Everett hop off the bed and go to his treat bag to take out one of Helga's arms.

Chapter 23

A Tragedy in Triptych
I

Children stood at the door in the kind of costumes that came in big plastic bags. The glum Aloysius stared at them.

Mamalee had badgered him to buy a big pumpkin she could carve, but Aloysius had "forgotten" or been "too busy." Yet the children had come.

Everett, only a toddler, watched wide-eyed from his high chair, his eyes dancing when the children cried, "Trick or treat!"

"I'm sorry," Aloysius intoned. "We have no candy."

"Wait, wait!" Mamalee came running into the room, a jar of homemade cookies in her hands. "We do have treats!"

Aloysius said nothing.

Everett beheld the children with delight, trying to form these magic new words. "Tw...twid..."

Aloysius turned to the boy, while Mamalee grinned at the visitors. "Please just say it again! I hardly heard you from the kitchen!"

The kids cried in near-unison, "Trick or treat!"

Mamalee giggled like a schoolgirl as she placed individual cookies in plastic baggies and lowered them into the bags, commenting on each costume.

"Tw...tw...twid o tweed!" Everett stuttered.

Mamalee spun with purest pride. "Oh, his first words!"

Aloysius's frown grew deeper, even when Everett smiled up at his papa with a giggle. "Twid o tweed!"

The children said their muffled thanks and disappeared into the autumn night, leaving Mamalee to go to Everett and pinch his cheeks. "Yes, baby! Trick or treat!"

"Twid o tweed!" the baby repeated, then and very often after.

Cooing, little Everett colored an arch-backed black cat in a coloring book while a record player behind him played Bobby "Boris" Pickett's "Monster Mash," which Mamalee had found for him after combing all thrift stores in a thirty-mile radius.

"Everett was some kind of prodigy," Candace would later tell Stuart and DeShaun as they hid in the dank recess of a café's rear staircase. "After that Halloween, his learning skyrocketed. But he only seemed to think about Halloween. Drawing, coloring, finger paints. Always Halloween."

Many nights, Mamalee lay in bed with the boy, reading from Everett's favorite Halloween story book: "Then the little ghost poked his head through the wall and said, 'Boo!'"

"Boo!" Everett would repeat, and when he did, Mamalee gave a laugh that was very natural and happy.

* * * *

On a hot summer day, four-year-old Everett, wearing a rubber witch mask not unlike one he'd seen among the first trick-or-treaters of his life, ran around in circles with a little broom between his legs while Aloysius clipped hedges nearby.

Mamalee, pregnant and happy, watched her boy from a rocker on the porch

Everett ran past his father, swiping his hand toward the hedges. "Chop! Chop! *Chop* off their heads!"

Aloysius clouded.

"I am afraid something is wrong with him," Aloysius told his wife, when he stopped to come up on the porch and drink some of her lemonade.

"Oh, Aloy," Mamalee disagreed. "Boys like monsters! They always have."

"No," Aloysius grumbled. "It's something more. This...obsession with Halloween. It was a time of sacrificing children, you know. Witches' rites."

Mamalee rubbed his arm and shoulder. "Not to him, Aloy. It's how he's learning. And he's so smart and talented! Can't you see?"

Aloy watched the boy ride the broom through make-believe moonlit clouds. "Do you pray for him?" he asked his wife.

Mamalee considered her answer. "I always pray for everyone." She put Aloy's hand on her swollen belly, and he seemed placated.

Chapter 24

Reverend McGlazer trudged to his office and sat with a heavy *plop*. Before realizing it, he opened the bottom drawer for the bottle he once kept there. This was an artifact from his seminary days, then his first tenure, at an Episcopal church in Buncombe County, near the Tennessee border. Catching himself, he closed the drawer without looking in it, a minor victory.

In those days, a bottle (or sometimes, *ahem,* a Mason jar, filled up in the hills from the still of a congregant) could often be found awaiting his attention. When these bottles began to have shorter shelf lives and more frequent trips outside the drawer, McGlazer was ousted from the position. He realized he had only gravitated toward Anglicanism for the relaxed attitudes its adherents held toward spirits.

Clicking on his desk lamp, McGlazer rubbed his eyes, recalling the incident of the flying candy. He dialed the sheriff's department to ask for Hudson and was told he was at the hospital. The desk officer explained about Albert and Norman. "Maybe I should go there, see if I can help." McGlazer felt stress scratching at his throat, making him thirsty for something amber and strong and smooth. He and the officer said their goodbyes, and McGlazer considered, as he did every October, having just a shot or so. Just as he did every October, he cleared his throat and shook his head, sending a physical signal to his brain that it was out of the question.

A muffled piano note sounded out in the sanctuary.

The old building was rarely silent, especially as autumn's temperature changes worked at its joints and foundations and corners. But music?

His flesh rose and tingled. The helpless terror of his close call with the flying candy rushed back, almost making him cough. He crept to the office door and eased his head out to see nothing out of the ordinary in the hall.

The note sounded again, a D on the piano—once and then sustained, then silent.

"Hello?" He asked himself what would a ghost encounter mean to his faith? To his sobriety?

The D note dinged, again and again, with increasing frequency.

If he checked the sanctuary, would he find a Halloween prankster, or the key playing itself?

Before he could stop himself, he went to the door and grabbed the handle. The notes repeated as McGlazer entered the corridor, and then the adjacent keys joined in as well. It became a banging, an attack on the instrument.

He opened the door trying to see into the darkened sanctuary. The sustain pedal remained active, vibrating dissonance throughout the rafters and walls, tinging like sleet off the stained-glass windows.

Then the pedal and the keys released, and McGlazer thought he had missed his opportunity to see an otherworldly presence. He almost *ran* to the piano in hopes he would see the keys move, feel something cold, see a wispy fog.

It was *there*—a black figure at the piano.

McGlazer's terror grew.

"*Whoa!*" called the pianist as he rose to a defensive posture. "Preach!"

McGlazer recognized the voice. "Dennis?"

Dennis relaxed. "Everything okay, Rev?"

"Maybe." McGlazer seemed disoriented. "How long have you been here?"

"Five, six minutes."

"You trying to spook the old preacher man?"

Dennis gave him a dark stare.

"You...had a relapse?"

"I just knocked back half a fifth of Diamante's." Dennis said.

McGlazer detected the slur in his words. "Well," McGlazer said, licking his lips, "at least you're here now."

"Yeah."

"So," McGlazer intoned, "where's that bottle?"

They assessed each other for a small eternity. Finally, Dennis raised a carton of cigarettes and a bag of candy corn. "How 'bout a coupla crutches?"

McGlazer held up a hand. "What about your bandmates?"

"Coming soon. We hit a speed bump."

"The boys at the old house on Gwendon?"

"It's under control, man." Dennis slugged McGlazer's shoulder. "Right now's smokin' time."

McGlazer followed Dennis back to the office.

* * * *

Dennis sat in a haze of cigarette smoke, staring at the candy spilled across the desk.

McGlazer brought him a cup of coffee. "Very hot."

Dennis raised a toast. "Coffee buzz, meet whiskey buzz." Dennis sipped, grimacing.

"What made you do it?" McGlazer asked.

Dennis used the cup to form an arc across himself that indicated *everything*. "I don't think I can handle this, Rev."

"It's been a difficult Devil's Night," McGlazer acknowledged.

"That? I can deal with that, man." Dennis's intense gaze was only more so under the influence. "If anything, it's helped keep my mind off shit."

He took another steamy sip and unwrapped a fresh sweet. "But this, this little lull, while we wait…" Dennis hung his head. "It *got* me, man. I tried. And I blew it."

McGlazer waited.

"What if I blow it tomorrow?" Dennis asked. "Hell. What if I *don't* blow it?"

"What would be wrong with that?"

Dennis leaned on the desk. "It would mean I'm just gonna blow it later. Only a lot bigger."

"You believe it's inevitable?"

Dennis slapped his own chest. "*Look* at me, man! I'm a God damned drunk. *You* beat it." A tear slipped from Dennis's angry eyes. "I can't."

Stronger than even just minutes before, McGlazer felt the pressure too, the need for refuge.

"They're gonna see now," Dennis said. "Ma. Stuart. Petey and Jill. They'll see they can't count on me."

"And you'll be free of your responsibility to them," countered McGlazer.

"What?"

"You'll be free and clear then? To drink whenever you want? To stay drunk, if you're so inclined?"

Dennis glowered at McGlazer. Then he sighed and slumped his shoulders.

"You know, Dennis, that's quite a good deed," McGlazer said. "Taking care of those boys, right after you found your equipment destroyed. Likely by them."

"Yeah, well. Toss one on the scales for good karma, huh?"

"You probably saved at least one life tonight," McGlazer said. "So maybe you can give yourself a little bit of a break on the relapse, huh?"

* * * *

Ruth walked along the side of the road, hugging herself against the plunging evening temperature, checking and rechecking the multiplying tentacles of her scheme.

An owl called from woods nearby. "Oh, shut up, you devil bird!"

Vehicle lights shone from behind her.

"Oh!" She unbuttoned her blouse by two. "Oh, Lord, please let it be a man."

As the lights drew closer, she waved, adding a scared-little-girl pout when the vehicle slowed.

It was two farmers, Lowell and Shep, to whom Everett had earlier waved before murdering Trudy. "Ho, Missy!" called Lowell. "You okay?"

"My car broke down. I could really use a lift," Ruth answered in a breathy voice.

"Car broke down? I don't 'member no car off the road back yonder." Lowell turned to Shep. "You?"

"I sure didn't see it."

"Well...Oh, no!" She breathed a damsel-in-distress breath of defeat. The driver lunged at the bait. "Whut?"

"I saw some hood types driving that way." She bit her lip like she was on the verge of helpless surrender. "I bet they stole it."

"Yeah, we seen some crazy kids out here too!" said the passenger. "Devil's Night and all. I believe one of 'em didn't have no clothes on."

Ruth put the back of her hand to her head and teared up. "Oh, I don't know what I'll do. It's just so *scary* out here."

"Well, don't worry now. We'll take you to the sheriff's. He'll look after you."

"Oh, I wish *some* man would!"

Lowell turned to passenger Shep with a fierce grimace. "Get out and let her in the middle."

"I can just scoot—"

"Let her in the God damned middle, Shep!"

Shep grumbled as he opened the door and stepped out. Ruth climbed in. "I sure hope there's room. You fellows have such broad shoulders."

"We'll get along just fine," reassured the driver. And they were off.

"I can't tell you how much I appreciate this," Ruth told them. "I mean, I just feel so vulnerable out here, especially with this being Devil's Night and those hoodlums I saw. Leather jackets and, and...sideburns." She closed her eyes and bit her lower lip. "I hope we don't run into them again."

"Well, don't you worry." Lowell gave her a smile. "We'll take fine care of you. Pretty girl like you, you shouldn't never have to be scared like that."

"I feel better already," Ruth cooed. "Except...well, never mind."

"Never mind what?" For a change, Shep looked her in the eyes. "What's wrong?"

"Well... Must've been at least four, maybe five boys in that car I saw." She shrank her shoulders, squeezing her breasts together. "If we were to run into them, I don't know if you could protect me."

"Oh, don't you worry. We got an equalizer, you might say," boasted Lowell.

"Really? Like what? A board with a nail through it?"

The men gave a confident chuckle, and the driver elaborated. "Oh, no. Much better than that. Shep, show her my little peacemaker."

"Well, it's really mine," said Shep. "We traded for that Conway Twitty record, remember? Original pressing. Worth a shitlo—"

"Shep, now, watch your mouth. The young lady don't wanna hear your potty talk."

Shep dug under the seat and produced a holstered long-barrel .38.

Ruth's eyes grew wide with wonder. "Oh, my word! That looks like something Charles Bronson might have!"

"It's seen some action, all right," bragged the driver, prompting from the befuddled Shep, "It has?"

"Well, we don't need to get into—"

"Do you think I could hold it?" Ruth asked with a bright grin. "Just for a second?"

Lowell and Shep were quiet.

"I won't point it or anything," she promised. "I just want to feel its, its *might* in my hands. Stroke it a little bit, you know?"

Lowell and Shep could not refuse now. "Why sure!" the driver said. "Shep, check the safety."

Shep did so, clicking it off, then back on, with a macho expression. "Yep. She's locked up tight, all right."

He handed it to Ruth, who accepted it, like she'd never held such power before. She unsnapped the holster. "Can I..."

Shep nodded. Ruth eased the holster off the weapon, eyes widening as she revealed its full length. "It's...it's just so big!"

"Well, I got a bigger one, at home. That's just for hairy situations like maybe tonight."

"I don't know why anybody would be fool enough to mess with you boys. ..." exclaimed Ruth. "You *men*."

"I hope your car turns up and all," Lowell began. "But maybe we could call the sheriff from, well, my place. It's just a mile or so past..."

"Ooh!" Ruth sang. "A fun little stop-off!" She gave a childish giggle, prompting the men to do the same.

Ruth put the barrel to the side of Shep's head and fired, blowing out his brains and the passenger window.

Lowell screamed, losing control of the wheel, running off the road.

Ruth jammed the pistol's smoking barrel into Lowell's crotch. "Do what I say or your little head ends up like his *big* head. You hear me, you God-forsaken pervert?"

"Yeah! Yes!" said the driver.

Lowell glanced over at Shep's head. The lower half lying against the dashboard, the rest..."What have you done? Oh, my Lord Jesus..."

"Don't you *dare* take His precious name in vain." She jammed the barrel farther into his groin.

The driver gave a yelp. "Ow! Please! That thing's still hot."

"So is hell, you fornicator," Ruth informed him. "You take the truck road into the next field."

"That's Hoke Natson's property. No...trespassing."

"You have already trespassed, sir. Now do what I tell you."

Chapter 25

Four scalding cups of coffee later, Dennis had found an even keel.

"The way the boy was acting. And your neighbor. Did you happen to see any candy lying around?"

"Huh?"

"Hard sweets in black-and-orange wrappers?"

"Nah." Dennis examined McGlazer through the haze. "Why?"

"I'm thinking there might be a connection to the strange seizures people have been having. Hudson agrees."

"No sh—uhh foolin'? Like, a bad batch?"

"Maybe," McGlazer answered. "I was waiting to hear from him."

"Maybe you should drive over to the hospital and catch him. I don't think you wanna get too cozy with the crew that's lending us gear anyway," Dennis said.

. "Oh?" McGlazer said.

"Let's just say, I doubt you have much in common with them. But don't worry. I won't let 'em burn down the joint."

McGlazer raised his hand. "Say no more."

As McGlazer stood, Dennis asked, "Hey. What about you, Rev? You ever find yourself pipe dreaming about some fine vintage?"

McGlazer sat back down, grateful for the opening. "When I was sixteen I had my first drink, and it was moonshine from the mountains," he said. "Straight out of the jar. I thought it was going to kill me. What does it say that that wretched devil's urine is what I find myself craving the most?"

Dennis crushed out his cigarette and lit two more, handing one to McGlazer.

"I'll have to smoke it on the go." McGlazer rose to put on his jacket. "I tell you, Dennis, I'll never understand why anyone would come to me for spiritual guidance."

Dennis snorted. "Yet here I am."

"Dennis, if I weren't your sponsor, you'd be mine."

McGlazer took a drag. "You know, this place will smell like cigarettes for weeks. Ruth is going to kill me."

"Tell me about it. Pedro and Jill are both all up in my a— uh, case about starting back."

They shared a long grim look, until Dennis said, "We're gonna make it through this Halloween, Rev."

"If it kills us," McGlazer agreed, turning to leave.

* * * *

Lowell's jaw throbbed. He realized he had been mashing his teeth together since everything went so terribly wrong.

He turned the truck into the sprawling pumpkin field, now just bare mud cast in dead gray under the autumn moon. Ruth directed him to a wide pit at the far edge of the field beside a tall pile of dirt. "Stop here."

Moving the gun barrel up to Lowell's temple, Ruth stretched across Shep's corpse and opened the passenger door, letting him fall out. "Get out and go get him."

Lowell did as ordered. Ruth got out behind him on the driver's side.

He gaped at her with shock as he went to hoist his cousin. "My Lord." He squinted. "This can't be really happening."

Lowell knew well the purpose of this hole, and the countless more like it that pocked the farmscape of Ember Hollow. Damaged and rotten pumpkins were 'dozed into them after harvest, the theory being that any unhatched squash beetle eggs would be buried too deep for spring revival.

"Take him over to the pit."

He complied, grunting as he took the remains of his relative to the precipice, a grimace of grief and terror on his face. "Now what?"

Ruth waved the gun. "Toss him in."

"Poor Shep." The driver scrunched his face at the mess of mushy pumpkins and mud. "I'm sorry, man."

He wept as he rolled Shep's body into the rancid mess and turned to Ruth. "Okay. I done what you said."

"Now you. Get down in there."

Lowell's face took on the weight of a decade's despair. "No. Come on."

"In Jesus' name *do it*!" Ruth shrieked.

He leaped in, finding himself standing to his thighs in the cold putrescence, the edge of the pit just higher than his head. "Shit, shit, shit…"

His gaze fell upon something that was not a pumpkin, and not Shep.

A bloated face bobbed up from the morass, slimy things writhing in the eye sockets and the ragged hole where a nose had once been. Lowell backpedaled from the noseless head of Angelo Betzler. *"Holy mother of Jesus!"*

"Shut your blasphemous mouth!" Ruth stood glaring down at him from the pit's edge. "Now. Get down on your knees and beg the Lord for forgiveness. Give your life to him."

"Wait…" pleaded the driver.

"Ask him to come into your heart."

"Come on, *please*!" he said through sobs. "I done that way back in Sunday school, ma'am!" Lowell's voice had become hoarse, pitiable. "I…I just need to start living it, is all!"

Ruth was unmoved. "That's not an option anymore."

"Wh…what about Shep?"

"He died so that you might see the light," preached Ruth.

"Oh, please, please, *please* don't kill me!" begged the farmer. "Please."

"Don't beg me. Beg God. Now get on your knees."

Ruth groaned in irritation. "I'll do it for you." Ruth closed one eye, keeping the other aligned with the pistol sight on Lowell's heart. "Lord God, this man is a sinner."

Lowell did fall to his knees, splashing the cold gooey mess onto his face and hair, and *did* pray. "Jesus, get me out of this. I'll pour out my shine. I'll throw away my cigars…"

Ruth raised her voice, to drown out Lowell's. "He is not worthy of your mercy or forgiveness, just as none of us are!"

"I'll tithe, and *then* some!" swore Lowell, louder still.

"But he knows he is a sinner and he knows this is his last chance to be with you in heaven!" shouted Ruth.

Lowell gave up on Jesus and addressed Ruth. *"No!"*

"Come into his heart and forgive him his wickedness."

He scrambled through the mess, reaching for Ruth's feet. "You ain't pure! This is the devil's wo—"

She shot him, and he fell backward with a splash, sinking into the mess.

"Praise be!" Ruth raised the smoking gun and her other hand to the heavens. "Thank you, Jesus, for moving in this man's life through me."

With an expression of peace, she went to the truck and left.

* * * *

Jill sat on the steps of the church's outer archway between Dennis's legs, holding out a church service program and slicing it into ribbons with her nails.

Dennis, hiding the signs of the mild headache from his micro binge, stroked her hair with one hand while dangling a cigarette from the other. Pedro leaned against the pillar, watching the church's graveyard gate.

Yawning, Pedro took a piece of orange-and-black-wrapped candy from his pocket that he had picked up somewhere. Standing still for too long had enervated the big bassist. He needed a sugar pickup.

Just as he tugged at the wrapper, a low rumble reached his ears.

The rumble was not a motor though, but rather dirge-like guitar notes, propelled by the unmistakable sonic assault of black metal blast beats, portending the red-tinted headlights that appeared in the distance.

Pedro tossed the candy away into the bushes, no longer needing it. "Funeral procession's arriving."

Dennis crushed his cigarette and lifted the slinky Jill to her feet, telling her, "I owe you for this."

She turned to him with an arched eyebrow and said, "Warm up your singing muscle, superstar," then spread two fingers under her mouth and flickered her tongue at him.

Scarlet Frost's van, a matte-black '70s Chevy with red and white runes spray-painted on the body, soon pulled into the grass of the church's yard, the artful dissonance going silent.

Tied to the front grille was an inverted cross made of two large cow bones, with a horned skull posted on "top."

The red headlights died, as doors opened and four longhaired twentysomethings emerged, dressed in spiked wristbands and belts, torn black jeans, pentacled jewelry, their faces unrecognizable in black-and-white corpse paint.

"Jesus *H*!" proclaimed Dennis. "Full regalia."

"Brutal," Jill noted.

Lead vocalist Darren leaped from the passenger side, followed by drummer/driver Horace, then ax men Wes and Madsen.

Pedro grinned. "You cats do not disappoint."

"Sorry to take so long!" said Darren. "We came straight from the gig." He hugged Jill.

"Thanks for coming, cuz," she said.

He ruffled her hair and said, "Anything for family," then scanned the faces of the Outlines. "So, your instruments have been destroyed. Grim. Grim…" He spoke with a thick Northern European accent.

"Wait." Jill cocked her head sideways at her cousin. "You guys are doing the Norwegian accent now?"

"Not us," corrected Horace. "*Him.*"

"It's about the music, Horace, you simpleton!" Darren's reproach was punctuated with a shove, and then he turned back to Jill and company, gesticulating as he expounded. "I want to be authentic. I want to feel it and mean it. You know?"

"Oh, yeah." Pedro was like a preteen boy meeting his rock gods for the first time. "We can dig it."

Dennis exchanged a fierce black-nailed clasp of hands with the diminutive metalhead. "Man, you cats are really pulling our asses out of the corpse grinder."

"Say no more, my friend! It puts broad smiles on our faces to help our fellow subversive artists."

Dennis looked at the other black metalers, finding no such broad smiles. Only sinister corpse-paint grimaces.

"So, where is the venue for the big show?" Darren asked.

"Movie theater in town square," Jill explained. "On top of the marquee."

Horace and the others murmured with appreciation.

"We'll go there now!" Darren proclaimed.

"Copy that," said Dennis. But as they moved toward their vehicles, Darren stood still, staring up at the church edifice with dreamy dark eyes.

"What's wrong?" asked Jill.

"I cannot lie," Darren began. "This place ablaze, crackling and crumbling. It would be glorious!"

As the Outlines gave each other doubtful looks, Dennis spoke up. "Yeah, well, that might stamp a veto on our contract, so we prefer it to remain flame free, if that's cool."

Darren turned to them with what might have been a sinister expression. "Speaking of *contracts.*"

"You're not about to demand my soul, are you, Darren?" asked Dennis.

"No, no, my friend. But we do have expectations. You have an executive coming to see you. No?"

"Yeah. Our Kanye-ass manager's picking her up in the a.m."

"Very good!" Darren clapped once. "I wish you much luck."

Pedro got the drift and asked, "You...want us to have her take a look at you guys? Is that it?"

Darren chortled like a maniac as he spun to his bandmates, who peered back from darkened sockets. "Let's all be realistic." A glance at their van, not to mention their attire, rendered this statement absurd. "No American record company will ever touch us." Darren puffed his chest. "And that's a point of great pride!"

"Right," said Jill. "So?"

"What do you want?" Dennis finished.

"*So simple,* my boy. I want you to play one of our songs."

The Outlines remained incredulous.

"One song? That's it?" asked Dennis.

"That will complete our agreement and erase your debt to us."

"I don't get it," said Pedro. "What's the punchline?"

"Yeah, man," Dennis said. "What do you gain?"

"Oh, my beautiful boy!" Darren said, putting his pale, sigil-tattooed hands on Dennis's face like a lover, gazeing into his eyes with near madness. "That voice. You sing like you are having such fun. Yet just beneath the surface...so much pain. Such weary wisdom. Like the lamentations of a fallen angel."

"But we won't even be here, dude," Madsen said.

Darren turned and snatched the lapels of his battle jacket. "*It's on TV,* you poser!" Then he returned his expectant blackened gaze to Dennis, as if awaiting the answer to a marriage proposal. Madsen, accustomed to the rough play, merely straightened his jacket.

Pedro and Jill shuffled about, as Darren continued to gaze into Dennis's perplexed eyes. "Yeah. Okay, that's reasonable," Dennis said. "Done."

"Supreme!" Darren spun to regard his bandmates with hands held out in messianic triumph—then slumped his shoulders with an exasperated huff, turning toward the church wall. "Wes, don't piss on this one, man! Show respect to our friends."

"Sorry." Wes zipped up and stepped away from the wall. "Habit."

Darren directed traffic. "All right, you guys, Let's get this gear moved so these kids can get some sleep!"

Dennis, grinning like the grille of a 1950 Mercury Coupe, gave Jill a lusty kiss and Pedro a hearty fist bump.

Chapter 26

Stella, comfy in flannel pajamas, switched on the television, sank into her recliner with her sewing basket and her half-finished fortune-teller scarf, and soon settled into the comfort of WEFC's weeklong Bela Lugosi marathon, well into the Hungarian actor's lesser years working under Ed Wood and various off-Hollywood hacks.

Bernard was away at his weekly poker game with friends from the factory. It was as much a respite for her as a social time for her husband, who tended to be so much smarter than average folk—including her—that it was depressing and lonely for him, as he had confessed.

Thus, this time apart was a form of marriage maintenance, and Stella savored it.

Her pet cockatoo, Catfood, cooed in her blanketed cage, as autumn's winds made flyby embraces of the quaint ranch house, soothing Stella into a contented fugue.

During a lull in the film, Catfood squawked and fluttered, bashing around in her cage like she had gone crazy.

Before Stella could rise, her scarf project wound itself taut around her arms, pinning her in the chair.

The bird continued its spasm, its human-like shrieks blasting into Stella's brain until she thought her knitting needle had also come alive and staked itself into her ear—but then she saw the implement fall out of her lap as the scarf tightened further, a flat python.

Then the chair's corduroy upholstery somehow became malleable, like quicksand, sucking her into depths that were as cold as well water, roiling up over her trapped hips and arms with a squelching sound.

As the alien muck closed over her face, muffling Catfood's cries, Stella knew it was a dream—*must* be—and fought to wake herself.

"*Wayg uhb!*" she cried through near-paralyzed lips, straining to raise her head to keep from suffocating. With great effort, she forced her eyes open—and beheld Bela Lugosi, cape pulled over the lower half of his face, stalking among the Styrofoam graves of *Plan 9 from Outer Space*. He turned to glare at her with his hungry eyes, as he pointed at a crooked wooden cross standing tall amid the props. A chain was wound around it like the scarf had wound around *her*, an ancient lock holding the links taut.

He lowered the cape, and it was Bela all right, and not the chiropractor whom Wood had hired to double for him after his death, for this was the *Land of the Dead*, which extended into Television Land, she realized, and this was not so surprising.

Bela parted his thin black lips and mouthed a single syllable: "Why?"

He extended his finger toward the wooden cross once more, and it was shaking, making the chain jingle. His emphatic movement must have carried supernatural force, for it yanked Stella from the dream and onto the floor, inches from the television.

Bela remained. But the film was *Mark of the Vampire*, not *Plan 9*, and his black-and-white image did not acknowledge her in the least.

Stella picked herself up, finding her limbs heavy with exhaustion. She went to Catfood's cage and found the pretty girl content and asleep, raising an eyelid before making a side shuffle toward Stella.

The unfinished scarf was splayed about the foot of the chair. Stella was not in the mood for knitting any longer, and certainly not for the scarf, nor the chair.

She went to her bookshelf in the bedroom and scanned the spines for the only book that mattered, praying that her husband had not tossed it during one of his frequent organizing rampages.

Relief washed over her as she found it—then came dread, for her next step was a drive to the cemetery.

* * * *

The weary Hudson dropped into his chair as two deputies wrestled with a man in a French maid's costume behind him. He took a deep breath, picked up the phone, and dialed.

Leticia and DeShaun worked at carving the last of at least a dozen jack-o'-lanterns, the finished gourds aligned along the counter like a platoon of orange lunatics, while little Wanda watched from her high chair, a mess of pumpkin pie smeared all over her face and a bib decorated with a cartoon bat captioned I DRIVE MY MOM BATTY.

Leticia wiped her hands and answered the phone.

"Hey, there, sweet thang," Hudson said in his best Barry White.

"Hi ya, love machine," she replied, making DeShaun roll his eyes at Wanda. She tried it too, rolling her head instead and making herself dizzy. "What's up?"

Hudson practically growled. "I'm...busy."

"Well, duh. How are those kids from the old house?"

"Doctor says they're gonna be okay, but I can't talk to them yet. Still one missing from their group. Some other weird shit happening too." The scuffle behind him grew louder.

"What is all that?" Leticia asked.

"You don't wanna know. Listen, I'm trying to track down Charlie Plemmons. Something funky is up with him and that girl Ruth from the church."

"Ooh! That girl is trouble with a capital crazy."

"Well, all things considered," Hudson assessed, "it's about usual for Devil's Night."

As the scuffle continued, something fell across Hudson's head. He snatched it off—a fishnet stocking. His face screwed up in disgust. "I gotta go. Hug the kids."

"Sure will. Rush it up, Black Dynamite."

"Ha-ha. Love you."

"Love you back." She hung up and returned to the table.

"Was that Dad?" asked DeShaun.

"Yep. Running late."

"Did he say anything about Albert and Norman?"

"He says they're gonna be okay."

"So weird," DeShaun said.

"That's why you are never allowed to set foot in that house again. Now get ready for bed."

"But I wanna show Dad my jack-o'-lantern," he protested, as he went to the counter and patted a pumpkin carved in a cartoonish image that could only be Hudson himself.

"He'll see it tomorrow when we get a candle in it. That'll be even better." Her tone took on an edge of mock anger, an early-warning system. "Now get your pajamas on and get in bed. You're helping me take these to the field in the morning."

"Can't I stay up a little longer?" DeShaun pleaded. "No way I can sleep after this crazy day."

"No. Tomorrow's a big day too, and a lot of people are counting on your help."

"I could just sit up and watch the Bela Lugosi scare-a-thon for a bit."

She turned to him with an agreeable expression. "What's the name of that movie where Bela grounds Son of Dracula to his coffin till the next ice age?"

DeShaun lowered his head in defeat.

"Now go get in your pajamas and brush your teeth, like I asked you to an hour ago! Or you can plan on staying at the community center with Miss Barcroft and me, watching all the little ones!"

DeShaun snapped his heels together and extended a Nazi-style salute. "*Sig heil, mein* furious! I mean, *fuhrer!*"

He marched away, goose-stepping, sending Wanda into a giggle fit.

"Oh, don't you start, little girl," Leticia warned, wiping the baby clean.

Chapter 27

A Tragedy in Triptych
II

Mamalee held Everett tight against her side, as she did every Sunday. During the course of mass, he had scooted lower, out of her controlling embrace. Then he could sit forward, fidget, and scan all the grim faces.

The head priest, Father Scalia, finished a reading from Matthew and began reciting a chant. He raised a cross, prompting Everett to bring his jacket lapel to his face and issue a defiant vampire's hiss.

The congregation laughed. All but Aloysius.

When the priest smiled down at Everett, it seemed like a look of patience, even adoration. But it was, in reality, something else.

* * * *

Aloysius went to the baby's room, driven by the new ubiquitous protective anxiety that was born alongside his baby girl.

When he found Everett standing on a stool, leaning into his new sister's crib and humming "Monster Mash," he was filled with dread. Newborn Candace gurgled and cooed but Aloysius did not hear it, his mind scrolling through any number of ways the boy might be mutilating his baby sister.

"What are you doing!" He snatched Everett up and tossed him to the floor, where the boy erupted into a fit of shocked crying. Aloysius ignored this and lunged to the crib, afraid to breathe. "My God!"

Baby Candace's face was covered in green and purple ink. Everett had colored her to resemble a little alien. The boy had even drawn little antennae on her forehead.

When startled by his strident father, Everett had shivered, accidentally drawing a haphazard lightning bolt on the baby's blanket. But Candace was quite unharmed: Everett had avoided his sister's eyes and mouth.

Still, Aloysius checked her over, frantic.

Mamalee, aproned and sweaty, ran in and hoisted the terrified Everett off the ground. "What is it? What's wrong?"

"The boy is possessed!" yelled Aloysius, pointing at Everett like a hanging judge.

"No, Aloy," Mamalee tried. "You're overreacting."

But her scowling husband would not be moved. "I won't let him hurt Candace!"

Candace joined her brother in bawling. Aloysius plucked her from the crib and skulked out, leaving Mamalee to calm and comfort the older child.

Chapter28

Bathed in garish underlighting, Bela Lugosi stalked into frame.

Sitting on the couch, Stuart paid little attention to the television, plucking at his sticker-covered acoustic guitar. He tried out a few lines from the song he and Dennis were writing.

"Turned thirteen without a warning
Woke up dead that Sunday morning
In the mirror, my worst fear
Overnight, I disappeared
My only consolation
Disintegration..."

His mother walked in. "Sweetie, you knew Dennis probably wouldn't make it home tonight."

"I know. I was hoping he would anyway."

She sat beside him and rubbed his shoulder. "He's doing fine now. You know that, right?"

"Yeah. Just...it's a lotta pressure." Stuart fiddled with the D string. "Like when Dad died."

"He was just a boy then, hon. Like you."

"Yeah. I don't think he'll drink. Not with Jill and Pedro around. But even so, I don't want him to feel it. The pressure."

"After tomorrow night, he'll probably be a big star!" She glowed at Stuart. "At least, as big as a spook...punky...billy...singer can get."

"Yeah. But what if he *does* get that contract? Won't even more people try to get him to drink and stuff?" Stuart wondered. "Maybe even worse."

"Well, that's why we have to stay close, babe." The widow stroked Stuart's longish hair. "That's our role, like Reverend McGlazer said. To give him so much love and support there's no time for anything else. So"—she turned him to face her—"we have to support each other too, right? Agree to always hold Dennis up, and hold each other up when our arms get tired."

Stuart furrowed his brow in thought. "This year, this Halloween, just feels so..."

"Hm." Mrs. Barcroft blinked. She knew, but wasn't sure how to phrase it. "Swollen?"

"Yeah. Like it's gonna pop."

"It is, Stuart." She hugged him. "Happy Halloween."

"Happy Halloween, Ma."

A willowy actress screamed from the television speaker.

* * * *

Pedro opened the scarred door to the cramped apartment he shared with his cat. "Watch for Joanie."

Jill and Dennis entered, on the lookout for Pedro's fat Siamese, Joan Crawford, in case she tried to make one of her occasional escape attempts.

The cat did appear, but she was far too distracted by the visitors to care about the open door. She essayed a sleepy, quacking meow as she trotted to the exhausted couple, rising on her hind legs to rub her cheeks on Jill's boots. "Aw, there's the good girl!"

Dennis took his turn, hoisting the feline for a cheek scratch and a kiss. "My best fan."

"Okay, you guys know where everything is," Pedro said in a tired slur. "I'll be on the couch. *Mi* casket is *su* casket."

He turned to them with a pained expression, eyes closed. "Just, could you please keep it to a low shriek please, Jilly?"

Jill pressed herself against Dennis. "Can't promise anything. My big man goes for the guts." She patted her lower belly.

"Aw, jeez. Spare me the gore," Pedro groused. "Just no caterwauling this time, how 'bout? Drove Joanie under the couch for a week last time."

"Oh yeah, bro," Dennis said. "That was me, sorry about that."

Pedro waved them off, then turned to stop them before they headed toward the apartment's only bedroom. "Hey."

"Yo."

"This is it, brother."

Dennis clasped Pedro's hand in a firm fraternal grip.

Jill lunged at Pedro to give him a fierce embrace. "You're the cat's tuxedo, Petey."

"God damned right," Pedro said. "All of us."

Jill released him and took Dennis's hand, leading him down the hallway. "Now let's go wreck Petey's mattress, Mister Killmore."

* * * *

Stella parked across the street from the cemetery's western side—the vast memorial lawn's rear—to avoid being seen. She was apprehensive enough about stumbling around in the old cemetery in darkness, much less being seen and becoming the center of rumors. Why, just imagine what Ruth would say!

This section of the road winding around Ember Hollow's memorial grounds hugged a bank so steep no one would even try to landscape it. Too many lawnmowers of both the push and ride varieties had careened into the street and its unsuspecting motorists.

The side on which she parked was the edge of a middle-class development whose entryway sign read EMBER MEADOWS, a memorial to the picturesque parcel that had been dozed to make way for the homes built over it.

Parking in this spot wasn't likely to draw attention, and a scarf—*not* the one that had "attacked" her—worn over her head would obscure her face from passing drivers.

She checked the flashlight, a heavy square black thing Bernard kept in the garage, then gripped the pocket knife—also Bernard's—that she had dropped in her pocket for protection. She rechecked all the doors to be sure they were locked, and then she realized she was stalling, that it wasn't getting any brighter or cheerier.

She made her way to the lowest point of the unfenced hill and clambered up, pleased that her youthful track-runner legs still carried their weight. At the top, most of her courage vanished when she beheld the rolling gray hills and the black monuments that jutted from them, markers that signified a rotting corpse just a few feet beneath.

No cars passed on the road behind her. Isolation cloaked her instead of the warmer coat she wished she had brought.

The grounds harbored the occasional tree, the burial plots located under their branches commanding optimal price for reasons that now struck Stella as absurd. The nearest was a dogwood with limbs low enough that someone could very well be squatting under them to watch her.

Never had she felt this daunted. Thousands of graves under a starless sky, and she had to find a simple wooden cross. The church was a vague, blocky void two hundred or more yards to her ten o'clock, and for this she was glad. There, she had witnessed the unknown, and there, she hoped, it would stay—at least for tonight.

She panned the flashlight beam across the first rough row of the field of fallen, praying that it would be just that easy. It wasn't.

She made a plan to circle around the outside, spiraling inward until she found the simple wooden marker, which, she was ready to consider, could very well be dead center, if it even existed.

At least it's distinctive, she told herself, hoping that Bela himself would not pop up from behind a stone to raise a cape-wrapped arm, the other drawn up beneath hypnotic sensual, satanic eyes.

Sweeping the beam, she cursed herself for overreacting at the sight of a tiny rabbit, which hopped away—probably not half as startled as she was.

"I should have come out here more often," she mumbled to herself, "learned my way around." As if this was bound to come up at some point.

The beam was drawn like a magnet to something dark sticking to a monument, a bat waiting to—what else?—become Bela, towering and intense, intent on whisking her away to some abandoned Universal Studios back lot.

It was just a wet leaf.

Nonetheless, Lugosi's alluring and alarming pale face flew to the fore of her mind's eye, soundlessly asking, *Why?*

"Why?" Stella said aloud, and the wind picked up, blowing past her face as if to draw her eyes to something to…her right?

The dogwood tree.

A warning. Her imagined hidden stalker was about to pounce.

She drew Bernard's pocket knife from her jacket pocket and clutched it as she directed the light at the tree, straining to see a human shape. "Why?" she asked the tree.

The wind blew the limbs across each other in her beam, taking a recognizable form, and her frightened mind sparked with recognition.

"Not 'why.'" Stella went toward the tree, emboldened by the smiling face of her Aunt Miriam replacing that of Lugosi. "*Y!*"

She opened the knife and walked to the tree, setting the flashlight on the ground. She cut a limb, then raised the light to do a quick scan around her before further trimming the limb into a *Y* shape.

Armed with the first dowsing rod she had touched since that long-ago summer visit to Aunt Miriam's cottage, Stella took a breath of resolve, turned off the flashlight, and tucked it under her arm, then held the rod in divining position, opening herself to whatever force made it work to guide her.

Wind blew, and leaves attacked her, one sticking to her hair and licking her neck with its damp stem before she smacked it away.

With each step, the pull of the rod became stronger, like a Great Dane out for its first walk in days. It dragged her in a near run to the towering obelisk monument and around it, lurching downward, almost bringing her eye-first into the top of the wooden cross.

Vibrating with such intensity it made her hands tingle, the rod split itself down the middle and went still.

Stella, both enraptured and terrified by the invisible power, released the two pieces of the spent divining rod, wondering if, as Ruth would proclaim, she was allowing something evil inside.

In any case, what she was to do next was clear: lift out the cross.

She took an underhand grip and again felt vibrations—much more powerful in the dense hickory—and in uneven pulses, as if two energies were at war within its molecules.

With a grunt, she lifted, her entire body radiating with what seemed like a mild electrical shock, growing in intensity.

The cross did not budge. Like *The Sword in the Stone*, it was immovable to all but Arthur—who she was not.

She released and stepped back, staring at the rough-hewn talisman. She saw no visual indication that it was tremoring. Stella thought how Bernard would raise his eyebrows high upon his forehead at such raving impossibilities.

She took in a cool breath and reset, squatting deep to get a better position. When she gripped the cross, it tremored harder than before, startling her. But the sense of urgency felt like life or death—hers, maybe everyone's.

Gritting her teeth and doing Lamaze breaths, she strained, ready to catch herself on her hands and rump in case of an abrupt release.

Instead, the cross floated, up and out. A sudden cold wind rose, seeming to pass *through* her, as the vibrations faded.

She stepped back to ponder the weightless cross, wondering if she was in another dream.

The nail through the cross-section extracted itself with a little groan and shot off into the dark.

Then the crosspiece separated itself and spun past her head like a boomerang while the post section shot up into the sky and arced out of sight, a wooden rocket.

Stella heard it thump down out in the woods, skimming leaves en route to becoming just another fallen branch.

She leaned over, squinting to see the inch-and-a-half-wide hole where the cross had been posted, wondering if she had just lost her mind, or her soul.

* * * *

A throaty high-pitched scream caused Pedro to shift on the worn couch that barely accommodated his bulky frame, unsettling Joan Crawford from his chest. He pulled his pillow over his ears and turned over.

* * * *

Jill, naked and breathless, collapsed onto Dennis's heaving chest. He squeezed her in his arms. "*Damn,* I love you."

She kissed him, deep and soulful, as she caught her breath. "I love you too, baby."

"Poor Pedro is gonna hate us," he said.

"Nah. This time tomorrow night, his new groupies will make him forget all about us."

They snuggled and kissed. Then Jill slid off to his side. "Case you can't tell, I'm really proud of you."

"Hm." Dennis beamed. "Almost there myself."

"You should be." She tagged his crooked nose with a long crimson nail. "See how much everybody believes in you, Dennis? Your brother, Pedro, and me. Even Darren and his, um…disciples?"

"It's do or die, you know." Dennis's face was grim but determined. "If this contract doesn't come through, I don't know if we can keep playin' biker dives till the next shot comes along. And I can't crash at Mom's forever."

"Hush." She nibbled his lower lip. "Forget about all that. You just be ready to play and sing your ass off tomorrow night. Dig?"

"Yeah, I dig." Dennis had planned to confess his little slip—but now decided it was a bad move. He would tell her after the show. "I want it for you too, you know. And Petey. And Stuart."

Jill pulled his arm around her shoulders and neck, settling against his side. "What is this? The Waltons? I thought men were supposed to go all corpsy after sex."

Dennis rubbed her shoulder then blew out the candle. "I'm not through with you yet, *girl!*"

He wrapped his arms around her again and buried his face in her neck, making her issue a delighted squeal.

Chapter 29

Hidden under tarps, the parade wagons sat in a semicircle as the pilot cars maneuvered into place to connect to them. Strong gusts blasted waves of noisy desiccated leaves across the grounds like ocean breakers while performers and participants stood mingling.

Reverend McGlazer, in costume as Lord Summerisle, complete with unruly wig, chatted with a trio of drivers, all in slick ducktail hairdos that were not part of a costume, at a table loaded with donuts and industrial-sized coffee urns.

Hudson Lott loped toward them, carrying an extra-large, ghost-themed travel mug. "Reverend, you got a sec?"

"Of course."

The drivers walked away toward the wagons.

"Trying to find Ruth." Hudson filled his mug at the urn as he spoke. "She around?"

"No, but I wish she were. I was hoping for her help today. Is something wrong?"

"I hope not." Hudson drained half the cup, ignoring the scalding. "Can't find Charlie Plemmons either. You haven't seen him, have you?"

"No," said McGlazer with mild alarm. "I hope they're both all right. Is there a connection?"

Hudson drank another huge gulp of the hot coffee and grimaced at McGlazer. "I was gonna ask you."

"No. Ruth is beyond reproach these days," said McGlazer. "She puts me to shame."

"Yeah." Hudson's voice was incredulous, but he didn't mention that he knew better. He topped off the giant mug, then raised it to McGlazer. "All right then."

* * * *

DeShaun, costumed as a white-haired kung fu master, tapped, blew on, then spoke into an unplugged microphone. "Ember Hollow, are you ready to *rock*?"

He mimicked audience excitement with a throaty hiss. "Ladies, gentlemen, victims of all ages, I bring you...the grave robber, heart throbber, shock-rock sensation feared throughout the nation!"

He assumed a deep guttural death metal growl. *"Staurt!"*

With a grand flourish, he thrust the microphone toward the glum Stuart sitting on the back of a pickup truck, costumed as a forties gangster in a pin-striped suit. He ignored DeShaun, tweaking tuning knobs on the borrowed bass. The instrument's body was sculpted into a Gigeresque nightmare of alien heads fellating gray and black serpent skeletons, the sort of thing that normally had Stuart grinning in awe. But he only sat and worked at it with listless concentration

DeShaun lowered the microphone. "Come on, man. Her folks probably decided she couldn't come at the last minute. Don't take it personally."

"Maybe," Stuart mumbled. "Weird that I'm so disappointed, isn't it?"

DeShaun sat beside him. "Nah. My folks are like that, all up on each other, kissing and hugging. Both of 'em. Makes me sick. Like, I really wanna throw up sometimes, man." DeShaun convulsed as though he was trying to clear away the very thought. "But yet, I'm kinda starting to get it."

Dennis, Jill, and Pedro appeared, giddy with preshow anticipation.

Dennis wore black shades and a black pearl snap shirt with the sleeves ripped off, his cheeks gaunted via Jill's makeup job.

Pedro's muscles strained the seams of a mesh tank top with a black Chalk Outlines patch safety-pinned to the front.

Jill, of course, was drop-dead stunning in ruined hose, a black corset, and a glittery hangman's noose necklace. "How's it coming, fellas?" she asked.

"All done," Stuart said, handing the bass to Pedro, who propped a boot on the tailgate and played a few notes. "Damn!" He remarked, impressed. "Perfect. Maybe better than mine, God rest its dark soul. And by ear, no less."

"I told you. Top shelf." Dennis's sneer reflected pride. "No one tunes mine but Stuart." He headlocked his brother, but the teen only gave a wan smile.

Jill stroked his hair. "Aw, sweetie. Sorry about Candace. Maybe she'll make it yet."

"And if she doesn't"—Pedro interjected, making a dismissive swipe in the air—"her loss, dude!"

"That's not gonna make him feel better, Big Mouth," chided Jill.

"You sure you guys feel like coming on stage with us?" asked Dennis.

"Oh yeah! No way we're missing that." DeShaun put his arm around Stuart and squeezed, making him grunt. "Right, Stuart?"

"Yeah…" Stuart conceded.

"All right then, Outlines," Dennis marshalled. "I gotta go warm up the pipes. Get your game brains on."

Pedro strummed a hard note on the bass and followed him.

Chapter 30

A Tragedy in Triptych
III

Aloysius sat across a massive oak desk from Father Scalia, head down in a supplicating, servile manner. Scalia's assistant, Father Wemble, sat nearby.

"You are right to be concerned. I believe it's important we get to the boy before he gets any older. We'll perform the rites of exorcism."

Aloy crossed himself.

* * * *

Mamalee answered the front door without a greeting, casting her worried face down.

The two priests stood there in full garb, Scalia holding a polished wooden box, Wemble carrying a large white-leather-bound bible. When Mamalee did not step aside, Aloysius came behind her and pushed past. "Thank you for coming, Fathers."

The grim-faced clergymen entered with curt nods.

Everett sat moping on his bed as Aloysius and the solemn priests entered his room. The silver cross Scalia carried reflected across the boy's face, its harsh glint making the boy wince. He looked up at his father, knowing this would be unpleasant, but never guessing it would be life-shattering.

Aloysius grabbed the boy's little arms, pinning him down on the bed.

Everett struggled, crying, screaming with greater strength than a small boy—but not enough.

Scalia crossed himself and chanted, looming over the boy as Aloysius and Wemble trapped his legs.

"Please stop!" Mamalee demanded. "You're frightening him!"

"Quiet!" ordered Aloysius.

"The demons in him are powerful," announced Father Scalia. "I'm afraid he will have to be bound!"

The priests deferred to Aloysius for permission, and he gave it.

He held the pleading Mamalee in a restraining embrace, as Father Wemble secured a leather strap, shiny and black like a malevolent eel, around Everett's wrists. "Make them quit it!" the boy pleaded to his parents. Baby Candace's cries rose from the next room.

"No matter what you hear, do not come in until we summon you," commanded Father Scalia.

"Yes, Father." Aloysius lifted Mamalee by the waist and scooted out the door with her.

"No, no, *no!*" Mamalee cried. "Please leave him alone!"

The priest slammed the door.

Mamalee, her face etched with heartache, rocked the crying baby Candace. She squeezed her eyes shut in denial as thumps and shouts emanated from upstairs.

Aloysius sat hunched over a coffee cup, staring into a deep scar on the table. Everett's cries penetrated through the doors and walls: *"No!* You stop that! STOP STOP STOP!"

In his powerful baritone, Father Wemble chanted Latin phrases to drown him out, but Everett only cried louder. *"MAMA!"*

Mamalee rose—but Aloysius slammed the cup on the table and glowered at her until she sat.

There was a long time of utter monstrous silence. Even little Candace was quiet, staring up as though expecting something to burst through the ceiling.

Then the faintest of sounds. Perhaps it was Everett emitting some agonized muffled moaning, or perhaps not. It was a sound that did not sound like a small boy. It was a sound that a grown man did not make in the presence of a child.

Mamalee covered Candace's ears, continuing to obey her husband, trusting that he knew best, that this would end with a new Everett whom Aloysius could love.

Then came a hoarse anguished cry, and another.

Not Everett. The two priests. And then a loud din of furniture breaking and thrashing and violence.

A new voice rose, one neither Mamalee nor Aloysius knew—raspy, low, and eerie.

Aloysius rose, dread painting his face. He blinked at Mamalee, showing uncertainty about this exorcism business for the first time since it had begun. "Fathers?" he called.

The low scratchy voice scuttled like a spider along gossamer sound waves, with a sinister sincerity.

Aloysius rose from the table and crept up the stairs. Mamalee held the baby close as she followed at a distance that almost felt safe.

Aloysius lunged to open the door to Everett's room, and froze. Mamalee kept her eyes closed as she cleared the distance.

Everett sat naked on the floor, blood smeared all over his face.

Seeing his parents, he smiled. "Mommy 'n' Daddy!" he pronounced in the raspy voice.

Just a few feet away, Father Wemble lay on his back, eyes glazed, blood spurting up from his open zipper, where his penis once had been.

Father Scalia was pantsless and on his knees, face pitched forward, blood pooling at his knees, senseless gibberish wandering from his mouth.

Mamalee saw her good roast knife, the one Everett liked because it reminded him of the plastic accessories at the costume shop, the one that had gone missing. It was just under the bed, where he apparently kept it hidden along with the scary drawings he knew his father wouldn't like.

Everett coughed as he pointed at something in the corner. "Very, very *bad things*!" said the boy in the kind of hoarse rasp that comes not from demonic possession as it turned out but from having one's throat violated.

The priests's crucifixes lay piled on top of two tubular red fleshy messes.

Scalia fell to his side, his face twisted by shock that could not be deep enough to block pain.

Everett made an inverted sign of the cross as he whispered, "Trick."

* * * *

For Candace the first understanding that something was wrong came on a Halloween night. Mamalee and Daddy had spent the weeks before packing.

Candace would recall Mamalee begging her father to take Everett trick-or-treating. It was the only thing Everett talked about, the only thing that made him happy. Mamalee made him a mummy costume, and he wore it every day until the big night arrived.

Aloysius told the boy over and over what he was to do. "I will choose a house. You just knock on the door, play with your toy knife for the count of ten, hold out your bag until they put some candy in it, then run back to me." Everett promised he would.

Candace was not allowed to go. She was to stay home with Mamalee, playing Halloween games on the bare mattress until Daddy and Everett returned, when they would leave in the big truck Daddy had rented.

Candace knew what Daddy meant by "play with your toy knife," but pretended not to. The year before, Daddy had taken Everett to a neighborhood where no one knew them and had let him join a group of kids. Everett did, and Aloysius followed them at a distance to watch. He saw them walk up to a house. When the door opened, the man who answered screamed, and all the kids ran away.

Aloysius ran to see what had happened and found Everett walking across the yard. Looking into his son's goodie bag, he saw one of Mamalee's good steak knives covered in blood. He realized that the man's scream was not a joke on the kids; it was a roar of pain and fear.

The addled father took Everett home and scrambled the family for a quick departure. As they hit the highway, Mamalee's crying alarmed Candace. "They will take him away!" she wailed. "Oh, my Lord they will take him far away, Aloysius!"

For once, Aloysius was kind and caring. "I'll never let anyone take Everett away, no matter what," he assured her.

Depriving Everett of Halloween was not an option. Mamalee could not take that from him, any more than she could let him be taken away. But on the following year's Halloween, the boy ran away in the neighborhood where Father took him. He found a garden spade. This time, kids were the victims. The boy's urge to kill was as strong as the family bond. There was nothing to be done except repeat the pattern, year after year.

Aloysius bought the truck, and moving every year on November 1st became a part of the Geelens family's lives.

Chapter 31

Slumped over in fitful sleep in the closet of her parents' bedroom, Candace slid to her side, bumping into several shoeboxes and raising a clatter.

Jarred awake, she remembered where she was, and why. She shrank against the wall, expecting Everett to tear open the door, meat cleaver in hand, and yell, "Trick or treat, Canniss!"

But beyond the closet door was only silence.

She peeked through the crack in the door. In her limited range of sight, her father's corpse still sat slumped beside the window, his construction paper smile glowing bright in the otherwise dim room.

Her head and limbs felt weary but manageable. She was lucid enough to realize she had hallucinated, and had maybe been drugged somehow. She hoped that whatever had caused the torturous visions had abated.

Which meant her father was dead.

For now, mourning was a luxury. She mustered a measure of courage and eased the door open, just an inch.

Everett was not in sight. His pillowcase was gone as well, if the wake of smeared blood leading from the room was any indication. She rose and took two tentative steps.

Fighting tears, she turned to the wall behind her to face another one of Everett's gruesome decorations.

Two mud-speckled severed arms nailed to the wall, dead hands holding either end of a construction paper banner that read, HAPEPIY HALLOWEEN!

Everett had lovingly centered the banner above Mamalee's head and articulated the bloody wreckage of her corpse as a linen-winged seraph, her tiny calloused hands nailed up in eternal expectation of toddling little boy hugs—or perhaps he had upgraded her to a ghost of herself, in fitting the theme of Halloween.

Candace stepped backward, stumbling over the mess of ceiling debris caused by Everett's descent. She fell, but got back to her feet and ran to the living room, where she lunged for the old black phone with the tangled cord. She held it to her ear, but heard only a silence as dead as her parents.

She ran for the front door and then outside, despair growing like a thirsty weed under the fickle autumn sun. She called for Bravo as she dashed to his doghouse, but he was gone.

Her breath hitched, reminding her not to cry as she wished for him to be safe, insisted to herself he was, and ran, ran, *ran* down her driveway, not with exhilaration this time but in desperation, knowing Everett's apocalyptic potential.

* * * *

Reverend McGlazer looked around one last time for Ruth before raising his megaphone to address the waiting crowd. "Thank you, everyone. The time is here! Any questions regarding parade route or responsibilities?"

The participants stood silent like monks.

When the sound of a familiar motor puttered onto the field behind McGlazer he brightened, recognizing it as Ruth's. "Just a minute please, everyone!"

Ruth stepped from her car, haggard and leery as she pulled her khaki raincoat around her, not knowing she had costumed herself as Barbara from *Night of the Living Dead*. McGlazer suppressed a smile at the irony as he went to meet her. "Ruth! I was worried about you! And Hudson Lott is looking for you."

He tried to hug her, but was met with a cool recoil. "You know how I feel about this," she said with a low and imperious tone. "How God above feels about it. I only came to give you one last chance to call off this demonic affront."

He motioned toward the waiting paraders. "Ruth, you know it's far too late for that."

"Well, then." Ruth sniffed. "You've made your choice." She turned to walk away.

"Wait! Ruth, I could really use your help today. I'll pay you if you like."

"My soul is not for sale, Reverend. Goodbye."

"What about Hudson?" McGlazer asked.

She ignored the question and stalked back to her car, leaving McGlazer pawing at his inner pocket for the long-gone flask.

Just as Ruth left, another familiar car arrived, answering a prayer he hadn't prayed. It was Stella, appearing even more exhausted than he felt.

* * * *

Guiding his BMW out of the airport parking lot, Kerwin was all smiles. He regarded his passenger, record company executive Cordelia Cantor, with all his usual subtlety.

Corporate and sensible in a tailored blouse, yet utterly stunning with Botoxed lips and an enhanced bust, she spoke with a high-end British accent that might have occasionally dropped a notch toward Cockney.

As the Outlines' demo played from the stereo, Cordelia studied the passing landscape with a condescending wistfulness. "So many fields and farms. It's beautiful out here. If perhaps a bit lonesome."

"Yeah!" bellowed Kerwin. "Well, a guy like me, used to the big city, I find it a little square. Was a case of right place, right time with these kids."

"I'm not surprised." Cordelia turned to show him an elegant smile. "Many great performers rise from humble and isolated settings. Nothing to do but create, I suppose!"

"Oh yeah! My guys can create!" Kerwin shouted over the stereo. "They create the hell out of this shit! I mean, it's an odd kind of music I know, but…"

"The world needs a fresh sound. And I wouldn't have agreed to come all the way down here if I didn't see their potential."

"Yeah, yeah! Right on!" Kerwin spun toward her, almost tossing off his glasses. "I told 'em that!"

As Cordelia flipped through her folder on the Outlines, Kerwin looked over her shoulder. "So…" he tried. "How does your husband or boyfriend feel about you taking this trip?"

She tossed a strawberry strand away from her left eye. "I rarely have time for my dog, much less a love interest, these days."

"Oh? Well, gee, that's a shame. Maybe I could take you arou—"

"This chap Pedro," she interrupted, holding up the band's publicity picture, her manicured nail jabbing the bassist's chest. "Is he attached?"

"Oh. Him." Kerwin's expression soured. "I don't know. I always thought he was, you know, in the closet."

"Of course." Cordelia put the photo down. "I could never become involved with a client in any case."

"No?" Kerwin had found his smile again. "By 'client' do you mean, like, strictly the musicians?"

"Actually, I mean anyone. Period." She made a dismissive wave of her pampered hand. "Married to my work."

Kerwin tried to hide his disappointment.

"Then again, I have my carefree moments," she said, prompting Kerwin to laugh with her, almost convincingly.

* * * *

"With the crowd they're expecting, I'll need someone to stay here at the church to man it as a sort of emergency station," McGlazer told Stella, his hand on her shoulder as a subtle convincer. "After all, you're a trained EMT."

"But don't you think you'll need me to help with the parade?"

"We have so many volunteers now I'm not sure what I'll do with all of them. Up here on the hill, you'll have almost a bird's-eye view, as the parade makes its way back toward the staging field." McGlazer took his hand away, but she didn't feel any less pressured. "It'll be hard to hear down there while Dennis is playing. You might be needed to make a phone call or something. Who knows?"

She was already feeling apprehensive, far above and beyond her disappointment with being disinvited from the parade.

"I know it's a sacrifice on your part," he admitted. "Believe me, it will be much appreciated."

"Just me? Can't somebody else stay too?" Bernard, busy with a contract deadline, would never agree to keep her company. She never would have imagined speaking her next words. "Ruth maybe?"

McGlazer's frown was her answer. "I all but begged her to help. She wouldn't budge. You know how she is." He gave her that tithes-and-offering-time look. "I...hope it's not about your...the..." McGlazer struggled.

"Ghost," Stella said. "I thought you believed me." She wasn't inclined to share her experience from the cemetery just a few dark hours ago.

"I never *didn't* believe you," McGlazer defended. "The parade is, well, overwhelming..."

"I understand," relented Stella. "I'll be fine."

Chapter 32

Candace found the door of her nearest neighbor's house hanging open. Her despair growing, she stopped in the front yard, staring into the doorway, at furniture and dust motes that were quiet beyond silence.

"Mister Fullbright?"

No answer. She scanned down the street and didn't see a soul. No music played, no leaf blowers buzzed, no dogs barked.

She turned back to the Fullbrights' front door and peeked her head in, seeing no one. But the phone sat on an end table beside the couch.

Candace dashed for it, lifted it, and moaned in despair. Then she caught sight of something outside that made her heart sink deeper.

The telephone pole that bordered the Fullbrights' property had been chopped down.

Mr. Fullbright, having tried to stop the perpetrator, lay dead nearby, his upper half separated by several bloody, gut-strewn feet from his lower, his shotgun still in his cold dead hands, a construction paper mask of a sad moose stapled to his face.

Candace dropped the phone. She backed toward the door, then turned to run, stopping at the edge of the next yard, where the windows of the house were splashed with blood.

Another house: a wrecked body lying on the walkway, the conical hat of a garden gnome driven through his or her stomach, another custom mask.

Next house: a woman's face pierced by the pointy teeth of the picket fence it lay on, a chicken mask flapping around the wound. A broken body lay across a front porch rail, Halloween lights wrapped around its neck.

"No…" Candace imagined mile upon mile of corpses, perhaps the world over, all sporting construction paper masks, all part of Everett's fevered Halloween celebration. "Everett, no…"

She realized that Everett would—and maybe even *could*—remake the world as a vast Halloween mural.

She hid both sides of her periphery as she ran, crying, into the road's horizon. "Not the parade! Not the parade! Not *Stuart!*"

She ran till her breath was ragged, trying not to see the unending crime scene on both sides.

In her periphery, she glimpsed a pair of older kids, Omar Lindstrom and Peggy Pike, pre-pre-engaged as of last Thursday, posed in an embrace, their entrails twined like a pigtail braid. They shared a single mask: a buck-toothed, bright-eyed chipmunk.

She screamed, falling to the ground, scraping and twisting her knee, turning her face away from the grotesque tableau.

As she crawled toward the other side of the road, she spotted a bicycle parked at the edge of a driveway.

Her resolve renewed, she stood and limped toward it.

* * * *

Under the demon dusk, a 1965 Chevy C-10 pickup, its bed filled with pumpkins, puttered toward the tunnel of high treetops just beyond the bullet-holed sign announcing Ember Hollow town proper, dead ahead.

Everett, in his senselessly composed costume of vampire's cape, executioner's hood, and shark grin, ambled in the middle of the road on a direct course toward the tree tunnel.

The C-10 pulled alongside him and stopped. Everett was set to raise the fondue fork hidden up the sleeve of his father's coat—until he saw the dead man in the passenger seat.

Enrique, farmhand by trade, theater artist by hobby, was the truck's passenger, dressed like a fresh corpse. The rubber scar across his neck glistened with fake blood. It was a two-for-one getup, celebrating both Halloween and Dia de los Muertos, the Mexican Day of the Dead.

"Hola señor! Habla Español?" Enrique asked.

Everett beamed at him, entranced by the fantastic makeup.

Enrique looked at the driver, Guillermo, whose costume, a sinister diablo, bore the same exquisite artistry. No less than four months ago,

Enrique had glued real goat horns onto a plastic mask, cast from a gelatin mold of the ever-patient Guillermo's face.

The devil mask was made with separate teeth from a high-end costume supplier. A heavy flowing crimson cape, plastic trident, and sharp black glue-on nails completed the look. Everett was awestruck.

Despite his mask's sinister grin, Guillermo was friendly. "Eh, do you go to parade?" He popped a thumb toward the pumpkins piled in the truck bed.

Everett admired the mound of orange beauties.

"Need a lift, *amigo*?"

Everett climbed into the back and settled in with joy in his heart, hugging a pumpkin in each arm as Guillermo accelerated.

* * * *

The young mother canoodled her daughter's nose, forgetting that she had on blue makeup till she saw it smeared on the little girl. She smiled at Elaine Barcroft, taking a tissue from her purse to wipe the mess.

"Oh, leave it," Elaine said. "We're going to be painting faces anyway."

"Oh, that's right." The mom stood. "You be a good girl for Mrs. Barcroft and Mrs. Lott, okay, Tina?"

The little girl nodded, though signs of separation anxiety were blooming on her little face.

"Come here, Tina!" Leticia chimed, grabbing Tina's hand and leading her away before the tears could come. "Wait till you see all the fun stuff we're going to do tonight!"

As a babysitting team, Elaine and Leticia were as tight as the Outlines were as musicians. They handled temperamental children and picky parents with equal aplomb, one reassuring where the other had to be firm, and vice versa. They had spoken of opening a day care but decided that their own families were far too important—and needy.

For Ma, losing a husband had made her cling to her two boys. She could not consider anything that might distract her from them, no matter how independent they became.

As for Leticia, Mr. Barcroft's death had shaken her as well. Her husband was a law enforcement officer after all, and operating under an umbrella of controversy thanks to the incident with Naples. She took the role of mother *seriously*.

As little Tina joined her age mates, Elaine and Leticia came together for consultation. "Is it me, or do we have about twice as many kids this year?" Leticia asked.

"A lot of folks are coming in from farther out of town. I hope Hudson and the deputies don't have a hard time."

Leticia nudged Elaine. "You do know why all these people are here, don't you?"

Elaine knew, but was almost afraid to acknowledge it.

"They're coming to see your boy."

Elaine held her hand to her mouth, awed by the notion that her son was on the verge of becoming a rock star. "Let's turn on the TV," she said. "It should be on the news soon."

Leticia made a funny *O* with her mouth and hugged Elaine's arm. "Kit Calloway! Yum yum!"

"Uh-*huh*," agreed Elaine. "To go, please!"

* * * *

The local station broke from its telethon of Hammer Studios horror classics for an update from Main Street, where Elaine and Leticia's crush, Kit Calloway, wearing a tie silk-screened with dancing mummies, smiled into the camera with just the right whimsy. "Hello, viewers and booers! I'm on Main Street in downtown Ember Hollow—make that *Haunted Hollow*—where hundreds have gathered for the beginning of the annual Pumpkin Parade!"

He turned to the costumed crowd behind him, and they whooped, raised their hands, and made monster motions.

Calloway turned back. "As you can see, we're having a great time, and eager to see Ember Hollow's own Chalk Underlines perform!" Although he misspoke, the crowd cheered.

"If you can't make it out to see the festivities yourself, don't worry! We'll be bringing you frequent updates throughout the evening!"

* * * *

Hudson Lott and most of the other deputies were concentrated at the parade's starting point.

Hudson resisted the temptation to lean against the light pole behind him. Under the browning sky, he watched the parade-goers gather by the hundreds at the edge of the street, milling, dancing, mugging in their elaborate costumes.

Figures in family-friendly costumes—local school mascots, firemen, and deputies—walked along the barricade, handing out candy, T-shirts, glow bracelets, and school supplies.

From a darkened alley just two blocks away, Ruth emerged, costumed as a rag doll. The outfit was well made, despite her disdain for Halloween, and somehow both enticing and frightening. The dress hugged her lean form, except for the puffy short skirt and frilly petticoat ending at the tops of her thighs.

An orange yarn wig with pigtails jutting at angles from her head curtained a greasepaint-paled face. Ruby red lips blended into a drawn-on stitch smile that arched to her cheekbones. The novelty glasses, round lenses tinted to look like big buttons, did not add the element of harmless whimsy that Ruth imagined they did. However, they did render her a stranger to all but the most scrutinizing passerby.

Despite the need for anonymity, she made sure to place her crucifix over her costume where she could touch it.

The gingham bag at her side was more than an accessory. It held several handfuls of tainted candy, as well as the .38 she had taken from the ol' boys who now rotted in a pit of pumpkin guts along with that filthy Angelo. Another box of the special candy sat hidden behind a dumpster.

She hopped the barricade and walked along the line, joining the pre-parade warm up crew. "Here we are, brethren!" she called as she handed out little orange-and-black-wrapped horror shows to adults and teens. "Have a blessed evening!"

An eight-year-old girl in a cow costume ran toward her, hoof-gloved hand held out for a "treat."

Ruth leaned close, her insane smile and dead button-eye glasses making the child recoil. "Why *hello*, little one!" she crooned, taking baby steps toward the little girl. "Can you say please?"

The child's mother walked up behind her to stand quiet and uncomfortable.

"Oh, well," Ruth crooned. "Here you go anyway."

The child looked up at her mother, who said. "It's okay,"

The girl took the candy, and Ruth grinned like a joker in a rigged deck. "Bye-bye, now!"

Then came a startling sound of screams from the four-way intersection a hundred yards away. People in the crowd craned their necks, murmuring.

First a man, then a woman, then a dozen average folk of all ages appeared, panicked. "It's coming! Get away!"

"Agh! It's horrible!"

More screams and exclamations, then amplified shrieking laughter, followed by—silence.

Ruth caressed the outline of the pistol against her hip in the gingham bag.

A staccato cadence rose, as something heavy punched the pavement with a doomsday rhythm.

Chapter 33

Higher than the roof of the shoe shop on the corner, a silhouette appeared against the bronze sky. Its head was two times too big, its bearing was evil, and it wore an orange-and-black-striped top hat—a Halloween-inspired Uncle Sam.

The onlookers, familiar with this character from parades past, shouted and whistled at the character known as The Night Mayor.

The insane babble came again, accentuated by grating feedback from an amplifier. Enacted by a man on stilts wearing a long orange-and-black-striped tuxedo to match the top hat, The Night Mayor rounded the corner, raising his oversized white-gloved hands to wave acknowledgment of the cheers and hoots.

The ghoulish giant was flanked on four corners by "dead" majorettes marching in orange leggings and black-buckled boots, spinning and twirling plastic legs and arms with the same expert precision they did batons during halftime performances at high school football games.

The Pumpkin Parade had begun.

The lead Toronado rumbled into view, crawling like a *Dune* sandworm as it pulled the first exhibit—a massive black cat with a devious grin, its yellow eyes, old-fashioned kerosene lanterns burning behind wax paper, glowing bright. Its mouth opened to reveal kids costumed as mice, cowering in pretend fear and agony, rodent souls doomed to a feline hell.

The crowd cheered as the squeaking mice tried to escape, only to be trapped in the cat's foam rubber teeth. Again and again, the act repeated, drawing raucous approval from the crowd.

On the cat's back was a kitschy flashing argon sign that read, EMBER HOLLOW PET AND LIVESTOCK SUPPLY.

A few yards behind this, rode a troupe of skeleton horsemen, astride black horses draped with blankets with a pattern of bones that made them look like equine skeletons. Lady GoDieVa, a skeleton in a tight leotard, tossed candy and packets of doggie treats from a black wicker basket.

Farther down and across from The Grand Illusion, a crowd more interested in the featured attraction than the parade cheered and strained against the barricade, fists and lighters rising, their homemade placards—cardboard guillotines slicing the air—reading, I'M A CASUALTY OF THE CHALK OUTLINES! WANTED: THRILL KILL JILL FOR SEX CRIMES AGAINST MY EARDRUMS and KENNY CAN KILL ME ANYTIME!

* * * *

Stella wore her homemade fortune-teller dress, sans the never-to-be-finished scarf. She was determined to be a part of the festivities, even if all by her lonesome. She had modeled her outfit after Maria Ouspenskaya's costume in *The Wolfman*, in which the diminutive actress had played the mother of a character played by Bela Lugosi.

She dropped off her coat and the latest issue of *The Beautiful People* magazine in McGlazer's office, holding her head high and faking a yawn as she sauntered to the end of the hall. She opened the door to the sanctuary, and, in no hurry, entered the sanctuary and switched on its light.

No, sir. No fear whatsoever in Stella's heart tonight, for she had no *reason* to fear, and of course no one and nothing would see just how unafraid she was.

By God, she had endured a midnight trip to the boneyard, all by her lone. What had she to fear from a mere settling foundation?

She didn't need all the sanctuary lights. She was *alone* of course, and wasn't afraid of shadowed corners. She experimented with the panel of switches until she found the lights over the piano, and left only that one on.

Stella sat at the bench, propped the hymnal open, and began to play. Soon she was immersed in choosing and practicing Sunday's numbers. Nothing was going to happen to her tonight, because that was ridiculous.

Her neck and back muscles relaxed, and she believed the story her actions were selling her mind.

Then that D key played itself, and Stella's courage flitted away like a moth sprung from its chrysalis.

* * * *

Stella scrutinized the piano key. She touched it with a trembling finger, pushed it, released. For a minute, maybe three, she waited for some response.

She got it. The lights went out.

Stella sat rigid in the darkness, trying to quiet her breathing, hoping the ghost would be so kind as to turn the lights back on. When it did not, Stella rose, praying that no cold fingers would brush her cheeks, no glowing figure would float up from behind the piano.

She reached in her purse and cursed. Her keys with the miniature flashlight attached were still in her coat—which was in McGlazer's office. Stella made her way up the aisle to the door behind the pulpit and choir benches, pricking up her ears for the reassuring low rumble of people down on the street, just a few hundred yards away.

Then the D key played again, echoing, building to a machine gun cadence impossible for human fingers.

Stella stifled a scream, reaching for the doorknob even before she stepped up on the platform.

The piano was playing an actual tune now, very fast, but with an almost brutal melancholy, and somehow familiar. But Stella didn't want to hear any more of it, didn't feel any need to solve the mystery. She only wanted out of this accursed place.

She stumbled the last few steps to the door, sparking a terrifying vision of falling and breaking her ankle, unable to escape this so-called sanctuary. But she made a deft recovery and found the knob via sheer luck or some sixth sense and, thank God and all his saints, it *opened*.

She entered the hallway, found the light switch, and breathed relief as the fluorescence fell upon her like an angel's wings. Then the door from the sanctuary slammed behind her, trapping her in this narrow corridor with the echo of her own short, shrill scream.

The lights flickered, randomly alternating from one fixture to another, up and down the hallway.

At least Stella could see—but when she took a step toward the office door, it almost slammed on her reaching hand. She bolted down the hallway, to the left-turning corner that led to more Sunday school rooms, and beyond that, the door to the gym, where many blessed doors waited.

But that section of the hallway went dark entirely, while two lights flickered above her.

She heard doors slamming, opening, and slamming again like thunder in that dark tunnel, and turned back toward the sanctuary door. Now the doors in that section were slamming as well, the lights in those rooms strobing like spring lightning.

When the office door opened and slammed with deafening staccato to her left, she dashed through the unmoving door to her right, never realizing, till that door also slammed shut, that she had just been herded like a sacrificial lamb.

* * * *

Candace pedaled like mad, glancing up at the ever-darkening sky, the empty and desolate fields stretching on either side of the road toward lines of yellow and red trees.

She churned the pedals with all she had.

Soon, she passed the pocked sign that read DOWNTOWN EMBER HOLLOW 3 MILES.

Discouraged, she pulled over to take a break, gulping for air.

Just as she crossed her arms over her handlebars and rested her head, a low rumble came across the plain. Candace raised her head, listening as a scrap of hope unfolded in her pounding heart.

Turning, she saw headlights in the distance behind her. It was a truck. A big one.

Energized, Candace pushed the bike forward and pedaled again, building speed.

As the headlights of the eighteen-wheeler drew closer, Candace positioned herself near the edge of the road. Now she could see its haul: a trailer with perforated aluminum walls, behind which was sporadic movement. Poultry cages, filled with turkeys.

The driver slowed as he passed—and Candace took the opportunity to grab the rear bumper.

She held on with a death grip, terrified of losing hold and careening into the ditch. The little darting beaks and curious eyes of next month's Thanksgiving dinners investigated through the ventilated rear door.

She strained to keep the handlebars steady with her right hand, raising her feet from the fast-spinning pedals. She had lassoed a furious bull.

Wind blasted her in the face, carrying with it stray feathers and the stench of trapped fowl. A tiny round eye pressed close and focused on her through one of the cage holes, perhaps sensing a shared fate.

* * * *

Everett examined the jack-o'-lantern he had carved during the short ride.

The pickup wheeled into the vast grass field reserved for parade parking, already nearly full. The world across from the field was a long row of asphalt lots with dumpsters, rear delivery doors, cargo bays, and alleys. On the other side of that—something loud, something festive.

A middle-aged lady attendant wearing an orange vest stepped up to the truck as they pulled in. She was either impressed or appalled by the costumes. "There's a few spots left over by the creek," she told them. "Be sure and lock up."

"*Si,*" acknowledged Guillermo. "*Gracias.*"

Everett stared at the uncostumed attendant with confusion, forgetting the fresh-carved jack-o'-lantern in his lap, the bounty of orange fruit all around him. The sound of the parade met his ears and drew his attention, filling him with the kind of excitement normal children feel on Christmas morning.

Guillermo guided the pickup through the labyrinth of cars and parked. "They start before!" Enrique complained, as he and Guillermo stepped out.

"*Si!*" said Guillermo, pointing where a watch would be, if he wore one. "It's gonna be late, I said you!"

Everett tossed away the soggy, tattered executioner's hood and put the jack-o'-lantern on like a helmet, inhaling the smell of raw pumpkin. He climbed down from the bed and regarded the two men.

Enrique's makeup was failing, the thick scar across his throat peeling off to reveal clean, unmarred skin beneath. Seeing Everett's new mask, he raised a thumb. "Oh! *Muy* nice, *mi amigo! Primo! Mucho* scary!"

Everett leaned closer to examine the throat scar, understanding with grievous disappointment that it was false.

Reacting to Everett's scrutiny, Enrique turned to his side mirror. "Eh, I need glue! Is *arruinada*!"

He pushed the scar back in place with one hand, as Guillermo tossed him a bottle of spirit gum. Enrique set to work reapplying the scar appliance, as Everett walked around him, observing.

"You want some?" Guillermo offered. "We ha' more scars. *Y sangre* too."

"Nn...not...dead?" Everett asked.

"Heh. No *muerte,* no." Enrique shook his head. "Heh-heh."

Everett reached up and pulled another scar off the man's forehead.

"Hey! No, no!" Enrique's patience for the weird gringo was growing thin. "What do you *do*? It taked a long time!"

Everett examined the deception as Enrique took it back, then at the deceiver, and drew a meat cleaver from his treat bag.

"Whoa!" Enrique took a step back from Everett. "What do you..."

Everett lunged at him and snatched the fake throat-slash scar away, raising the cleaver, insisting, *"Trick!"*

Enrique cried out and fell to his back.

Guillermo rushed around to intervene, throwing his mask down in anger. "No! *Estancia lejos!"*

Now it was Guillermo who had Everett's attention. "Trick?"

"Es no divertido!" Guillermo scalded, reaching for the cleaver. Everett slashed it across his throat. A wide ribbon of blood splashed across Everett's pumpkin face.

Guillermo stumbled backward as he issued a gurgling scream, staring down at his companion with confused terror.

Enrique watched him fall to his back, gurgling and kicking.

"Guillermo?"

Too shocked for rage, too deep in denial for terror, Enrique felt Everett coming closer. He could see the seed of murder blooming in the soulless orbs within the jack-o'-lantern.

"Me deje solo!" Enrique cried.

Everett held up his red-slick gleaming cleaver. "Dead is *trick!*"

Enrique bolted. "Help! Help me!"

Everett raised the cleaver, calling, "Dead is *treat!*"

Rising from her lawn chair, the attendant peered over the sea of cars, seeing only Enrique's bobbing head.

"You boys simmer down! I don't play that shit!" Grumbling, she went back to her seat, spitting as she lifted her newspaper.

The tatters of his costume trailing like streamers, Enrique screamed as he raced toward the noise and people and safety of numbers, where *policia* would be.

As he streaked past her, the attendant lowered the paper, rising to call after him, "What are you boys playin' at? Huh?"

Hearing a grating giggle, she turned around to find Everett, now garbed in Guillermo's devil mask and cape, regarding her with a tilted head and inhuman eyes. Everett dropped the cleaver in his bag, only to replace it with a hammer. Then he drew a paper mask from his pocket, a pink-cheeked beauty queen.

"Dead is for *everyone!*"

The attendant took off at a run, pursued by Everett—the game of victim and monster that he never tired of.

Chapter 34

Ruth the Rag Doll scanned along the parade as it advanced.

Her gaze settled on a wide float with several lithe dancers cavorting around a spiderweb-covered sign that read, THE DANCE MACABRE FEATURING THE EMBER HOLLOW DRAMA ACADEMY MODERN DANCE TROUPE. The platform was pulled by a 1971 Hemicuda, covered front to rear in plush brown fur and trailing oversized pennants reading WOLF WAGON! The hirsute-faced driver and a model in a fur bathing suit howled and waved, receiving imitative calls of response.

Ruth ran alongside the float and hopped on, helped up by the well-muscled dancers, even while they gave her quizzical looks.

Ruth did her best to imitate the moves of her stagemates, while tossing handfuls of candy in all directions. She jumped off the other side and disappeared into the onlookers, having such fun.

* * * *

The room opposite the office was where special-needs children spent Sunday school time. Abutting the sanctuary, it had no windows. There was no need for a phone.

It was a blackened trap, and Stella was its captive. The light switch didn't work, and the door would not open.

Whatever the ghost (what else could it be called at this point?) had in mind for her—perhaps just the tormenting terror of being alone in the dark—it seemed preoccupied with playing the fast tempo yet *oppressive* series of notes it had begun when she ran from the sanctuary. The notes repeated, and Stella realized she was being tortured.

She reached into her purse, feeling for some memento as a charm or talisman. She found a canister of mace and raised it in both hands, recalling how secure it had made her feel when she walked in darkened parking garages and the like. Against a ghost, or whatever this thing was? Maybe it would hold whatever power she *believed* it did.

Stella tried to remember what she had learned from the book about communicating with the dead. Now she wished she had memorized the damned thing, or at least kept it in her purse. She recalled that the book confirmed something she had heard often on television and even from Ruth: that Halloween was the night when whatever veil existed between the worlds of the living and dead thinned to nothing, allowing spirits to enter our world at the height of whatever power they possessed.

If this spirit needed to accomplish something on Earth and Ruth's ritual had somehow muzzled it, it would not be happy.

Then there was the dream, and the wooden cross.

The entity needed it removed to escape. And he used Stella to do it.

The repetitious tune became more frenzied, building to some crescendo.

As it grew faster, Stella recognized "Rumble in Frankenstein's Castle," by The Chalk Outlines.

* * * *

Candace blinked tears and dirt from her eyes as she peered around the rear of the truck, still fighting like mad to hold on with one hand and steer the bike with the other.

The lights of the town center glowed just beyond the tunnel of molting trees.

Candace did not spot the pothole that jounced the truck and then met her tire with shocking force, tearing her away from the bumper. The bike careened, both tires blown flat. She veered hard to regain some kind of control, but it was too late. She crashed into a patch of rocky earth at the edge of a pumpkin field.

Candace rolled and bounced and rolled some more, until the momentum spent itself. She lay still. When her breathing settled, she sat up. Her knees were scraped and flecked with dirt, her hands raw.

She lay still again and cried, becoming acquainted, then intimate with a physical pain that matched her lifelong despair.

But still, she had to stop Everett.

She got up and limped toward the tree tunnel.

Chapter 35

McGlazer was having fun with his Summerisle shtick, joined in the truck's open rear compartment by four church volunteers sporting campy paganesque getups. The ghouls behind in the Cemetery Terrorium were all performing better than rehearsed. The parade passed the fans behind the barricade, true punkers who sported devilocks, skull-painted faces, spiked bracelets, T-shirts with logos reading The Crimson Ghosts, The Other, Spookshow, Black Flag, The Coffin Shakers, and, of course, The Chalk Outlines.

A wall of artificial fog billowed from the theater lobby doors, reducing the vista to a gray blanket in all directions. Excited yelps punctuated this foreshadowing. Then a wall of sound rose and grew ever louder, Dennis/Kenny Killmore, holding a prolonged note.

The note ended, as light beams pierced the fog.

Up on the marquee, Pedro burst through the haze, stopping at the edge as he hit a single crushing note that drew screams of delight from young females, aggressive whoops from their men. Pedro released the note and pumped his devil horned fist into the sky.

Dennis's sensuous voice targeted eager ears like a heat-seeking missile. "One. Two. Three…"

Jill's drumbeats punched the air, a lively rockabilly beat soon to be joined by the return of Pedro's pulsing bass.

The fog cleared, thanks to powerful industrial fans at the corners, giving spectators the full visual force of the performance.

Dennis's rapid-fire three-note riff filled the gaps, followed by breathless vocals.

* * * *

On the platform, DeShaun ran to the edge and cavorted in his kung fu master getup, making snake- and mantis-like movements, while Stuart walked to the other end. By contrast, he only waved, tossing T-shirts and guitar picks but—just not into it.

Hudson came to the barricade across from the stage, joining Monahan and Yoshida in keeping overzealous rockers from getting too close.

* * * *

Enrique, his zombie costume decaying to reveal his vitality, scrambled out of the long alley between Felcher Fabrics and The Bestaurant, trying to catch his breath.

Turning the corner he barreled into the rear of parade watchers, shouting, "Hey! Asesino! *Psicópata!* Please! *Ah...ayuda!*"

Of course, they ignored him. He grabbed the nearest sturdy man by the jacket. "You must hear now! *Mató a* Guillermo!"

"Okay, we get it!" replied the man. "Scary shit!" The man pushed Enrique down.

Through the legs of the parade-goers, the fear-addled immigrant spotted a deputy, Sergeant Shavers, standing in front of a store window, chatting up a blond in a bar-wench dress.

He fought through the crowd, unaware that Everett was stepping out of the same alley, wearing Guillermo's *Satanás* mask, the red cape pulled on over his Dracula cape.

Everett caught his reflection in the store window and waved at himself. Mirrors had been rare in his world.

Then he turned to examine the backs of countless heads that waited to meet his hammer.

Everett caught a glimpse of what they were watching and became bewitched.

* * * *

Pedro mugged at the audience as he beat the hell out of his bass. Dennis held sway with Jagger swagger and Madsen's goblin Gibson.

DeShaun crouched, vaulted and kicked like the Silver Fox himself, Whang Jang Lee, while Stuart tossed swag between long scans of the road beyond the parade's tail.

He spotted a familiar figure beyond the rear of the crowd. Candace.

She was dragging herself toward the parade. And she looked like hell.

Stuart shoved his armful of giveaways at DeShaun and ran to the marquee doorway. DeShaun spotted Candace too and mouthed her name at Dennis. He gestured for DeShaun to go.

Chapter 36

Stuart burst from the theater and jumped the barricade, bolting past the deputies shouting at him and alongside the crawling floats, unstoppable. Yards behind the last wagon Candace staggered, her eyes showing as much alarm as her body did fatigue.

With the passing of the parade's last float, people condensed toward the marquee and the Outlines, leaving an empty street.

Stuart covered this span with all he had, running till he reached Candace. He took her arm, checking her scraped knees and hands as he walked with her to a bench well away from the parade route, and draped his suit jacket over her shoulders.

"What happened?"

Candace buried her face in his shoulder and cried. Stuart waited till she raised her head. "They're all dead."

"Dead? Who?"

"Mama. Daddy. The neighbors. The whole street…" She surveyed the crowd with wild eyes. "Soon…everyone."

Stuart rechecked her to see how badly she was hurt, wondering what the symptoms of shock were.

DeShaun arrived with a bottle of water. "Everybody okay?"

"Not by a long shot." Stuart had taken on Candace's panic. "I think you better go get your dad."

* * * *

"Alejar a!" Enrique forced his way through the crowd and was jostled back for his rudeness. "Move away! I must talk to *policia!*"

He raced across the street, shoving through a swath of medal-covered war veterans, all dressed as hobos for the parade.

Shavers spotted Enrique. Assuming his erratic behavior was due to tequila or two, and eager to impress the bar wench, he puffed up his chest. "Hey!" He grabbed Enrique and dragged him away from the marchers. "What's wrong with you, son?"

"Un loco mató, eh, cutted *a* Guillermo!" Enrique couldn't bring himself to mimic a stabbing or slashing motion.

"What?"

"He, he *corto el cuello!*" Enrique shouted. "Cutted him!"

"Boy, I do not have time for this!" Shavers pulled Enrique toward him by the collar—but found the "prankster" yanking back. The terror on his face made Shavers go cold.

"Es insane, this mother!" screamed Enrique.

"Watch your language!" The sergeant struggled with Enrique's grip, stunned when the skinny Hispanic grabbed his radio and screamed into it. "Guns! Get all God damned *armas*! One for both hand, mother!"

Shavers wrested the radio away.

The barmaid watched this unfold, sucking the strange, delicious candy she'd been given by the rag doll. She saw a tiny black tentacle emerge from Enrique's neck, which the deputy somehow could not see.

Shavers shouted, "You want to go to jail, boy?" Enrique jostled Shavers like a madman. *"Si!* Take me in jail! Lock me up!"

Shavers keyed his radio. "Hey, Hudson, you there?"

But Hudson, watching the moshing, roiling crowd, could not hear his radio over the music and crowd noise.

* * * *

Kerwin wheeled into the overflow lot, stopping to speak to the reflective-vested attendant. She sat stiffly in her chair, a crinkled paper beauty queen mask on her face.

"Hey there!"

Next to him, Cordelia leaned into Kerwin's space to take in the sight. "My word! You people really do get knee deep in this Halloween business, hm?"

"Uh, yeah," Kerwin responded, annoyed with the attendant's lack of response. "Any good spaces?" he asked.

No answer.

Cordelia's face showed a bored kind of delight. Kerwin sensed that something was wrong but was too afraid of blowing the big deal to delve any deeper. "Well, sleep tight then!"

He smiled at Cordelia for the one thousandth time, as he drove into the field.

* * * *

Candace worked to control her breathing as Stuart brushed dirt from her clothes and hair. "What about your brother?"

"Everett." The hard wisdom in Candace's eyes was too much like that of someone very old. "*He* killed them. He killed them all, Stuart," she said with a grim conviction that raised his goose flesh. "And he's not going to stop. He's *never* going to stop."

Tears filled her eyes. "He's *here,* Stuart. I know he's come."

Stuart took her hand and stood, feeling very vulnerable. "We have to tell my brother. We have to warn everybody."

Chapter 37

DeShaun shoved his way through the costumed throngs toward his father, his apologies doing nothing to prevent angry curses, threats, even shoves.

Making it worse was a strange feeling coming off the collected mass, like a fast-approaching storm. He had to ignore this and remain focused on maintaining a course to his father.

Erratic movement ahead of him. Someone stumbled, and the people around, perhaps unnerved by the odd behavior, were quick to clear a circle. DeShaun realized he could not prevent a collision with the thrashing woman, and he feared that if he fell he might not be able to get back up for several precious seconds.

He raised his arms in time to keep from being head-butted. As the woman, dressed as Slave Leia from *The Empire Strikes Back*, turned, DeShaun saw that is was Mrs. Nettles, his teacher from sixth grade. "Sorry, Mrs. Nettles."

She stared not at him but *through* him, her eyes full of terror. What she saw was DeShaun's false white beard and eyebrows dissolving into thick billowing smoke that formed amorphous devious faces.

She screamed in his face, flailing and falling backward into others, creating a domino effect.

"Jeez!" DeShaun tried to help her up, but she became more and more entangled with others. He realized something was very, *very* wrong with not only Mrs. Nettles but a growing number of parade-goers. Giving up on helping her. he worked his way toward his father.

* * * *

Rag Doll Ruth paced the sidewalk beside the spectators, praying that her scheme would work. It wasn't long before her prayers were answered.

She spotted a preteen boy lying in a fetal position on the sidewalk scratching at his cheeks, to the dismay of his alarmed parents. Not far from this, an old man in a wheelchair gaped at his hands, violently shook them, and then shook them harder, terror blooming in his weathered features.

"Thy will be done, Lord," she prayed. "Make them beg for thy mercy. And turn thy glorious face away from them!"

* * * *

"Dee-scrip-chee-*own*! Can you describe him?" Shavers, unnerved by the strength of the thin man, made a series of senseless gestures, but they weren't needed.

"He wears *calabaza*!" Shavers stood immobilized. "A big-ass jack-o'-lantern!" Enrique insisted.

Enrique dragged Sergeant Shavers toward the parking lot where he had watched his beloved partner die. With growing dread, Shavers shouted once more into his radio. "Hudson Lott! Please respond! Chief Deputy Hudson Lott!"

Just a few yards away Everett cried tears of joy as the majesty of the Halloween parade unfolded before him.

The float for Home Sweet Home Appliances passed in front of him, its washer and dryer mock-ups bursting open every few seconds to reveal a zombified fifties housewife blasting a humanoid sock monster with a Super Soaker. A child sitting on the float in a witch mask waved at him and tossed a detergent sample in his direction.

He dropped his hammer and clasped his hands together. "We all trick! We all treat!" His face had an expression of pure, childlike joy.

* * * *

Outlines crowd favorite "Freakshow Radio" filled the air, enthralling old fans and making enthusiastic new ones. Few could resist moving their hips, head, or hands to the energetic punk-rockabilly sound.

DeShaun had long since tossed away the beard and now worked his way along the edge of the barricade, shouting, "Emergency!" every few feet to prevent irritated shoving. He spotted his father standing with his back to the crowd, almost in reach, if he could just...

A man in a motorcycle jacket and corpse paint flailed in the street, screaming and swatting at invisible things. He ran toward the parade display before him, sponsored by Frenkel's Exterminator Service, where a cute eight-year-old girl with a water-filled canister spritzed bug-costumed actors as they chewed on huge furniture props.

The "bugs," seeing the crazed biker, ceased their mock death throes and converged to protect their little executioner.

Hudson went into action, tackling the man to the ground. DeShaun's reaching hand missed by a second. The crowd swelled against DeShaun, mashing him into the barricade, where panic and pain double-teamed him.

"Dad!" DeShaun called, but the clamor was too much.

The song ended, prompting an eruption of cheers and clapping. Then Stuart's hands closed around DeShaun's arm, dragging him out of the crushing ruckus. "Come on!"

Together they battled back the crowd and squeezed into the street.

The Outlines played on. Now that it was darker, the high-wattage lights blasting their eyes prevented them from seeing the disturbance on the street below.

Hudson was trying to restrain the biker-jacketed man, turning his arm behind his back and pinning him facedown, when he heard DeShaun call to him, saw him running closer. "DeShaun! Get your ass back over the barricade! This is dangerous, son!"

In this pocket of relative silence, he heard the radio squawk. "Hudson! Answer, God damn it."

With his free hand, Hudson keyed his radio. "I'm here!" He waved DeShaun and Stuart away, as the man on the ground cried, "The invasion has begun!"

"There's some kinda killer running around here," Shavers said. "I've got a body and a witness!"

"Shit!" Hudson exclaimed.

Stuart turned to DeShaun. "It's Candace's brother! He's psycho!"

Turning to check on Candace, Stuart saw her pressing herself against a shop wall far behind the barricade and the unpredictable crowd.

Mrs. Nettles had plummeted into full-blown, stark-raving paranoia, running and swinging around in a frenzy, knocking people down. In the melee, a large man in an orange prisoner jumpsuit lost balance and fell against Candace.

Stuart ran to help her, followed by DeShaun.

Hudson's collar, foaming at the mouth, bashed his forehead on the ground, screaming, "You can't take my brain if it's ruined!"

Hudson turned him over and embraced him to prevent further injury, keying his radio. "Sergeant, you there?"

"Here," came the answer. "Witness seems to be saying our perp is wearing a pumpkin on his head. Repeat, perpetrator is wearing a *God damned jack-o'-lantern*!"

"We need to shut this thing down," Hudson said.

Up on the stage, Dennis, oblivious to the burgeoning fracas, addressed the crowd. "This next one is a special request."

Dennis brushed back his sweaty hair as he talked to his fans. "It's a cover of an epic soul freezer by our buddies in Scarlet Frost. It's called…'Wind of Winter's Dawn.'"

Pedro played an extended note that was both melancholy and menacing, dissolving into Dennis's sludgy riffs.

Jill banged a voodoo beat, and Dennis sang, closing his eyes.

"Cold the fog lay upon the bog
where rests the maiden mourned
Her heart remains ever in twain
in a cage of bones adorned
Years she watched with ache she matched
Her pregnant grief unborn…"

Kerwin, escorting Cordelia toward the parade through a breezeway, stopped cold upon hearing the uncharacteristic strains of soul-crushing, dirge-like black metal. "Shit! What are you guys doing to me?"

"This doesn't sound like the demos you sent," Cordelia noted.

"No." Kerwin covered his panicked expression with a sly grin. "They, see, they're playing a goof on their poor old manager. Yeah, that's it! Come on. It'll start jumping in a sec."

He rushed her toward the street.

* * * *

DeShaun and Stuart jumped back to the crowd side of the barricade just as a furious brawl broke out. Bodies, fists, and screams filled the air as more and more people converged. The boys ran to cover Candace.

Just a few yards away, the parade accordioned on itself. A lavender limousine towing a float for Turner's Wedding Rentals halted across from this pocket of chaos. Amid the lace, frills, and latticework of the display, the performers, costumed as ghost bride, groom, and parson, craned their heads toward the ruckus.

A teen girl in a Barbie costume ran toward the wedding scene, setting her hair on fire with a lighter as she climbed aboard, screaming, "My hair! It's eating my *mind!*"

The faux phantom wedding party tried to circle and corral her, but she wallowed amid the decorations, which caught and carried the flame.

DeShaun and Stuart guarded Candace on either side. They dashed along the shop walls until they found an open alley and sprinted into it, leaping over trash and boxes.

"What's wrong with these people?" DeShaun wondered.

"Some kinda mass hysteria," Stuart guessed, trying to catch his breath.

Candace stopped them. "It happened to me last night!" she exclaimed. "I saw...*evil* things. Everywhere."

"What about Dad?" DeShaun huffed.

"And Dennis."

The big man in the orange jumpsuit came around the corner, his hands and chin smeared with blood. Eyes burning with malice, he ran toward them, bellowing like a hippo, his plastic ball-and-chain prop bouncing behind him.

The kids ran around the corner, much faster than their pursuer. Seeing a panel delivery truck, they dashed to the far side and huddled together, covering their mouths as the man ran past. They heard him stop a few yards away, puffing.

He spun, roaring. They knew he was onto them somehow. They dashed around the back of the truck, where DeShaun tried to raise the sliding door—but found it locked.

"Shit!" Stuart said, as they all searched around for shelter.

Pointing at something along the back walls of the shopping center, DeShaun whispered, "Over there!"

Chapter 38

Kerwin and Cordelia arrived at the rear of the undulating crowd. The black metal dirge droned on, scorching Kerwin's ears. A brawl broke out just a few yards to their left, the combatants snarling and snapping like wild dogs.

Cordelia squealed with fright, but Kerwin ignored them, He craned to see the Outlines, mumbling, "What the hell is *wrong* with you? You stupid little shits!"

A beer glass flew from the crowd and broke at his feet. "Hey! Watch the suit!" he shouted.

The perpetrator, a man in a caveman costume—appropriate given his size and build—homed in on Kerwin, muscling past the other parade-goers. Kerwin found himself at a loss for words for once, just before the caveman decked him.

Kerwin scrambled up and pushed Cordelia in front of him. "What the hell are y—" she protested.

Salvation of a kind came when someone scrambled onto the convertible Corvair pulling a float for Double S Sporting Goods, tearing at the driver's oversized baseball cap like it was a rabid cat, then pounding it, still on the driver's head, into the steering wheel. The Corvair veered toward the barricade, accelerating on its way to bashing the wall of humanity, including Kerwin's Neanderthal assailant, who was thrown to the ground.

On the street, balls of all sports and sizes sailed from the float, bouncing and rolling in all directions.

* * * *

Sergeant Shavers, having left the bawling Enrique wrapped in a blanket in the back of a cruiser, returned to his post, just as the candy began to work its effect on him...

The costumed patrons all seemed to mesh together, then melt apart again, glowing lava lamp globs of sinister threatening faces.

His radio squawked and startled him, a disjointed chorus of distorted mocking voices assailing his senses. "Suspect is wearing a *pumpkin*! Suspect-pect is wearing-*ring* a pumpkin-KIN!"

The fur-suited girl from the Wolf Wagon ran toward him, calling for help, blood from a head wound trailing down her cheek. But her furry bikini was too much for Shaver's tainted psyche. He saw only a snarling, disembodied jackal head rocketing toward him, streams of hell trailing from its eyes. Screaming, he raised his pistol. Before he could fire, the massive spider exhibit fell from the careening Great Gardens wagon, yanking the vehicle to its side and crushing Shaver.

The spider landed safely away from everyone.

The terrified bikini girl cried louder as vehicles collided, piled up, and crashed through the barricade and into the storefronts, fire hydrants, sidewalk benches. A telephone pole fractured and leaned, suspended by sparking wires.

Watching the catastrophe from her planter perch, Ruth threw her head back in delight, praising The Lording.

For Everett, the tableau was heartbreaking. The most beautiful thing he had ever witnessed, dashed to ruins before his very eyes. His fingers formed claws.

* * * *

A mushroom of fire caught the attention of the Outlines. Opening his eyes from deep immersion in the song, Dennis stepped to the edge of the stage and beheld the mayhem below.

"Where's Hudson?" Jill shouted.

Dennis shielded his eyes and scanned for him—just as a half-empty bottle of Diamante's Deep Dark Rum came hurtling from the crowd and smashed into his forehead.

Dennis lurched forward headfirst. He collapsed onto the edge of the stage, his momentum carrying him over, and he plummeted to the ground below.

Jill screamed.

Chapter 39

DeShaun led Stuart and Candace to a short wooden staircase behind the Kronos Cafe. It was boarded in on the front side, but there was a narrow space between the stairs and wall into which the kids scuttled.

They crouched low in the tiny space. DeShaun squinted through a crack between the boards to see the crazed fat man kicking boxes and trash cans nearby. "He's going the other way. I say we stay here for a minute. Maybe he'll forget about us."

"Then what?" Stuart asked.

"We have to help our families," DeShaun said. "We can't bail on 'em."

Stuart looked at Candace, at the exhausted, anguished, terrified expression on her face. "I'm so sorry, Candace."

"What's the deal with your brother anyhow?" DeShaun asked.

Stuart slugged him in the shoulder for the impropriety.

"It's okay," Candace said. "You guys have to know. *Everybody* needs to know."

* * * *

Everett grew sad, seeing the beautiful Halloween decorations burning, people throwing away their wonderful masks, bags of candy spilled and discarded like trash.

The gush from the broken fire hydrant washed loose basketballs, baseballs, bowling balls, and golf balls into the street and sidewalks, toppling already dumbfounded parade-goers. The pilot vehicles accelerated to avoid pedestrians, hydroplaned, and turned sideways, smashing into one another as they flung the floats and hapless passengers about.

An elderly woman, frozen in place by sheer terror at the edge of the street, was smashed between two colliding platforms.

The HAUNTED HOLLOW banner draped across the street erupted in flames, dripping molten plastic onto running and fallen people.

Hay bales and gas from punctured tanks erupted into towering blazes. Loud booms and clouds of erupting flame rose from all directions.

Chapter 40

"Miss Leticia, Miss Elaine, I'm scared!" Little Tina stood in her pajamas near the television, where she had gone to wait her turn for tucking in on her cot. "This isn't real, is it?"

Tina must have seen the parade on television. Her question raised a lump in Elaine's throat, the one that her maternal instinct had already planted hours ago.

She and Leticia went to see, walking to keep from appearing too urgent and frightening the girl further.

"Go pick out a pillow and blanket, sweetie." Leticia guided her away, then joined Elaine.

"Oh Lord…" They crowded against each other as they watched the footage.

"Helen, what we are witnessing is real. We see a fire spreading over here…" Kit Calloway's mellow baritone betrayed his fear.

The camera turned to focus on a pillar of flame—then came a loud *boom*.

The camera made a rough pan back to Calloway. Alarm twisted his handsome features. He turned and ran. The shot became an incoherent blur and then—static.

Then Kit's colleague Helen was on screen at the station, looking like a well-tailored deer caught in headlights. "W…we've lost our feed. Apologies to our viewers, we…hope to have some kind of update in just a few minutes. Please stay tuned. Emergency services are on their way, and they have asked everyone to stay away from the parade site!"

"What are we going to do?" Elaine asked.

Leticia hugged her. "We're going to stay right here with these children because they need us. And we're going to pray."

* * * *

Candace blurted the important details that Mamalee had related to her the day before; about Everett's early childhood strangeness, the assault by the priests—his first Halloween night violence.

Candace, her eyes focused on nothing, finished. "Every year we move to a new place and stay until Halloween comes. We set Everett free on Halloween night, and he goes…'trick-or-treating.' The next morning, we move again. Mamalee and Daddy hope…*hoped*…that one day, he would grow out of it. Now, he's grown, all right. And he's strong. And he never got better. Only worse."

Candace sobbed. "I…I try not to make friends, but…you guys…"

* * * *

Candace touched Stuart's cheek like all the grown-ups had at his Dad's funeral. He hugged her, and glanced at DeShaun. There was no judgment in his eyes, only compassion.

"Jeez," Stuart mumbled. "I thought *I* had problems."

"We all do now," Candace said, sniffling. "Mamalee told me yesterday, before I left, what those priests did to Everett, how he got so messed up, I realized it means he'll never stop. Maybe he can't."

"That's why you were scared of the church," Stuart said. "What happened to Everett…Wait!" Gears turned in Stuart's head. "Maybe if we can all get to the church, he won't come there. And DeShaun's dad can catch him."

"Yeah, but how are we g—"

DeShaun's query was cut short by their massive jump-suited assailant, crashing his head into their hiding place through the enclosed wall of the staircase. He roared, and the three escapees scrambled to crawl out the way they had entered.

Candace made it out first. As the pursuer charged around the staircase to pen them in, Candace switched into defensive mode and sprang out to face him, raising a weathered two-by-four. "You get away from my friends!"

She smashed the board into the man's shoulder, knocking him back. "You don't scare me, you stupid creep!"

The maniac was stunned. She swung again, landing a cornerwise strike to the shin that drew a shrill cry.

"I've seen scary, mister," she shouted, "and you're not it!"

She smashed the board over the fat man's head, sending him to the ground.

As Stuart and DeShaun came to Candace's side, their assailant stirred, blinking up at them with confusion. Then he began to bawl like a baby.

Candace tossed the board away and grabbed Stuart's wrist. "Come on!"

* * * *

Keeping the wayward biker pinned, Hudson examined the strobe of running bodies and saw Pedro and Jill running onto the street, then McGlazer climbing down from the still-moving truck, toward...

Dennis's feet, sprawled at an alarming angle on the courtyard just below the stage.

Hudson yanked the handcuffed prisoner up to his feet and dragged him toward the street's edge, where he hoped the addled partyer would be out of harm's way—more or less.

"Sorry to do this, buddy!" Hudson said, and knocked the man out cold with a short left hook.

* * * *

"Come on, baby. You're gonna be okay." Jill rocked like a mother comforting a baby, as she held the unconscious Dennis on her lap, alarmed to see blood slickening the grass beneath his head.

"Somebody help!" Pedro yelled. "We need a doctor!"

But there was only running, anarchy, panic.

Reverend McGlazer joined them and checked Dennis's vital signs. "We may never get through this mess in time," McGlazer said. "But Stella is an EMT. She has her kit at the church."

"We'll get him there!" Pedro stooped to lift Dennis in his arms.

McGlazer stopped him. "No. We can't move him."

"What are we gonna do?" Jill asked.

"Apply pressure to his wound," McGlazer said. "Here, use my jacket."

The insane crowd closed in rapidly, and *worse*—converged, as if with a single purpose.

Hudson appeared. "What's his status?"

McGlazer told him about Stella.

"We need to get her down here. Take the next street over," advised Hudson. "Situation's no better ahead, I don't think." He turned to Pedro and Jill. "You two are officially deputized. Protect Dennis."

As McGlazer darted away toward an open alley, Pedro patted the unconscious form of Dennis, looked at Jill, and stood. "'Bout time. Haven't had a good rumble since that Planet Six gig."

* * * *

The fire was an octopus of flickering, flailing tentacles, growing by the second, as burning patches of hay and paper rose into the air to rain embers and renew the cycle.

Witnessing the chaos ruining the parade, a heartbroken Everett fell to his knees and wept. Then, through the roaring flames and cries of pain and terror, he heard someone laughing.

Not with innocent joy, as he had when he found this giant celebration. It was *spite*. That haughty snicker of smug superiority, reminding him of those priests, relishing their power over a little boy.

Someone was enjoying this.

Everett's teary eyes found a figure dressed like a wonderful rag doll, standing on a brick planter, throwing her head back to address the sky. "Thank you, Lord!" cried the woman. "Praise your holy name!" she said.

Everett followed her gaze to the sky, but saw nothing. Nonetheless, she was talking to the sky like the priests who had raped him. Even a child could surmise that she had something to do with this calamity. And there was no greater a child than Everett.

He took up his hammer and walked toward her.

Chapter 41

"Burn, Sodom, *burn!*" cried Rag Doll Ruth, enraptured.

Then she saw a strange figure coming through the wall of flame.

Once through the wall, the figure stopped, regarding her with a sinister and threatening smile. It was the Devil himself, clad in a flowing red cape, bearing a bloody hammer.

Ruth's joy plummeted. "Y...you've come."

Terror gripped her. By rote, she spoke the words that no one else could say. "You are not welcome here, ye old serpent!"

Everett's glittering eyes were fixed on her. Blood dripped from his hammer. Heat from the flames behind him distorted his devil mask into a shimmery dream-demon face.

Ruth removed the button glasses and threw them away. She took the gun from her candy bag. "Get thee *gone,* Satan!"

She fired at him with shaking hands, missing once, twice.

Everett was delighted. A new game to cheer him up.

Ruth backed up, almost falling off the planter—but caught her balance and hopped off. "Lord help me!"

She shot again and again. The third bullet passed through Everett's shoulder—not even slowing him.

Everett walked through another small island of flames, oblivious to them.

Ruth stumbled back against the storefront, screaming, her gun hand shaking. For the first time since her conversion, she felt a sense of utter and complete abandonment. "Help me! Somebody *help*!"

As Everett drew closer, he raised his hammer—then stopped.

Ruth's crucifix necklace flashed in the firelight.

The talisman filled Everett with fear. He saw the priests, his would-be exorcists, one smiling before shoving the boy over and ripping down his pants, the other glancing toward the door as he held up his crucifix, bellowing chants in Latin.

Everett dropped the hammer. Now it was he who backed away, whimpering.

Ruth saw the reflection of the cross on Everett's face and realized it had immobilized him. Grabbing the little graven image with thumb and forefinger, she got to her feet. "You...you *tremble* before God, prince of liars! Before the power of the cross of Jesus!"

As she advanced with the cross thrust out, Everett withered, fell to his back, and covered his face.

"That's right, you foul demon! You have no power over the righteous! You have no power over me!"

She raised the pistol with her right hand, thrusting the cross pendant till its clasp dug into the back of her neck. "I cast thee into the lake of fire!"

Everett rose and turned, trying to run away. Ruth fired, emptying her last three rounds into his back, as she bellowed, "In Jesus's holy precious name, I rebuke ye, Satan!"

He fell to all fours, crawling away from her. She raised the pistol for the coup de grâce. "There shall be no escape from His wrath!"

She fired—but the hammer clicked dry. "Oh, Holy Spirit." She reached into her bag and withdrew the box of shells to reload. "Guide my hand." She snapped the cylinder home and raised the gun.

Everett tried to struggle to his feet.

Ruth shot him once more in the back, sending him sprawling headlong into the wall of flames.

She lowered the weapon, watching the flames consume him, pleased by his helplessness, as he crawled further into his own destruction.

"Don't you ever come back, Lucifer! For I vanquish ye to the lake of fire forever! In the name of Jesus!"

* * * *

McGlazer ran up the hill, picking up speed at the sound of gunshots.

He opened the door to the sanctuary, finding it dark and quiet. "Stella?" he called. "Where are you?"

Heading to the back entry from the sanctuary into the hallway, he heard Stella's harried cry: "Leave me *alone*!"

McGlazer flipped on the hallway lights—no sign of her. He opened the nearest classroom door. "Stella?"

He tried the door to his side, but it would move only a few inches. He reached in to click on the light and was met with a blood-freezing scream—and a blast of pepper spray.

McGlazer stumbled back, smashing into the wall.

"Leave me *alone*!" Stella emerged, pepper spray held ready for another burst.

"Stella! It's me!" McGlazer called.

"Reverend?" Her voice was hoarse, shaking. "Oh, thank *God*!" She lowered the pepper spray. "I've been scared to death." She hugged his arm. "I'm so sorry!"

"Get me a wet towel or something!" said the blinded minister.

"The…presence is back, Reverend!" Stella exclaimed, as she walked him to the restroom a few doors away. "I know how it sounds. I swear something is here! I'm not just—"

"No time, Stella. Dennis is badly hurt. He's down on the street. We'll call for help, and then get your gear. We'll have to run. The roads are blocked."

* * * *

Down on the street, Ruth scanned for any more pockets of wickedness the Lord might need her assistance in eradicating. Toward the church, she spotted DeShaun, Stuart, and Candace working their way through the cemetery, and her righteous anger rocketed. "Vandals!"

She checked the pistol's chamber, running toward the kids with the gun outstretched. "You will *not* defile the house of God!" She squeezed off a round.

The bullet pinged off a tombstone six feet from the kids, stinging their faces with flying bits of marble. Candace squealed as she pulled the boys to the ground.

Taking a quick glance toward Ruth, Candace rose, dragging the boys by their collars. "Come on!"

They crawled behind a wide gravestone, off which another round sparked with a loud whine.

Ruth stormed through the front gate, flames raging behind her in the town square. "Face your judgment, ye demon-filled monsters!" She fired again.

* * * *

McGlazer and Stella stopped, almost at the door. "I hear shooting," Stella whispered.

"Right outside," McGlazer said, dabbing his eyes with the towel.

He squinted toward the fire exit door, and Stella went to it, opening it an inch or so.

She saw forms hiding behind a grave marker. Then she spied a lithe figure coming up the drive, loading shells into a gleaming revolver. "There are kids out there," she said in low tones, "and the shooter's coming this way!"

"I'll have to draw fire. You get them in the side door!" McGlazer ordered, blinking at her.

"Are you crazy? It's not much safer in here." Stella's tone was hard with conviction.

"Just get to Dennis somehow. He's in front of the Grand Illusion." McGlazer stepped out, running toward the assailant, waving his arms. "Hey! Up here! Leave them *alone!*"

Ruth turned, raising the pistol. Recognition formed on her face as McGlazer came closer. "Reverend?"

Through the residual fog of the mace, recognition dawned on McGlazer's face as well. "Ruth! What are you doing?"

Ruth giggled, eager to caption the horrific tableau behind her. "I'm cleansing Ember Hollow, Reverend!" she said. "Isn't it beautiful?"

Chapter 42

"Go time, boys!" As the crowd surged toward them, Hudson and the rockers tightened their ranks like Spartans. The crazed parade-goers snarled and slavered. "It's *these* monsters! *They're* cooking us!" came a cry from deep in the roiling brood of madness.

"Man, they're multiplying like rabbits," Pedro noted.

"Or rabid rats," added Hudson.

Jill roared, a lioness ready to protect her fallen mate.

* * * *

"Ruth?" McGlazer came close to her, obstructing her view. "My God. What has happened to you?"

"I've been *anointed*!" She spoke with breathless exhilaration. "Now I need you to move aside so I can exterminate some godless vermin."

From the side door, Stella waved to get the attention of the terrified youngsters.

"You can't shoot them!" McGlazer shouted. "Have you lost your mind?"

"*No,* Reverend McGlazer." She stabbed an index finger at her crucifix. "I've gained my soul." She raised the pistol to his face. "Now step aside. And repent."

"I can't let you, Ruth. This has to stop now."

Ruth caught sight of the fugitives running for the church behind McGlazer, and this renewed her righteous rage. She shrieked as she raised the pistol, trying to aim around McGlazer. He maneuvered in front of her and held out his arms. "No!"

The kids dashed inside. "They're in!" Stella screamed. "Come on, Reverend!"

McGlazer turned and dashed for the door, praying he wouldn't take a bullet in the spine before he could make it.

"I warned you!" shouted Ruth.

McGlazer dashed past Stella—who took a second to flip off Ruth just as she slammed the door shut.

* * * *

"It's okay!" In the darkness, Stella hugged the kids like they were her own, watching McGlazer with desperation.

"You can't risk trying to get to Dennis," he told her. "Take the kids and hide."

"What about you?"

McGlazer took a heavy copper cross from a corner display behind the choir pews. "I'll stop her."

* * * *

Brushing at his suit, Kerwin half rose from behind an overturned papier-mâché clown.

Most of the crazed parade-goers had surged toward The Grand Illusion to attack the Outlines, far off to his right. He crept in the opposite direction, keeping his focus on a handful of straggling maniacs across the street. They were rolling on the ground and moaning in puddles left from the burst hydrant.

Approaching an alley on his left, he did not see the figure emerging to smash him in the face, sending him onto his flesh-padded ass.

Kerwin found Cordelia standing over him, scratched and dirty, her tailored clothes torn, fury in her fire-lit face.

"You used me as a bloody *shield*, you sodding little coward!" Her accent carried a good deal more Cockney now.

"No! I was just..." Kerwin's capacity for quick lies failed him, as the enraged executive loomed over him. All that came to him was "My suit!"

Out on the street, at the edge of the fire, a smoldering figure rose, shrugging off remnants of a charred heavy red, still clad in the protective black cape beneath it.

"Then you left me there and ran away to *hide*!" Cordelia accused.

"I…I thought…thought…"

"You thought you could save your own worthless skin, you sleazy wanker!"

"It's not my fault!"

She kicked him, each blow emphasizing a word. "You…can…*forget*… about your band…ever…getting…*signed*!"

Kerwin cowered in fetal position, never seeing the smoking figure creeping up behind Cordelia. "I'll see to it that you *never…ever*—"

She stopped, midkick. A muffled giggling came from behind her. She tried to turn, but couldn't. A smoking gloved hand was tangled in the top of her hair.

Struggling to butt-scoot away, Kerwin could not see the figure behind her. But he saw the assailant's other hand come up, the one that held a thin carving knife. Cordelia scratched at the iron-like claw in her hair, her false nails popping off and skittering on the wet concrete.

The knife pierced the side of Cordelia's neck, through to the other side.

Cordelia's eyes flew wide and then rolled to white, her twitching fingers dabbing at the horrible point dripping her blood.

Everett sliced forward, cutting through Cordelia's larynx and spraying a shower of blood onto the trembling Kerwin, coating his beloved suit in slick gore.

Cordelia fell to her knees with a distorted scream.

Kerwin, whimpering, turned over to crawl away.

Everett followed him. The charred psycho was only a step away, giving off a cloying odor of burned meat and melting polyester, something like sulfur.

Kerwin turned to face the stalker, whose visage, a plastic devil mask melted around a painful-looking grin, left him breathless. By sheer instinct, he resorted to his second greatest talent—coercing, lying, begging. "Listen, fella! I can help you! I can set you up for life, my friend!"

Kerwin's back met a cold brick wall. He was cornered—but the devil man didn't make any motions to attack. Instead, he dropped the carving knife into his trick-or-treat bag, which he set to the side.

"Yeah! That's a good…uh, burned guy!" Kerwin encouraged. "Look, whatever you're on, I can get you much, much more!" he promised.

Everett reached into his back pocket to get his new favorite toy: the claw hammer. The motion was casual enough that Kerwin did not grow alarmed until Everett raised the tool over his head.

Kerwin opened his mouth to scream, just as the hammer descended claw end first, tearing off his bottom jaw and sending it clattering onto the sidewalk.

Kerwin didn't have the release of a scream. A sickening gurgle would have to do, and that continued even after he lost consciousness.

Everett liked the way this man celebrated Halloween, but he didn't like the man himself. He was somehow like those men from church, the ones who had hurt him.

From up on the hill at the end of the street came the sound of the wicked rag doll's screaming. *She* ruined the parade. *She* hurt him. *She* made a big mess of Halloween! He would teach her, though. He would show her trick *and* treat.

* * * *

"Ruth! Stop and *think* about this!" McGlazer shouted, as he moved a heavy oak pew against the inner foyer door and leaned his weight into it. "Ask God for guidance!" This was a stalling tactic at best. Ruth had keys to every door.

He heard Ruth growl—a near-demonic sound. The outer foyer door slammed open. The inner foyer doorknob rattled. Then—the cocking of the big pistol's hammer. McGlazer dove to the floor as a shot rang out. Splinters sprayed above him.

Ruth shoved her way inside and stopped in a slab of moonlight that revealed her demented countenance, made worse by her smeared doll-face makeup.

She raised the pistol as McGlazer came to his feet. He threw the brass crucifix at her but, his focus still blurred, missed. The cross flew through the foyer and skidded out onto the front step.

Ruth lunged to retrieve the cross, lifting it as quickly as she could. "Oh, I'm so sorry, precious Lord." She stroked it. "I *swear* I will be thy vengeance for that blasphemy!"

She eased it down against the entryway wall, then charged and scrambled over the pew—only to be tackled by McGlazer. The pistol fell from her grip and slid out of reach.

She screamed as she did battle with the minister, yanking away the Summerisle wig—and a sizable hunk of his hair.

McGlazer dropped her with a punch to the forehead, enjoying the satisfying thud as he scrambled for the gun.

Ruth grabbed a vase of flowers from the high dais holding the sign-in book and smashed it over his back, then dragged him out of the way by his foot so she could crawl under the pew to get the pistol.

McGlazer recovered enough to pull the pew down across the back of her legs. Her striped hose recalled the Wicked Witch of the West, her kicks and screeches adding to the effect.

But she had the gun, and she was able to twist just enough to fire three rounds through the upturned pew. The third punctured McGlazer's side.

He fell to his back, clutching the wound.

She struggled out from under the bench and stood over McGlazer, snarling like a jackal. She yanked her wig off and hurled it at the floor. "I knew you were hopelessly backslidden." She dropped to straddle the Reverend's chest. "But I can't let you hinder my holy works!" She smashed the butt of the pistol into his face.

Chapter 43

Ruth caught her breath as she glowered down on McGlazer's unconscious form.

The man who was such a part of her life, the one who never insulted or hurt her. She became sorrowful, touching his cheek. "Oh, Reverend. I once dared to think you could...want me. That we could be together, saving Ember Hollow and the world. Sometimes, I daydreamed of having you lay hands on me. Healing me down below. I would be a virgin again. And then I could give my blood to you."

She licked his blood from her finger.

McGlazer moaned as he stirred—sending Ruth back to wild-eyed rage. "No!"

She smashed him again with the gun. "You're too late!"

She stood, straightening her clothes. "Maybe in heaven," she offered, and headed into the church.

* * * *

Stella gathered the kids against her, hiding under McGlazer's desk.

"What do we do if she finds us?" Stuart asked.

When Stella offered no answer, DeShaun filled the breathy silence. "Man, I've never been this scared."

Candace stared at the office door with dread.

The desk shook.

"What the hell is *that*?" asked Stuart, recoiling.

Stella scooted back against the wall. "Oh, God. It's the ghost! It's going to bring her right to us!"

"Ghost?" DeShaun said in a hoarse falsetto. "There's a *ghost* now?"

The desk bucked like a bull. The wall cracked. Pictures and certificates fell to shatter on the floor, one just missing Stella.

Suppressing a scream, she rose and pulled the kids after her. They all rushed through the office door, just as the ancient wall crumbled in on the room, a bursting dam of masonry and darkness.

* * * *

Hudson pounded rushing attackers to the ground, hoping Pedro and Jill were at least half as effective in neutralizing the crazed townies. The wild flailing of pale tattooed arms in his periphery was promising—as was was the sound of Jill's cries, like a Valkyrie gone blood-crazy. She kicked a two-hundred-pound man, and he crumpled like an accordion, falling face forward.

The crowd surged, multiple hands clutching and tearing at them, driving them back.

Hudson gritted his teeth, terrified he would have to kill one of the townies, or that they would kill *him* and the rockers. He thought of his family, as he checked up the street to see if, by some miracle, reinforcements were coming and spotted the Ember Hollow Fire Department's parade display—their biggest engine, soap-painted rather artlessly with monster faces. Hudson had a hallelujah moment. "Pedro! Can you guys keep 'em busy for a minute?"

"A minute would be stretching it!" answered the bassist, as he snatched an attacker by his neck and pants, pressed him over his head, and threw him like a sack into three on-rushers, sending them all to their backs.

Hudson shoved an on-rusher back into her fellow crazoids hard enough to knock down four of them, then turned and knelt to check on Dennis. The rocker didn't look good, his face pale against the black patch of blood-muddy grass beneath him.

Jill's studded boot halted the advance of crazed town councilman Randall Trotter.

Hudson was grateful when Pedro flew over him to intercept the latex-garbed dominatrix whose studded paddle was arcing toward his head. The deputy took the opening and bolted toward the fire truck.

* * * *

Ruth burst into the hallway. "I'm coming for you, *hellspawn*! I'm coming to exterminate every last God damned one of you! In Jesus' precious name!"

In the darkened gymnasium, Stella eased shut the door from the walkway, whispering, "Stay quiet, kids."

The heavy wooden gym doors cracked and splintered, shaking in their frames—and robbing Stella of hope.

"Shit!" DeShaun whispered.

"Exit doors!" Stella called, determined to save the youngsters, if not herself. "Go!"

The kids ran across the hardwood floor to the doors—which refused to open, no matter how hard they kicked and shoulder-bashed them.

The ghost was like a game master, pushing all the playing pieces toward each other for some sinister finish, Stella realized.

"We're trapped," Candace said with strange calm.

The cross painted in gold on the wall over the court blistered and peeled. The brick behind it crumbled like dried mud.

Candace tensed, grim realization dawning on her face.

What now? wondered Stuart.

Chapter 44

Hudson dashed to the truck and hauled out the thick hose, pointing it toward the melee. The tank's capacity was a thousand pounds. Hudson hoped it was at least half-full.

"Get down!" Hudson shouted to his crew.

He secured a solid grip and a wide stance and opened the nozzle. A good kick—then the stream was smashing into the rioters like rocket thrusters, sending them off their feet and sliding backward.

Hudson choked down on the pressure, maintaining just enough to keep the parade-goers off their feet once they were clear of his friends.

"You're the *man!*" Pedro shouted to Hudson, as he turned to check Dennis.

Hudson said a quick prayer that Stella would be along soon—and that DeShaun and his friends were all right.

* * * *

At the church's entryway, the crucifix that McGlazer had thrown at Ruth began to smoke—then twisted and contorted on itself, becoming a meaningless lump.

In the sanctuary, the wooden cross over the pulpit creaked, then disintegrated to a pile of splinters.

The cross on the roof broke off from its own weight and fell to the ground, where it exploded in a cloud of dust.

* * * *

Stuart and DeShaun watched Candace, fearing she had cracked from the strain.

"She's trapped too," Candace murmured.

Ruth came to the door and kicked its broken pieces out of the way. She stalked inside. "Silly sinners. Don't you see? Yahweh is guiding my hand. He's *driving* me." She poked her crucifix again. "To destroy all of you blasphemers."

Stella pushed the kids together behind her. "Leave them alone, Ruth."

"Oh, no, *no,* Jezebel." Ruth's smile was rapturous. "I shall bash their heads against the rocks! It is the will of the Father."

Candace stepped from behind Stella, glaring up at Ruth without fear.

"Candace, *no!*" Stella tried to restrain the little girl, but Candace pulled free and strode toward Ruth, stopping only when the zealot lowered the pistol to her face. "Ah, ah, *ah!*" mocked Rag Doll Ruth. "What's your rush to die, little sinner?"

Stella pleaded, "Ruth, please! Take me inst—"

"You are *no martyr!*" Ruth screamed at her. "But *you* can be first, little witch."

Candace didn't care about the gun. She just peered into Ruth's eyes. "I tried." She was sad. "I know I was too late, but I tried to warn all of you."

Ruth cackled. "What are you babbling about?"

Candace lunged, her hand like an arrow, and snatched Ruth's crucifix necklace, ripping it from her neck.

Ruth pistol-whipped her to the floor—but Candace barely reacted. "He won't ever stop," she said.

Ruth was perplexed by the strange girl's enigmatic words. Then, perhaps smelling burned flesh and plastic, she spun, breathing the word *no.*

In the doorway stood the silhouetted, devil-horned form of Everett Geelens, damaged child, Halloween enthusiast, and mass murderer.

"You...you *can't be!*" Ruth croaked.

She reached for the necklace that was no longer there. Turning, she tried to take it back from Candace, who scooted out of her reach. Everett was behind Ruth, his hammer held high. "Trick!"

He brought the hammer down, breaking the wrist of her gun hand.

The gun clattered to the hardwood floor. Her hand went limp, hanging at a sickening angle. Ruth cried out as she fell to her knees, then rolled to a fetal position.

"He doesn't know dying is real," Candace said, though no one could hear her over Ruth's scream.

Everett knelt beside Ruth. He raised the steak knife he had used to kill Cordelia just minutes before and drove it through Ruth's ruined wrist, pinning her to the polished wooden floor. The pitch of her wail became higher, harsher. With the hammer, Everett drove the knife deeper.

Ruth reached across to remove it, but Everett sat on her torso, grabbing her good hand to pin it as well. He took

another long knife from his bag, then hammered it into her left hand. Ruth's cries filled the room with anguished madness.

Everett took off his devil mask, hissing as it pulled melted plastic from his burned flesh. He positioned it on Ruth's face, then drove in tiny finishing nails, his rasping laughter growing louder.

Everett drew from his pocket the bag of orange-and-black-wrapped candy that Angelo had left for the Outlines at the spooky old house. He unwrapped one piece *"AND* treats!"

He stuffed the candy in her mouth, then another piece, and ten, *twenty* more, till her cheeks were swollen, her cries of horror reduced to muffled gasps.

Chapter 45

Dennis was dimly aware that the crushing, swirling blackness of the battlefield around him had collapsed, beaten down by a shocking blast of arctic wind.

Not wind—water.

Somehow he had fallen into some black ocean full of mermaids and mermen who were determined to rip the Outlines limb from tattooed limb.

One of 'em must have put a boot to his head. It throbbed with the pain of a thousand Carolina moonshine hangovers.

Oh, yeah—not a boot but a bottle. And not an ocean—Main Street, in the midst of a freezing freak typhoon.

But there was Hudson down the street, blasting the gnashing attackers— addled townies, not merfolk—with a fire hose. A few still had mean hands on his bandmates, though.

He had to clear his head, get in the game. Jill was feral and Petey was strong, but neither was all that quick, and that was where he came in.

He rolled himself to a stand, wiping the blood from his eyes. He swayed, left, right—and back to center. Took a breath, gave Hud a high wobbly thumbs-up, raised his fists.

* * * *

Candace buried her head in Stuart's chest. He hugged her tight and turned his back to hide her from the sight of…whatever the hell was happening to Ruth.

The rag-doll-clad killer convulsed, orange foam erupting from her mouth like the ol' Coke-and-Mentos gag. She vibrated like a jackhammer, her eyes growing, inflating like balloons. Her ears curled in on themselves like wilting rose petals.

Blood shot from her nose in high-pressure streams that painted the floor some twelve feet away.

Bubbling foam rose from her mouth and flew toward the ceiling, turning to thick clouds of orange smoke, like a parachutist's signal. Her hair waved around her head, as if she were underwater.

Her ballooning eyes burst, splashing black ichor. Then the back of her head banged and *bangedandbangedandbanged* on the hardwood floor at an impossible speed, until the staccato sound was a sustained note, something like a D note.

The opening in the back of her skull crumbled away enough for her brain, reduced to a mushy glop, to fall out and be flattened by her last flailing smash—and she was still.

Everett squished his feet in the gooey mess, having enjoyed the evening's grand finale.

Stella hugged the kids, whispering to Everett, "Stay away from us. Please."

Candace pulled away from Stuart and turned to face her brother. She cleared her throat and took three slow steps toward him.

"Candace!" called Stella.

Candace had no fear in her eyes. " Shh!" she said. "This is family business."

Everett drew the crumpled alien mask from his pocket. "Canniss." He reached toward her.

Candace closed her eyes. Everett dabbed blood from his bullet wounds on the back of the mask, then stuck it to Candace's face, saying, "I luh…luh…love you."

Candace opened her eyes. "I love you too, Everett."

Everett rocked on his feet, fighting some urge.

"Candace," Stella whispered. "I think you should come to me, baby."

Candace took a leery step back—and Everett followed.

Stuart made a move toward them, but Stella, with the strength and quickness of maternal instinct, pulled him back.

Everett's gaze fell to the hammer on the floor. Then his gaze rose to the ceiling.

Following him, the others saw a white mist descending.

It settled to a stop between Candace and Everett, then sharpened, gaining definition.

Everett clapped his hands with delight—it was a really *real* ghost!

It was the shade of a man, imposing and regal, wavering between degrees of distinctness.

Stella felt something familiar about it, something powerful.

The face of Wilcott Bennington formed. He had maneuvered her—*used* her. He had endangered these children, and her.

Bennington floated toward Everett, who was even more pleased than he had been with Rag Doll Ruth's spectacular demise.

The ghost opened a shimmering maw. "*Die now*," the town father intoned in a commanding voice.

Everett's smile faded. He touched one of his bullet wounds and inspected the blood with understanding.

Candace sat on the floor Indian style, and Everett eased himself down to lie his head on her lap. She stroked his burned and bloody head and said, "Happy Halloween, Everett."

"Hap......" Everett trailed off.

The ghost became vague, almost imperceptible, as the exit door, immovable just minutes ago, clicked with an echo and creaked open. Bennington, fading to mist, floated toward it.

Stella followed, wishing she would see the mist settle into the massive obelisk. She had helped to complete this night's work. She needed that symbol of closure.

As soon as she set foot outside the door, a large shadowy figure met her head-on.

Stella shrieked, prompting the others to as well.

The lights came back on and the dark figure, Reverend McGlazer, stumbled into Stella's arms, issuing a cough.

The kids went to help hold him up, Stuart saying, "Rev?"

"I'll live," he rasped. "Just beat to hell. But Dennis..." He paused for another cough. "Get down to the street. Go now!"

Everett lay still, peaceful. Candace gave his empty vessel one last look.

* * * *

Hudson and Pedro squatted on either side of Dennis, who sat on the grass propped on his elbows, smoking a cigarette while Jill dabbed at his head with a bandana. The wet street bounced firelight across their grim, tired features.

The crowd, shocked to their senses by the cold water, wandered about, recovering from their hallucinatory rage, sitting, shivering, and holding one another.

As Stella and the kids limped forward, Stuart spotted his bloody brother and ran to the scene. Jill pulled Stuart into an embrace with his brother, saying, "Oh, sweetie! So glad you're all right."

"I *knew* something would happen to you without me around to babysit your sorry ass!" Stuart said to Dennis.

"Yeah, yeah, good to see you too, loser." Dennis winced. "How 'bout we don't mention this to Ma?" he said. "She worries."

"Yeah, good luck with *that*," Stuart replied. Dennis took the cigarette out of his mouth and flicked it away. The night's worries were over.

Stella appeared, taking over the bandana and applying pressure to Dennis's wound. "Looks like it just skimmed you," she said.

"Lady," Dennis said, "please tell me you brought some aspirin."

DeShaun ran to Hudson and they hugged harder and longer than they had since DeShaun was a toddler. "Man, am I glad to see *you*," said the boy. "Same here," Hudson said. "'Cause you're grounded starting right now."

Candace was happy for them all, for their places in loving families. She didn't want to think of herself and all she had lost. She wanted to feel the way young girls were *supposed* to feel on Halloween. She wanted magic and safety and meeting people and having fun with friends.

She sat with her back against one of the Indian laurel planters, ready to close her eyes for a second, maybe even cry—when she was startled by a familiar sound. Something emerged from the shadows and barreled toward her and she got to her feet—to welcome it.

Bravo, her best friend ever, jumped up to put his big paws on her shoulders and lick her face. His paws were cold with mud, his coat was a matted mess, and he stunk to high heaven—but he had found her.

She *did* have family still, and she knew she could always count on him.

And she knew, somehow, that they would need each other, very soon.

There were still dark things in Ember Hollow, waiting, festering, focusing on her and her friends—and her town.

Grim Harvest

Don't miss the next chilling novel in the Haunted Hollow Chronicles . . .

Coming soon from
Lyrical Press, an imprint of Kensington Publishing Corp.

Keep reading to enjoy a sample excerpt…

An excerpt from *Grim Harvest*

If not for the nature of his crime, Nico Rizzoli might not have been in the van, on his way to Hutchinson Correctional in Kansas, where his reputation and influence would theoretically carry less weight than the Craven County system in North Carolina, where he was practically a superstar.

Upon learning that an associate had ratted out the Mid-Atlantic Fireheads motorcycle club for their meth business, Nico had eschewed flight for fury.

He tracked down the informant and, using a length of steel pipe he had selected, measured, cut and taped himself, he smashed the poor bastard's ribs to jelly right in front of his girlfriend and mother. Nico reasoned that healing from ruined ribs would be a long and agonizing process, versus head trauma, which potentially offered merciful blackouts and memory loss. As a bonus, his women would sob about that crazy shit to every square in sight, for years to come.

He kept at it till the cops came, then fought all the way to lockup, cursing the boys in blue for not letting him finish. He had wanted to gelatinize the man's legs as well, you see.

But sitting here in the transport shuttle van amongst a bunch of morons doing time for possession and robbery and other pussy-ass bullshit, Nico wasn't thinking about the past. He was more interested in the future; specifically—any minute now.

Nearly midnight, and they had already been on the road for ten hours. The extradition agents would be getting bleary-eyed and slow.

"You go' stop at Boogie Burger, or what!?" inmate Georgie "The Juice" DeWitt asked Extradition Agent Higgins through the steel mesh partition, the shackles on his wrist and seat armrest making him stretch. "I'm 'bout to starve my ass off."

Neither the driver nor his partner answered; they had been instructed to have minimal communication with DeWitt, as he was notoriously short-tempered and easily riled.

"*Huh!?*" DeWitt persisted. "I need some goddamn *food!*"

"Shut up," Nico said.

DeWitt turned with early stage rage on his face, which vanished when he realized it was Nico talking to him. DeWitt took his seat and proceeded to shut up.

Normally Nico didn't bother talking to lesser cons for any reason, but he needed distracting noise kept to a minimum, so he could hear the familiar roar of beefed-up Harleys driven by his brothers.

Although intensely focused and purposeful—Nico Rizzoli might have made quite a politician if not for his violent nature—he was not above or beyond feeling something that could pass for love. His old lady Ruth, the most passionately devoted chick he had ever banged, undoubtedly had his heart.

Now she was dead. On Halloween night, just trying to make the world a better place; trying to do God's work. Ridiculous as that was to him, the bottom line was that something that belonged to him had been taken away, and that shit did not fly. Nico would find out the how and the who, and in the process, he would wipe this little jerkwater called Ember Hollow right off the map, along with the big deputy who had assisted in his arrest.

Nobody takes what belongs to Nico Rizzoli. Not even God.

Nico rubbed the tattoo on his forearm; the one he'd had inked just the day before. He liked the way it itched and stung. The inker -somebody had named him Mozart because they though the composer was a painter owing to the "art" in his name- had a picture of a ragdoll Nico had ripped from an encyclopedia in the library, and Mozart didn't blink an eye when Nico told him that was what he wanted.

Ruth had loved rag dolls for some reason. Had one from when she was a girl that she wouldn't let him toss. To Nico, it came to represent her. She talked to the thing, and even brought it to lockup with her when she came to see him.

He wanted to slap the tattoo, just to amp up the sting a bit, but that was for later.

Or maybe sooner.

The beautiful sound of a six speed 1690 cc engine—*his* bike—reached his ears before anyone else heard. Nico went ahead and gripped the armrests, bracing himself. He smiled at the doomed dipshit seated beside him, who cluelessly yawned and settled his head back to doze.

The roar of two other bikes joined that of the Fatboy. Perfect.

Agent Higgins looked in the side mirror, but he wouldn't see them yet. They were riding dark; coping just fine in full-on blackness.

"Funny," Higgins said in his Georgia drawl. "Thought I heard hogs."

"Whut, you mean pigs?" asked his partner, Agent Dutton, a Detroit-born city boy.

"No, dumb ass," Higgins said. "Harleys, man."

Higgins rubbed his eyes, and both fell back to their complacency; a short descent.

Came the sound of the bikers gunning it, and in less than a second, they were beside the van. A couple of inmates stirred in their seats, muttering unease. Nico nodded down at his brother Rhino coming up just outside the window on the Fatboy, the only one riding solo. Rhino returned the gesture and roared far ahead.

The second bike zoomed in place next to the van's driver's side, while the third bike eased up parallel to Nico.

Both these machines carried huge, hair-covered passengers behind their smaller drivers. They were already rising to crouch on the seats with the confidence and agility of trapeze artists, or seasoned predators.

"Hey, what are these assho…?"

The two hirsute passengers leaped in unison, hooking into the side of the van with their claws like magnets.

Agent Higgins screamed and swerved the wheel, as his window exploded in on him, a huge hairy hand finding his throat like a guided missile—and tearing it out.

Agent Dutton had his pistol out, but he would never have a chance to use it, for the van careened off the road and into a scrabbly patch of wasteland, where it flipped onto its passenger side with a groan, the gun lost in the chaos.

Nico held onto his armrests, chuckling at the sound of steel mesh tearing away from his window. The glass broke, and a slavering snout was in his face, growling and snapping.

"Yeah, yeah." Nico pulled at the chain that fastened him to the seat, and his liberator, Aura, bit it in two, her hairy breasts rubbing across Nico's face. She gave him a lick, bit his eyebrow just hard enough to draw blood, then clambered in to go to work on the passengers.

Nico slid out of his seat and landed feet-first on the left side of a skinny inmate first-timer he knew as Ratso. The boy cried at Nico for help, but -just for kicks- Nico booted him in the face instead.

Blood splashed across Nico and everything else, as Aura went about wasting the other prisoners, showing off for him. The other lupine Berzerker, Pipsqueak, wrenched the front partition apart and slashed into the hoarsely-bellowing DeWitt, destroying a lot of meat as he worked his way to the man's heart, only to spit it out on finding it blackened from cigarettes.

Aura dropped a brawny arm on the passenger side windows at Nico's feet, but he kicked it away. Pipsqueak went after it. He and Aura briefly scuffled over it, their massive hindleg claws digging into what was left of the inmates as they clambered for traction.

"Knock it off!" Nico called. "Let's roll."

Pipsqueak had something to show him. He dropped to all fours to turn toward the front. Nico followed, flinging his long, blood-soaked hair out of his face.

Pipsqueak growled and bit Higgins to draw a cry of pain, then leapt out the driver window to get out of Nico's way.

Nico looked Higgins over. "Damn boy," he said. "You ain't gonna make it."

Higgins was hanging at a forty-five-degree angle, spilling blood onto the squashed corpse of Dutton. Deep claw marks had separated Higgins' face and throat into sections. His left arm was hanging on approximately halfway; tendons and cartilage still holding where muscle and skin had given way.

Higgins was weakly feeling around for his sidearm. When he found it, Aura muscled past Nico and clamped her teeth shut on the guard's head, squashing it like a grape.

She rolled onto her back and smiled her toothy smile at Nico, clearly expecting a rub on her fuzzy belly.

"Never gonna happen girl," Nico said, as he unbuckled Higgins. Aura rolled away as the messy bag of meat fell where she had been. Nico stepped up on Higgins and climbed out, followed by Aura.

He and the wolves went to the three bikes waiting there. Smiling, Rhino, slid back to let Nico drive his Fatboy.

Acknowledgments

Michaela Hamilton believed in me and in this series. She took a chance, and I'm determined to make her proud.

My wife Jennifer Greene never wavers in her support and honesty.

My mother Daisy Jones tolerated me drawing monsters on the wall as a toddler and made sure my brothers and I got to trick or treat when we were old enough—and long after we were too old. She lauded my horrific artwork and remains patient with my oddball outlook. She is a saint.

April Courtney Gooding, who may well be the Supreme Beta Reader of this or any universe.

And lastly—all the Halloweeniacs, metalheads, punkers, greasers, and alt folk, whose passionate spirits I hope to touch.

About the Author

Photo by Scott Treadway

Patrick C. Greene is a lifelong horror fan who lives in the mountains of western North Carolina. He is the author of the novels *Progeny* and *The Crimson Calling*, as well as numerous short stories featured in collections and anthologies.

Visit him at www.fearwriter.wordpress.com.

Printed in the United States
by Baker & Taylor Publisher Services